TRIAL BY TOWN

SHARON FERNICOLA

TRIAL BY TOWN

Sharon Fernicola

Lambertsmill Publishing

Dedicated to my dad, who taught me to love a good murder mystery, one Perry Mason episode at a time.

PROLOGUE

The courtroom was closing in, seemingly getting smaller and smaller. She fought for each breath; the outburst was inevitable. "No! Oh God no!" Mrs. Keans screamed in disbelief. "How could you? You—"

She never finished her words, collapsing to the floor from the weight of her sorrow. She continued to moan and wail, the sounds resonating from a place deep within. They came to her aid, trying desperately to console her, but the almost unrecognizable screams only intensified. Even the blare of the ambulance siren couldn't drown out her anguished cries. Racing to the hospital really didn't matter. No earthly medicines could ever heal her despair.

CHAPTER 1

Katie loved the mornings, particularly the routine of getting ready for the day; the smell of her husband's aftershave on her favorite towel, and especially the aroma of freshly brewed coffee. Or cappuccino, as he called it. Matt was serious about his coffee and meticulously made certain each day was greeted with the proper combination of Italian ground beans and a secret brand of bottled water he used only for this special event. She was just about to apply mascara when she heard his *"Ahh."* That was his sip of approval. "Hon, coffee's ready."

She smiled; as if he needed to tell her. She could hear that it was ready. "Be right there."

Katie finished applying her mascara. She didn't need much time. She was a natural beauty, blessed with features that promised to keep her looking young well into her later years. A little blush, a comb through her auburn shoulder-length hair, and some lipstick. This all served to accentuate her most engaging quality, her green eyes. People often asked her if she was wearing "those new type of colored contacts." One more quick look into the mirror and she was ready. Although she didn't agree or really understand, her friends envied her appearance and style and particularly her simple maintenance practice that made her look like a teenager rather than the twenty-eight years she recently celebrated.

Matt was reading the *Wall Street Journal* but tossed it to the side as she entered the kitchen. "You look sensational," he said. "Will you be home for dinner? I'd like to grill some salmon and asparagus tonight."

She walked behind him and gave a quick peck on the cheek. "I'm almost certain the case will settle this morning, so, if all things go according to plan, I'll even bring the wine."

He pushed away from the table, turned around, and embraced her. After six years of marriage, they still had the passion and playfulness of newlyweds.

"Baby, you're the greatest," he emoted, giving his best Ralph Kramden imitation. He tilted her back in his arms and was poised to give her an ardent kiss on the lips when the mood was broken by the sound of the phone. It startled them a bit and they both laughed. "I'll be right back, so don't go up to Trixie's," he said as he went to answer the phone.

"You know," she yelled to him as he walked away, "not everyone watches *The Honeymooners.* Some people actually quote Shakespeare, King, Churchill, Kennedy."

Truth be told, one of things she loved most about him was his sense of humor and his unfailing ability to see the lighter side of life. She was actually a closet Abbott and Costello fan, but never let on. After all, she thought, every good marriage should have one secret.

Katie could hear him talking excitedly, but because he was on the other side of their large apartment she didn't have a clear understanding of the conversation. She remained in the kitchen and relished her first, and best, cup of coffee of the day. She began thinking about how fortunate she was to have Matt Russo in her life. He was successful in his own right as a principal in a computer technology business. And, aside from having those handsomely Italian chiseled good looks, he was also an incredibly nice person. "A rarity these days," she muttered softly. Unlike herself, he was raised in a large Italian household that held family values above all else. At first, she was terribly awkward around his parents and his seemingly endless stream of relatives. Even people who weren't kin were considered family and were often bestowed with the title of *zia* or *zio*. As time passed, and to her amazement, these incredibly warm and wonderful people welcomed her fully.

In stark contrast to Matt's warm and supportive family, Katie's parents had always been emotionally distant. Her in-laws struggled to grasp her hesitation about starting a family, unaware that she had grown up without a nurturing example to follow. Deep down, she feared that she might be missing the maternal instinct altogether.

Katie never had a role model. She tried to explain to Matt's family that growing up, her own mother was stern, manipulative, and generally disinterested. Her father was equally unapproachable. Her parents gave her medicine when she was sick, fed her when she was hungry, and provided heat on cold nights. But, as for affection, that was a commodity in short supply. Both parents were products of a stern and wealthy background where the dollar was given more respect than people. Katie sadly could recall their business meetings and social gatherings taking precedence over her school plays and dance recitals. Although she learned to accept that her parents were unlike those of her friends, their neglect was nevertheless quite hurtful.

As Katie matured, her relationship with her parents was civil, at best, but it deteriorated rapidly at the announcement of her career choice. She had worked hard on her studies to try to obtain some semblance of approval, so she was particularly hurt when they proclaimed their dissatisfaction with the path she selected. Funny, she thought, after all these years she could still recall in detail the very moment she told them of her decision to work for the DA's office rather than accept a position with Deis Associates, a financial company with close ties to her father's business. She tried to explain that she wanted to first learn the law from the prosecutor's vantage and then, ultimately, become a defense attorney for legal aid. "How could you do this to us?" was her mother's response, while her father's, "I won't allow it," ended the conversation.

Motherhood was not something she had ever even contemplated until she got to know and experience Matt and his family. Admittedly, she was a little proud of herself for at least thinking about it. Although Matt's family tried hard to conceal their disappointment, she knew that not having a child was tantamount to not believing in the pope as the spiritual leader of the Catholic community. She tried to explain to them, particularly Matt, about her fears of motherhood. What if being a terrible mother was genetic? What if she really didn't have any maternal instincts? What if, what if...

She poured another cup of coffee, wondering to herself how in the world her thoughts could have possibly turned to this topic. "Stop thinking," she muttered to herself, then quickly spun around, hearing Matt approaching but still on the phone.

"I'm so sorry," he said. "Please, let us know if there's anything. Yes, she's right here. I love you too. Hold on. Katie, it's the Professor's wife. She said he needs surgery."

Katie's face changed completely. Bad news was something she never took well, especially when it involved a loved one. She reached for the phone and began frantically, "Phyllis, what's happened? Is he all right? What do you need?" She fired off her questions with the same intensity and manner usually reserved for a cross-examination.

"Easy, Kate," Phyllis said. "He's being cared for, but he'd like to see you. He needs your help."

"Consider it done" Katie said firmly. "But please, tell me what happened."

Phyllis explained how she found him on the floor at the bottom of their staircase. "Fortunately," she said, "Maria, the housekeeper, and I were both home, so we were able to immediately notify emergency services." She paused, carefully considering her words. "I won't lie, Sean has other health issues, so I am concerned, but he's too stubborn to let this get him down."

Katie's heart was racing, but she tried to maintain her composure, not wanting to upset Phyllis. "I'll be there, Phyllis. Please tell him I'll be there."

Matt had sat by her side the entire time, holding her hand. The Professor meant a lot to both of them, particularly Katie. Her overreaction to anything threatening to the Professor was highly irrational but utterly understandable. He meant the world to her.

She handed Matt the phone. "The Professor needs me, Matt, and I must be there for him."

"Without question, just tell me what I can do to help."

"Just give me a hug."

CHAPTER 2

It was 6:00am and Katie was already seated at the desk in her law office trying to get organized before her assistant Tessa arrived. She wasn't usually in this early, but yesterday's phone call prompted her to get things in order as quickly as possible. She was in court all day yesterday, so she hadn't yet told Tessa about the Professor or that she would need help in rescheduling her cases over the next several days.

Katie tried to be her usual model of efficiency, but her mind was so focused on the Professor that she found herself repeatedly shuffling the same case files. She paused for a moment, took a deep breath, and leaned back in her old, but comfortable chair. *A gift from the Professor*, she thought to herself. She took a sip from the cup of coffee she was forced to purchase from Ruby's Deli next door to her office. Her grimace was a clear indication that this liquid had no business calling itself coffee. As she tried to get refocused, she caught a glimpse of the photo prominently displayed on the entrance wall. It was of herself, Matt, and the Professor. She stood and walked toward it. As Katie gently touched the photo, her eyes began to well. "The two most important men in my life," she said aloud.

She began to reminisce. *"June 2nd, I think it was a Wednesday."* Katie had just moved into her new office after deciding to go into private practice with two friends she had made in the DA's office. Matt was helping her unpack the dozen or so boxes when the Professor dropped in for a surprise visit. Rather than the obligatory plant, he came bearing pizzas and wine. Katie's partners, Thomas and Zoe, were delighted to meet the legendary Professor, and were only too happy to forego the unpleasantness of setting up the office for good eats and even better stories. As the day came to a close, Zoe took a picture to "permanently record our very first visitors." Neither partner minded when Katie asked for it to be hung in the entranceway.

Katie walked back to her desk but still could not concentrate. "I just can't seem to help it," she mumbled as if she had to justify her feelings to someone. "If it weren't for him, my entire life would be different."

Katie had first met the Professor her freshman year of college. She was still undecided between majoring in law or economics, so she registered for the introductory course for each. A quirk of fate, the usual professor who taught the basic law class became ill just prior to the start of the new term. So, Professor Sean Kyle Jr. reluctantly volunteered to help for "just this one term and no more."

As Katie related the story, the Professor entered the class late and considerably disheveled. There had been an ice storm just a few hours prior to class, and apparently the maintenance department had yet to take the necessary safety precautions in the faculty parking lot. As the Professor walked from his car, he unexpectedly encountered a rather large patch of ice and unceremoniously fell flat on his posterior end. At least that's how the Professor told the story. For the next hour of class, rather than refer to the text material, the Professor spent the entire time explaining the basic elements of law with regard to suing every employee of the maintenance department. The class was educational, informative, and extremely entertaining. The students actually gave him a standing ovation at the conclusion. From that point on, Katie was hooked.

As the semesters progressed, Katie enrolled in every class that the Professor taught. He was an imposing figure, particularly as he walked the academic halls. Gray streaks threaded through his hair and beard, framing the wire-rimmed glasses that perpetually slipped down his nose as he cast a skeptical gaze over the case briefs. Tweed was the wardrobe of the day, complete with elbow patches. He often terrorized first year students with his deliberate and bellowing voice. But Katie came to recognize and understand his myriad of personalities. Sometimes the lovable curmudgeon, sometimes the impatient taskmaster, and sometimes the court jester. Regardless, he lived and breathed the law, and when he spoke of it, he was eloquent and full of passion. To Katie, he was never more powerful than when he delivered some of his prior court summations to the class. He was an artist. The courtroom was his canvas, and he used words to paint a picture just as skillfully as any artist using a brush.

In addition to helping her grow as a lawyer, the Professor helped her grow as a person. Like so many new students, she entered college reticent and filled with doubts, many put upon her by her own family. But somehow, in his classes, she found a safe haven. He recognized her talent and provided an outlet for her to flourish. By the second year, it became apparent that he was her mentor and biggest supporter. In some ways, she found in him the paternal support and affection that was sorely lacking during her formative years. Despite a few jealous whispers, their relationship was definitely special, but always proper and above reproach.

Katie smiled as she recalled how the Professor had served as matchmaker for her and Matt. He denied it, of course, but it was too coincidental for anything but a planned rendezvous. The Professor had asked Katie to meet him in his office, but when she arrived, he asked her to wait in the outer office as he completed an important business call.

"Do me a favor," he called out. "The computer repair man is supposed to be here shortly. Would you please ask him to wait too."

She left his office and took the seat nearest the door. A few minutes later, the repairman came in. Actually, he was more of a repair boy. Katie tried to tell him about the Professor's phone call, but she was tongue-tied. She was staring into the most gorgeous face she had ever seen. He had dark wavy hair that framed his face, deep brown eyes that held a quiet mischief, and a smile that stretched from ear to ear, revealing a single dimple. And, fortunately, he was clearly enamored with her as well.

The two fumbled through a twenty-minute conversation when finally, the Professor emerged. "I still need to complete my call, but I would appreciate if you could both wait a little longer. I took the liberty of ordering a pizza. I hope that's agreeable." At that point, their fate was sealed.

Katie's reminiscing was interrupted by the sound of a key in the lock and chatter. "Good morning, Katie, you're here early," Tessa said as she dropped an armload of newspapers and files on her desk.

Thomas was right behind her holding a box of Krispy Kreme donuts. "Hi, Katie."

"Good morning, Thomas, and please pass one of those gooey ones this way. Tessa, I'm sorry to be so abrupt, but I'd like to meet with you now. I'm due in court this morning and I'm going to need your help."

"Sure, what's the matter, Katie? Are you okay?"

Katie spent the next hour explaining about the Professor and reviewing the case workload for the balance of the week. Tessa listened intently and gave the, "It will be okay," in all the appropriate spots. She may have been young, but Tessa gave Katie the support and calmness she needed to get through the conversation. Hiring her as a legal assistant was one of the best decisions she, Thomas, and Zoe had made. Her addition to the office was immeasurable.

"Listen, Katie, don't worry about a thing here. You've helped a lot of your colleagues through some rough spots. I know they'll be more than happy to get the chance to return the favor. By the time you get back from court, I'll have everything worked out. I promise." Tessa's confidence was a welcome relief.

"I don't tell you this enough, but I couldn't do my job without you. Thank you, Tessa. Thanks so much for everything," Katie said sincerely. She picked up the Verga file and quickly placed it in her briefcase. "I've got to run or I'll be late. Judge Kym loves to find any excuse to hold lawyers in contempt."

Tessa gave Katie a gentle farewell, her voice calm and reassuring. "Katie, everything's going to be all right. Try not to worry."

Katie finally smiled as she closed the door behind her.

CHAPTER 3

Harlem River Drive, George Washington Bridge to I-95 North. According to the GPS, about a two-and-a-half-hour drive, and, although traveling alone, Katie felt comfortable that the rental would get her there safely. With the maze of the city behind her, she started to ease into the drive. The radio was set to light music—Streisand, hopefully, and golden oldies. The window was cracked to give access to the aromas and sounds of a mid-June morning.

Pulling things together last minute wasn't nearly as difficult as she had imagined. Tessa had been right. Colleagues Ali, Libby, and Tyler were only too happy to cover her current cases, while another, Nicholas, even went so far as to volunteer his time on her behalf at the legal aid department. Katie never really appreciated just how well liked and respected she was. Matt was also a tremendous help in getting her prepared, both physically and emotionally. After some discussion, they both agreed, for business reasons, that it would be better if he stayed at home to complete the Noone project. The profit from that job alone could cover the expenses of adding a baby's room to their condo, *"should it be necessary,"* she thought. At that moment, she realized it was more than a passing notion; the dilemma of starting a family had taken root and refused to let go.

Exit after exit, and then finally the sign for Keansbury, Connecticut. "Ah, there it is," she said aloud. "Only two more miles to go." The trip thus far had been uneventful, and if it weren't for such an unpleasant occasion, she would have actually described it as enjoyable. She knew the days ahead would be somewhat emotional, so she took Matt's advice and used the driving time to unwind and get grounded. She cleared her mind of her cases and the baby decision and just sang as loud and off-key as possible to the words of every song that the radio stations played.

Keansbury, Next Exit. She veered toward the right, took a quick glance to check the GPS, and turned effortlessly onto Highway 601. Straight ahead, not too much farther. She was anxious to see the Professor and, by now, equally looking forward to stretching her legs and getting a bite to eat.

The ride on 601 was a bit different somehow, Katie thought. It felt and looked different. The closer she got to her destination, the surroundings seemed to alter. It was so subtle that, at first, she hadn't noticed. What started as a semi-major highway now had the look of a quaint out-of-the-way road. It narrowed to two lanes, with barely enough room for opposite traveling cars to pass one another. Trees lined either side of the highway, perhaps Italian cypress. They were tall and regal-looking, and she laughed to herself when she compared them to British guard's bearskin hats. They were lovely, but just seemed somewhat out of place and overstated.

Katie had never been to Keansbury, so her impressions and expectations were based on previous conversations she'd had with the Professor. She had envisioned a small, unpretentious town; however, she decided to reserve her opinion regarding the people themselves. Katie wasn't one to prejudge, so she chastised a friend who declared with certainly that any small town outside of Manhattan surely was a breeding ground for the unsophisticated and monotonous.

Katie's recollection was that the Professor's grandparents had settled in Keansbury, moving in with a distant relative who served as their sponsor. Although most of the other details were sketchy, she did remember the Professor saying that he himself was the first member of the family to ever attend college and that he ultimately left Keansbury to attend law school. However, he kept their family home and considered it his primary residence. After graduation, he successfully practiced law in the city and ultimately transitioned into teaching full-time. He and Phyllis split their time between their New York apartment and their Keansbury home. After his retirement, he and Phyllis decided to establish permanent residency here. Some were surprised by his decision, considering him a New York City force, but he assured everyone that they would be very happy and content in this community by the ocean.

WELCOME TO KEANSBURY
OUR FAMILY CARES ABOUT YOUR FAMILY
ESTABLISHED 1945
FOUNDER PETER KEANS I

As she passed the handsomely crafted sign, she realized that what she had perceived as a black border was, in fact, black material draped carefully from end to end.

She lowered her window, "Excuse me, sir," she shouted. "Would you please tell me how to get to Keansbury Community Hospital?" Fortunately, it was only minutes away. She drove by the Keansbury Middle School and made a left at the Keansbury Post Office. She had been too tired and too nervous about seeing the Professor, that she failed to notice that every sign and lamppost was draped in black. Katie turned into the hospital parking lot and pulled into a space next to a van; *Keansbury Florist* adorned its side in large gold lettering. As she opened the car door, she immediately inhaled a lovely fruity aroma. *"Could that possibly be coming from the van?"* she wondered. Anxious to see the Professor, she stepped out of the car, stretched for a moment, then reached in the back for the small wrapped gift. As she walked toward the entranceway, she had a sense that things were quiet. "You're in a hospital zone," she muttered, but it was more than that. Everything just seemed too quiet, almost stagnant. She got a shiver. "I must be more tired than I thought." A young man held the door open as she entered the lobby.

An elderly, pleasant-looking woman was seated at the information desk. "Good morning, I'm Cecelia, how may I help you?"

"Good morning. Professor Kyle's room, please," Katie said politely.

The woman responded cheerfully, "Oh, you must be Mrs. Russo. Welcome to Keansbury. Mrs. Kyle told me to expect you, and you're as pretty as she described." Katie could feel her face blush. "Straight ahead to the elevators, dear."

Katie noticed the woman wore a black armband on her left sleeve.

CHAPTER 4

Katie walked quickly but quietly down the long hospital corridor. It was pale blue and lined with pictures of the hospital's construction and dedication ceremony. She reached the two elevator banks and pressed up. She began rubbing the left side of her temple, a habit that someone had pointed out to her that she did whenever she became somewhat overwhelmed.

She was getting anxious now and impatient for the elevator to descend. As she shifted from one foot to the other, she noticed the opposite wall. It was filled with photos of people; descendants of the Keans, to be exact. The display started in the upper left-hand corner with Peter Keans I, a name she recalled from the town's welcome sign. The rows continued in an orderly manner from left to right, with each photo becoming more sharp and crisp as photo technology improved over the decades. She read the names of each generation: Peter Senior, Peter Junior.

"Bing."

"Ah, finally." She twirled around and stepped aside to let two elderly men exit the car. She pressed floor four and the doors closed. She hadn't noticed that the photo in the lower righthand corner was draped in black.

Another *"bing"* and the doors opened. She looked straight ahead but couldn't seem to move. Her heart was pounding and her mind was racing, but her legs weren't working. She leaned against the side wall as she held firm on the *Open Door* button. A deep and slow inhale and a calming exhale. "You can do this," she said to herself. "He'll be all right. He needs you."

She finally exited and read the room numbers painted carefully on the wall. Left, then straight to the VIP wing.

As she passed the nurses station, a young woman smiled and said, "Good morning, Mrs. Russo. Down the end of the hallway, last room on your left."

"Thank you," Katie replied, wondering just how many people Phyllis had informed of her visit. One more rub to the temple. She was only a few yards away when her heart rate began to intensify. She began the "what ifs"... *What if he's sicker than she was led to believe? What if he doesn't recognize her? What if he asks something of her that she can't do?* What if, what if... She placed her hand on the room door handle when suddenly it swung open and Phyllis appeared.

"Kate!" she screamed. "Oh, Kate." Phyllis always referred to her as Kate. The two women embraced and kissed. Phyllis gently led her away from the Professor's room to a waiting area just down the hall. "The doctor is running a few tests. It won't take long. How about a cup of coffee? I'm buying."

Katie was surprised by the waiting room. It resembled a chic cafe. No snack machines here. The coffee was prepared every few hours and served in silver urns with a variety of milks and sugars neatly arranged nearby. Assorted pastries were also available and kept fresh under a crystal cover.

"Kate, you take it black with sugar, right?" Katie nodded. The two women exchanged a few minutes of small talk when Katie finally punctuated the conversation with questions about the Professor.

"Phyllis, please tell me what really happened. Is he getting the best care here?" She could feel herself lapse into lawyer mode.

"Kate, I believe he's getting the best care possible. The doctor wants to run a few more tests and then we'll all make the best decision on how to proceed. As for what happened, there's not much more than what I told you on the phone. About two months ago, I found him at the bottom of the stairs. He doesn't recall exactly, but somehow, he tripped and tumbled down the entire flight. He complained about his hip, which turned out to be broken. Unfortunately, things are complicated by his severe case of diabetes.

Katie always thought of the Professor as invincible. Perhaps that's what had been worrying her so much. The inevitable realization and acknowledgement that he *wasn't* invincible.

Katie looked up and noticed a professional-looking young man exiting the Professor's room and heading their way.

"Excuse me, Mrs. Kyle. I'm all finished. You can go back in now." Turning toward Katie, he introduced himself. "I'm Doctor Christian, Professor Kyle's physician."

Phyllis smiled, "Ah, Doctor Christian, this is our dear friend, Mrs. Kate Russo."

He extended his hand. "So, you're the famous Katie I've been hearing so much about. It's a pleasure to finally meet you."

"How do you do?" Katie's greeting was perfunctory; her true concern lay with the state of the Professor's health. "Doctor, how exactly is the Professor? Is this the best place for him, and what do you plan on doing next?"

"Am I a witness for the defense or the prosecution?" Doctor Christian said without skipping a beat.

A slightly tense moment was quickly diffused with a sincere

apology from Katie. "I'm sorry, Doctor. I'm tired and I've been so worried about the Professor that my concern got the better of my manners."

"I'd like to know too," Phyllis said as she put her hand on Katie's arm.

"I fully understand," the doctor said compassionately. "I can assure both of you that we are all doing everything we can to get the Professor well just as quickly as possible. As you know, we are recommending surgery to either repair part of the hip or to replace it entirely. The tests we've been running will help us make that decision. As you also know, we are working very hard at keeping him as strong as possible to minimize the risk of any complications before, during, and after surgery. And, Mrs. Russo"...she noticed he addressed her formally..."if I believe for one moment that another doctor or facility would increase the chance of his full recovery, I give you my word that I will not hesitate to take the necessary action."

Well, score points for the doctor for being direct and without ego, Katie thought to herself. "Thank you," she told him sincerely. "I appreciate your candor." She and Phyllis both felt reassured.

As he turned to leave, Katie quipped, "Oh, and, Doctor, in answer to your question: for the defense." He gave a mild laugh and left.

"I think I like him," she said to Phyllis.

"Me too." "Kate, are you ready for a visit?"

They walked back toward the room. "Listen, Kate, Sean's been through a lot these past few months and it's taken its toll. I just want to forewarn you; he doesn't look exactly like he did the last time you saw him."

"Let's go," Katie said without hesitation. "Let's go see our favorite man."

Katie pushed the door open with her quivering hand. She positioned herself to allow Phyllis to enter, but Phyllis stopped.

"Why don't you two spend some together," Phyllis said. "I need to call my sister and Sean's nephew to give them an update."

Katie was able to muster a silent okay. She turned and walked into the room and was immediately struck by its size and appearance. Except for some medical machines and equipment, it could very easily have been mistaken for a hotel suite.

"Phil, is that you?" he asked somewhat weakly. She was partially hidden by two rather large betel palms.

"No, Professor, it's me, Katie," she said as the tears she tried to hold back began flowing uncontrollably. She stepped into full view of the Professor.

"Katie, I knew you'd come." This time his voice was stronger and inviting.

Although forewarned, Katie was taken aback by the thinness of the Professor. He was sitting up in bed with a sheet pulled up to his chest. From what she could see, his face was drawn and tired, and his once thick gray hair and beard seemed sparse.

The Professor gave a reassuring grin. "Not quite the same as before, huh?" he said, aiming to soften the concern in Katie's eyes.

"You look as handsome and charming as ever," she said with a delivery that any jury would accept without question. She dispensed with the formalities and rushed over to his bed, gently wrapping her arms around his neck. He responded in kind, but she could feel his unsteady grasp. After a few moments, she pulled away so as not to tire him any further.

"Katie, child, you're as beautiful as ever. Now, stop that crying," he demanded. "I'm not dying. Besides, you're beginning to look like the Pillsbury Doughboy right around your eyes."

She laughed as she reached for the tissues on his nightstand to dry her face. She wanted to say so much, but didn't for fear of becoming weepy again. She placed the small gift on table. "I thought you might like something to read." It was a how-to book on playing cards. Although he enjoyed a spirited game of poker and rummy, he was a terrible player and a worse bettor. She recalled how in college her four-of-a-kind won her a homework-free weekend.

"Thank you." His voice changed as he spoke to her. It was sincere and serious. "Katie, it's really so wonderful to see you again. And thank you so much for coming so quickly. It's heartwarming to know that I could count on you."

"I love you, Professor."

He squeezed her hand and motioned for her to sit in the chair next to his bed. "Katie, I want so much to spend time talking to you about your work, Matt, and everything else in your life, but as you can see, time is not on my side. Until I get this hip problem taken care of, I'm afraid my energy and attention are rather limited. So, forgive me, my dear, for just focusing on the reason I asked for you to come here. I promise we'll spend more time later just catching up."

"Of course. I know you care, so please don't worry about anything but what's on your mind. Besides, I must admit, I'm anxious to finally be able to do something for you for a change."

"All right then, let me first give you some background." She smiled as he said that. He was always being teased for making a long story longer while she liked things short and sweet. She grabbed for her purse and pulled out a pad and pen and began taking notes. This was her first real opportunity to help him, and she had no intention of forgetting or overlooking any detail.

"This is a wonderful town, Katie," he began. "We seem to possess the right blend of big-city populace, diversity, and industry along with small-town charm and friendliness. Physically, the town is almost secluded, and we like it that way. We're more of a large neighborhood than an actual city."

"You seem to be describing some type of utopia, Professor," Katie interjected.

"No, no, this isn't paradise. We have our share of problems, which I'll get to in a moment, but it is a wonderful place to raise children or to retire. I enjoyed it here growing up, and I've had gratifying years here since retiring from teaching and my law practice. Anyway, there is one thing that does make this town very unique, and that's its undeniable link to the founding family. Now, don't get me wrong, this is not a Peyton Place or some dictatorial country. However, everything, and I do mean everything, in this town is in some manner connected directly or indirectly to the Keans family. Peter Keans the First settled here about eighty years ago, and his son, Keans Sr., and grandson, Keans Jr., each have put their mark on the town's growth and progress. Sadly, that tradition has recently come to a tragic end."

Katie noticed a weakening in his voice and a tiring look in his eyes.

"Professor, would you like to get some rest now and I can come back later?"

"It's all right. Please, I'd like to continue."

Selfishly, Katie was glad he wanted to go on. She was intrigued by his story and anxious to know just how she was going to fit in.

"A little over two months ago, in April, Peter Keans Jr., aged 18, died. He was the grandson of the founder and the only child of Peter and Meadow Keans. His parents have been devastated by their loss. Senior was a very active participant in this town's import/export industry and continued growth. However, since his son's death, he's been a virtual recluse, and people are worried. Not just for his own well-being, but for the well-being of the entire community."

"Ah, the black draping on the welcome sign and the black armbands," Katie muttered.

"What?" the Professor asked.

"Oh, sorry to interrupt. I just realized I've been seeing black draping and black armbands, and I now realize they were out of respect for the young boy."

"Believe me, Katie, those symbols don't even begin to show the depth of mourning and grief the people of this town are experiencing. Or the worry about the town's present and future."

"Professor, please, what is it that I can do to help?" she said almost in a begging tone. The anticipation was getting to her as she rubbed her temple.

"Just another moment more, I promise. What I've omitted thus far from this story is how the young lad died. Katie, he was murdered."

The revelation left her momentarily speechless. Earlier, she had jotted a note in the margin—a reminder to ask the Professor what illness had claimed the boy's life. It had never occurred to Katie that his death might have involved anything beyond a tragic sickness.

"There's more, Katie. There's a young woman who has been charged with his murder. In essence, a crime of passion, or to quote the prevailing belief, a lack of passion."

Katie was once again going to ask the Professor how she could help when she heard the door open and people talking. It was Nurse Cathy followed by Phyllis. Phyllis placed her hand on Katie's shoulder as the nurse gingerly picked up the Professor's wrist to check his pulse.

"I'm sorry to interrupt," she said, "but Professor Kyle has had a long day and he really needs to rest now." She handed him a pill and a cup of water. "This will help you sleep."

Katie began to rise when the Professor motioned for her to stay seated. "Just a few more minutes, I promise," he stated firmly.

"All right," Nurse Cathy said. "But I'll be back to check on you, and you'd better be sound asleep." Her words were harsh, but they were clearly said with care and affection.

"Yes, sir," the Professor snapped back as she walked away with a smile.

"Professor, I'd better go. I'll come back tomorrow morning and we can finish then."

"Yes, yes, you're probably right. There is still so much more I need to tell you, and I don't seem to have the required stamina."

Katie turned to Phyllis to inquire about local lodging.

"Absolutely not," the Professor said as he mustered what little strength he had left. "You're staying in my home. It's roomy, comfortable, and on the beach, just as you like it. I've already made arrangements with Maria and Carlos Torres; she runs the household and he takes care of the property. You should have everything you need, but if you don't, they'll see to it. Please enjoy the space—my den is open and definitely worth a visit."

Katie didn't want to intrude and looked toward Phyllis for a sign of what she should do.

"He's the boss. I haven't heard him this forceful in quite some time," Phyllis said with a smile.

"Professor, I—" Katie tried to protest, not wanting to be a bother, but he interrupted her with further orders.

"Besides," he continued, "Maria has already prepared one of your favorites, grilled chicken, mashed potatoes, and French-style string beans. I'll keep the dessert as a surprise. You can have a wonderful dinner, take a nice relaxing steam, and end the night with a cup of Earl Grey with lemon. And please feel free to roam around the house, especially my den."

His thoughtful awareness of her preferences and routines gave Katie a shiver of surprise. "Professor," she said with a smile, "it's uncanny how well you understand me. And you went to such trouble without even knowing if I'd stay. Well... I will. I'd love to accept your offer and stay in your home."

The Professor pointed to the nightstand drawer. Phyllis reached in to retrieve directions to the house as well as a spare set of keys and handed them to Katie.

"Make yourself at home, Kate. I'll be staying here tonight and the rest of the week at my sister's home in town. Here's her number if you need me. Otherwise, Maria will take great care of you."

"Katie, will you come and see me again tomorrow morning around 10? I promise to be more alert, and I promise to fill in the rest of the story. All right?" the Professor asked.

He was nearly asleep, and his words were now slow and slurred. Katie bent down and gave him a kiss on the forehead.

"I'll be here at 10 sharp," she said softly. "Now you get some rest and don't worry about me." She turned toward Phyllis and the two women embraced.

"Thank you, Kate," Phyllis said very appreciatively.

Katie turned one last time to say goodbye to the Professor. With a frail motion, he reached out, grasping her arm and drawing her close.

"Katie," he murmured, his voice thin but urgent, "I know you. And I know you need to understand why I called you here."

She leaned in, her tone had an edge of impatience. "Professor, I won't pretend—the suspense is maddening. Please, tell me. What do you need from me?"

He shifted slightly, gathering what little strength remained. Then, just before sleep overtook him, he whispered, "The young woman accused of killing the Keans boy..."

"Yes?" Katie pleaded.

"I want you to defend her."

CHAPTER 5

She sat in her car for a moment, clumsily attempting to get the keys in the ignition. "Defend her?" She was sorry she kept pressing him for an answer. She would move heaven and earth to help the Professor, but taking over a case at this time would be a huge inconvenience and imposition not only on herself, but her clients, colleagues, and family. Her law firm was flourishing, inundated with cases. How could she justify stepping away, even for a moment? Of course, she would never tell him that. Katie wasn't one to overreact, so she decided to stop the histrionics and wait until tomorrow to hear the complete story.

She finally started the car and glided effortlessly out of the parking lot into the late afternoon traffic. Left at the light, then two rights. She was on Kyle Drive and assumed it was in honor of someone in the Professor's family. As she continued, she was much more aware of the town's grief, noting endless streams of black ribbons and trim along almost every building and sign visible to the public. The barber shop and cleaners each were for sale, and she wondered if that was related to the murder or just a mere coincidence.

Over the course of her career, Katie had encountered grief in countless forms, but never had she seen an entire community bound together by sorrow. She didn't know at the time just how profound and unifying that grief truly was.

The Professor had described the town as diverse, and as she drove through its center, the array of culturally distinct eateries made that truth immediately visible. Grandpa Silverio's, in particular, caught her eye because of the distinctive green, white, and red Italian colors over its entranceway. Spanish, Chinese, Mexican, all within a few blocks of one another. She made a mental note as to their locations in case she happened to still be in town through the end of the week. As Katie made her way just outside of the hub, she drove by two blocks of very uniform, but distinctive, homes. They seemed familiar to her, with their brick façade, neatly groomed gardens with white orchids, and Madonna statues respectfully displayed on the lawn. It occurred to her that this similar landscape could be found prominently in many European neighborhoods within the Manhattan boroughs. Her in-laws had often regaled her with stories of Western Europeans immigrating to the United States as highly skilled laborers. Their hard work and commitment to their new communities was often proudly displayed through their homes and property.

This locality appeared to be of Hispanic descent as Katie recognized a bodega on the corner with the daily produce specials announced in Spanish. The area was festive and bright, with storefronts adorned with vivid, eye-catching murals. Another mental note.

She turned onto Keans Boulevard. As Katie was nearing the Professor's home, she noticed the air becoming more intense with the ocean perfume, interspersed with that same fruity aroma from the hospital parking lot. The homes in this area were fewer, more scattered, and grander in scale. They sat regally on the ocean's edge with much of their architecture obscured by the encompassing vast property and naturally high dunes. Only those fortunate enough to sink their toes into the pristine beaches could fully appreciate their grandeur.

About a mile from her last turn, Katie noticed that atop one of the homes was a flag at half-mast. As she neared, she also observed a steady stream of cars entering and exiting the side road that appeared to lead up to that home. She decided to follow suit. As she made the turn, she was astonished at what she saw. Propped carefully along the entire property wall, stretching from the boulevard to the beach, lay a seemingly endless row of flowers, notes, pictures, and gifts. It was obvious that this must be the home of the young murder victim. Another fifty yards confirmed it, as she slowly passed the two pillars framing the Keans home entranceway. Photos of the boy and more flowers adorned the marble and stone slabs. She shook her head. His death was senseless, and she was not looking forward to meeting the woman who was responsible.

Katie continued to the end of the road, made a U-turn, and proceeded back onto Keans Boulevard. After a few minutes, she finally came upon the driveway to the Professor's home. She pulled her car up the long circular driveway to the front of the house. She stepped out of the car, walked back several feet, turned around, and gazed disbelievingly at his home. "It's probably the smallest of the castles in this town, but nevertheless, it's a castle!"

A few moments later, the door opened and a robust and pleasant-looking woman raced toward Katie, embracing her as if they were dear friends. "*Hola*, Señora *Russo. Bienvenida. Un placer conocerte. Soy María.*"

Katie responded with an equal excitement. "*Hola, María. Mucho gusto en conocerte.*"

Katie's words and enunciation were convincing, so Maria

continued an animated conversation in Spanish. Katie politely interrupted, explaining that her command of the language was limited. "*Excúseme, yo hablo solamente muy poco español.*" However, just like with Matt's family, a few familiar words and some poignant hand gestures were often more than adequate to communicate the essentials. Both women laughed, grabbed a few bags, and proceeded into the house. Once inside, Katie again found herself amazed. Given her background, she was certainly no stranger to opulence, but she nevertheless was awed by the elegance and sophistication of the décor. Perhaps, even more so, by the fact that the home belonged to the Professor—someone so noted for clutter that his students often claimed that if he ever cleaned his office, they would discover the bodies of Judge Crater and Jimmy Hoffa! It was certain that Phyllis led the way, either personally or through a decorator. Regardless, the welcoming charm was pervasive.

Aware that she was tired and most likely hungry, Maria gave Katie only a brief tour of the first floor just to get her familiar with the layout. Standing in the foyer and looking directly ahead was a very impressive circular staircase, natural white oak. To its left were the kitchen, dining, and family rooms, while the rear was mostly occupied by a game room, small conservatory room, and Jacuzzi. It appeared that another large area was under construction. To the right of the stairs was the Professor's den. Although curious, Katie decided to forego inspection until after dinner; she wanted to first settle in and get a bite to eat. Maria's quarters were on the main level, and the master and guest bedrooms were on the second floor.

With the tour over, Maria motioned for Katie to follow her up the stairs and to the left. "Your room, señora," she said as she held the door open. Maria had a much better command of English than Katie had of Spanish. The guest room was large, airy, and wonderfully inviting. Katie instinctively moved over to the curtains adorning either side of the bed and pushed them apart, revealing a balcony overlooking the beach and ocean.

"Under different circumstances, this could be one magnificent vacation," she remarked.

Maria got the fireplace started as Katie unpacked her bags. "Dinner in *cinco minutos*. Do you want to eat by the fire, *si?*"

"*Sí, gracias, Maria, muchas gracias.*"

Katie freshened up and slipped on her robe. More than food, she wanted to hear Matt's voice. He answered on the first ring, somehow knowing it would be her. They didn't like being apart, but at least hearing each other's voice was reassuring. He told her about his meeting that morning with Ms. Stephanie Merlin from the Noone Group and was very hopeful that the deal would go through. If so, it would be quite a coup for his business and would mean extra money. As anxious as he was to share his news, he insisted she tell him all about her day. He was like that, always placing her first. She needed to talk and didn't leave out a moment. His support and genuine caring had a very calming effect on her. Just as she said, "I love you and I'll call tomorrow," Maria knocked on the door and entered with a tray of grilled chicken—just as the Professor had promised.

She sat by the fireplace as she savored each bite of Maria's exceptionally prepared meal. Although she was pleasantly full, she was disappointed as the last morsel disappeared. Reinvigorated by the dinner and her conversation with Matt, Katie decided she had enough energy to explore the Professor's den sooner rather than later. She stepped into her slippers and quietly descended the stairs, not wanting to disturb Maria. As she approached the den, Katie hoped it would be more reflective of the Professor's personality, at least the Professor she knew and adored. Although she loved the décor of the entire house, she had a feeling that he had acquiesced to the choices of his wife. She placed her hands on the brass knobs of the two large oak sliding doors and, with some effort, pushed them apart. The room was mostly dark, punctuated only by the moonlight sneaking through the edges of the drapes. As she stepped in, she was immediately struck by the cherry-wood aroma of an oft-smoked pipe. This conjured up memories for her of being a very small child. Her father smoked a pipe, and its lingering scent seemed to keep him near despite his frequent business trips.

She brushed her hand along the textured wall fabric searching for a possible light switch. "Ah, here it is," she muttered. "Let there be light." And with that, the inner sanctum was revealed. Much to Katie's delight, the room was exactly as she had hoped. In keeping with all the other rooms, it was large. However, it was very much a traditional and stereotypical den, worthy of any tweed wearing, pipe smoking college professor. Books, possibly hundreds, lived snuggly on rows of shelves. There was a fireplace, filing cabinets, an oak desk trimmed in brass to match the door, and, of course, the requisite leather chair, regally positioned, making it seem more like a throne. She took a few minutes exploring each facet of the room. Finally, she walked over to the chair, spun it around, and sank in its plush, leathery texture. It was as comfortable as it was beautiful. She twirled around to face the desk and observed the room from the Professor's vantage. "Impressive," was all she could say. She was just about to call it a night when she noticed a folder on the desk with her name boldly written across the top. A note was attached.

Katie,

I hope by now you've settled in and like your room accommodations. If there's anything, anything at all, that you need, please ask Maria. She's a miracle worker!

*I'm assuming by now I mentioned the reason I asked you here.
There isn't anyone I trust or respect more than you, and it is
with that in mind that I'm imposing.
I'd like your help in representing the young woman.
More to the fact, just providing her with legal guidance. My
unfortunate medical condition has prevented me from
doing so.
In this folder, I've included all the information and
documentation relevant to this case. If you're up to it
tonight, please review the materials so we can discuss in
the morning. I've set up an early afternoon appointment
for you to meet with the accused at the sheriff's department.
At this point, I'm offering no personal opinions, thoughts, or
ideas. I'd like your fresh and unbiased viewpoint.
Katie, as I've undoubtedly told you earlier today, thank you.
Have a good evening and sleep well.
Love,
Sean*

She found it interesting, even a little amusing, that the
Professor had already assumed she would be staying at his
home and would have visited the den in the evening. She
laughed to herself about how well he knew her.

Katie tucked the folder under her arm, turned off the light,
and went back up to her room. She decided to peruse the
contents by the warmth of the fireplace. Besides, she needed her
reading glasses, which were still in her briefcase. As she curled
comfortably into the oversized lounge chair, she realized Maria
had brought a tray of tea, Earl Gray. She quickly poured a cup,
carefully rested her glasses on the bridge of her nose, and
opened the folder.

She looked through the contents to see what was included:

sheriff's report, coroner's report, and a transcript of the initial statement from the young woman, a Miss Jennifer O'Neill.

She started with a summary of the sheriff's report:

- Suspect: O'Neill, Jennifer, 18 years of age, single, Caucasian charged with premeditated murder
- Victim: Keans, Peter, Junior, 18 years of age, male, Caucasian
- *Stabbed once in the heart*
- *Suspect fixated on victim*
- *Victim rebuffed advances*
- *Location of murder scene, Pals Cabin*
- *Suspect apprehended fleeing scene, northbound Highway 22*
- *Murder weapon, knife, located approximately 10 yards from Lamberts Trail*
- *Suspects fingerprints and blood on murder weapon and at murder scene*
- *Suspect interviewed, statement obtained*
- *Suspect denied counsel*
- *Suspect pleaded not guilty*

Katie continued to work her way through several more pages of the sheriff's report, pausing now and then to jot notes in the margins. When she reached the end, she removed her glasses and sat still, absorbing the weight of what she'd just read. The evidence painted a troubling picture: the accused appeared to have been fixated on the Keans boy, though he hadn't returned her feelings. Authorities believed that she had lured him to the secluded cabin, at which time things took a violent and deadly turn. There were no direct witnesses to the crime, but multiple accounts placed the two together, previously arguing.

She reviewed the coroner's report next, which confirmed

that the cause of death was a result of one stab wound, piercing the heart and lungs. The young boy had no other signs of illnesses or any indications of substance abuse.

Finally, Katie reviewed a copy of Miss O'Neill's handwritten statement:

Peter Junior told me he was addicted to drugs. I tried to help him, but he rejected any suggestions I put forth regarding clinics and medical treatment. On the day of his death, I received a call from Peter asking me to meet him at Pals Cabin, 8:00 that evening. I assumed it was to talk further about his drug problem. When I arrived at the cabin, I knocked but no one answered. The door was unlocked, so I entered and called out. Again, no response. I tried the light switch, but nothing worked. Finally, as I was about to exit, I tripped on something, which turned out to be Peter's body. I saw a phone on the table, but it wasn't working, so I raced out of the cabin with the intent of getting help. I retraced my steps, racing down Rahway Road, the same path I took initially. However, this time the bridge on the road was blocked, so I crossed over to Lamberts Trail. As I finally reached the highway, I spotted the police and frantically asked for their help. The next thing I knew, I was taken into custody for questioning.

Katie closed the folder, placing her glasses on top. She made certain all the embers were out, closed the curtains, and finally got into bed. She placed her head on the pillow, amazed that so much had happened in only one day. "This shouldn't take more than a day, possibly two at the most," she whispered to herself. She would visit the Professor in the morning, meet the sheriff at 1:00, and meet with Miss O'Neill later in the afternoon. Hopefully, if the fates were with her, she would be able to work out some type of deal with the district attorney by end of day. As far as she could tell, there wasn't one piece of evidence to corroborate Miss O'Neill's sworn statement, but perhaps she could plead it down to manslaughter.

She turned on her side and closed her eyes. *This was definitely a day with twenty-five hours,* she thought as she began a night of well-deserved deep sleep.

CHAPTER 6

The morning was glorious and so was her mood. How could one not be infatuated with the ocean's spirit or its sweet aromatic breath? Although Katie had only been in town for one day, things already seemed familiar. Taking the beach route back into town felt comfortable and relaxing. She wanted to be at the hospital by 10:00, so she left early enough to allow for any unforeseen wrong turns. She pulled into the parking lot and was surprised that the ride wasn't nearly as long as it seemed the night before. She gave the receptionist an acknowledging smile and went directly up to the Professor's room. She knocked first, opened the door gently, and peered in to assure she wasn't interrupting an exam or an intimate moment with Phyllis. The room was empty except for a surprisingly animated Professor.

"Good morning, my dear. You look well rested. I hope you were comfortable. Did Maria take care of everything?"

She gave him a warm embrace and a peck on the cheek. "I'm glad to see you looking so well rested and in good spirits. As for being comfortable, your home is incredible. Not a bad place to retire to. As for Maria, I can just about move. After last night's dinner, I swore I wouldn't eat for days. But I dismissed that thought as soon as I saw the French toast she placed before me at breakfast. Pure magic."

He laughed and squeezed her hand. Then, as if a whiff of melancholy drifted over him, he said, "Katie, it really is so wonderful to see you again, so wonderful..." He trailed off. The moment passed and he was expressive again. "Would you like to get some coffee before we start discussing the documents you reviewed last night?"

She shook her head no and grimaced at the thought of ever consuming anything again. She really was stuffed. It also hadn't escaped her attention that he didn't ask her if she had even read the material. She didn't feel it necessary or appropriate to bring it up as an issue.

"Professor, I read everything, thought about it for a while, and then read everything again. It all points to her guilt. With the data that was available to me, there doesn't seem to be one shred of evidence that would substantiate any of her assertions. Not one. The best I could come up with is a possible argument for a lesser charge of manslaughter. Perhaps she didn't go to the cabin to kill him, but to change his mind about their relationship. She could have brought the knife as means of getting his attention or maybe to end her own life."

He listened attentively, nodding occasionally. "Unfortunately, I agree. I was hoping you would see something that wasn't apparent to me."

She walked deliberately toward the window, taking a moment to feel the warm rays on her face. She wanted to ask him about his interest in this case and needed a moment to find the respectful phrasing. "Professor, I know it's a paramount concern for you that each and every individual be afforded due process. Is there an aspect of this case that you find to be in conflict?"

"Very delicately asked," he said, smiling. "And to answer your real question, no, there is no personal involvement between Miss O'Neill and myself."

She could feel her face getting red, and it wasn't due to the sunlight.

"Professor, I—"

He didn't let her finish. "Come here," he gently requested. "It's my fault for not starting from the beginning. Last summer, I was working on an article for the *Harvard Law Journal.* I needed some assistance with research and editing, and without the benefit of students at my disposal, I had to place an ad in our local paper. Miss O'Neill was one of several that responded. I knew who she was, but little more than that. So, I did some checking and discovered that her grades were impeccable, and, in fact, her IQ scores were in the genius range. It was obvious during our interview that she was extremely shy, but nevertheless, very committed and focused. I gave her a chance and, to my complete delight, she was an outstanding assistant. Her insight and perspectives proved invaluable. Funny though. We worked together for three months, and I knew as much about her at the end of that time as I did at the beginning. She gave 150% to the work, but nothing else. After the article was published, there were a few smaller projects I worked on for which she provided assistance. When this awful tragedy occurred a few months ago, somehow I just felt obligated to speak on her behalf. I only had a chance to meet with her once, here at the hospital, before this damn hip of mine became an unbearable problem. As far as I know, since then, she's had two court-appointed attorneys, neither of which were retained. From what I've been told, the consensus was to plead guilty or temporary insanity. She refused both, remaining steadfast in her claim of innocence."

He paused for a moment, motioning for a glass of water.

Katie obliged immediately. She had been listening to his story with the same awe and reverence she had in college. Regardless of how simple or sophisticated his choice of words, he had a way of presenting them in such a captivating manner.

"Professor, last night you mentioned you wanted me to defend her. How is it that you think I can actually be of help?"

He took a few more sips before continuing.

"Katie, as with most violent crimes, there are multiple victims. Unfortunately, that's also the case here. I wouldn't be overstating it by saying that every resident of Keansbury has been affected.

"Whether this town can truly recover—or even move forward—is uncertain. But I believe its only chance lies in ensuring that justice is pursued both fairly and efficiently.

"At present, the situation resembles an open wound. The only path to healing is through the legal process: a plea must be entered, and, praying it won't come to this, a trial if necessary. My concern is that this process must be handled with care. She needs legal representation that is competent, impartial, and unshaken by the intense public sentiment. If she's found guilty, it must be because the evidence supports that outcome. If she's found innocent, it should be for the same reason—not due to a procedural technicality.

"That's where you come in. I'd like you to meet with her, speak to anyone you deem relevant, and help her reach an informed decision. If the circumstances were different, this might evolve into a lengthy case—and I wouldn't have asked for your involvement so directly.

"Under the current conditions, I believe the most constructive approach is to guide her toward an honest acknowledgment of responsibility. Ideally, the district attorney's office would then consider a plea agreement. If all goes as hoped, this could be resolved within days.

"Katie, I understand I'm asking a great deal—disrupting your life, even if only for a week. But the stakes are high. And I can't think of anyone I trust more."

Katie listened in silence, absorbing the weight of his words. The town's pain, the urgency, the trust he placed in her—it all settled heavily in her chest.

She glanced away, not to avoid him, but to steady herself. The request was enormous. The responsibility, even more so. And yet, beneath the gravity of it all, something stirred—a quiet resolve. She didn't know if she could fix what was broken, but she could try. Not for the town, not even for justice, but for him.

She took only a few seconds to respond. "Professor, it would be a privilege to help any way I can."

She had a few more questions, but decided to wait until later. Some of his earlier energy was draining, and she could see he was tiring. She also knew that there had been a lot of restrained emotion behind his words. He wasn't just an attorney; he was a member of this community. He, too, was a victim.

"Professor, I'll let you get some rest. I'll do what I can today and I'll speak with you later. Is there anything you'd like before I go?" She moved the water closer, rearranged the pillows, and closed the curtains to block out the sun. His eyes were already closed. It was about noon when she exited the lobby. Her meeting wasn't until 1:00, so she decided to drive to the ocean. Hopefully, she would be able to find an area where she could sit and meditate for a while. Some personal grounding was necessary before having to encounter the cause of so much agony. She pulled out of the parking lot thinking about what the Professor had said. He wanted someone who was unbiased. How could she be unbiased? How could she not feel contempt for the person responsible for hurting him?

CHAPTER 7

The sheriff's office seemed almost sedate by comparison to the usual commotion in Manhattan police stations. A young officer quickly came to her attention and introduced herself as Deputy Sheriff Jessica Wong.

"May I help you?"

"Yes, thank you. My name is Katherine Russo and I have an appointment to speak with the sheriff and then Miss O'Neill."

"The sheriff said you would be coming in this morning. He'd like to meet you first, if you wouldn't mind."

"Not at all," Katie replied.

Katie was escorted to his office and promised he would be with her in just a moment. While waiting, she glanced around the room, mostly at the photos and awards displayed prominently on all four walls. In particular, there was a baseball team picture that was draped in black. She moved closer to read the inscription.

"That's our softball team, the Keansbury Krew. We came in third place last year. The best we've ever done."

She hadn't been aware of his presence, so she was startled by his booming voice.

"I'm Sheriff Patrick Michaels. I'm sorry, I didn't mean to make you jump. Please, have a seat."

He was a big man with gentle features and a sincere handshake. And, as she was made aware, a very strong voice. She formally introduced herself and they exchanged the customary pleasantries.

The sheriff's voice became more subdued as he again referred to the photo. "We made it all the way to the finals. That picture was taken on the day we won with a perfect game. Our pitcher was young Peter Keans."

He switched his attention from the photo to her. "Mrs. Russo, I spoke with the Professor, so I understand why you're here. I just want to make certain you understand how difficult the situation is for the people of this town."

"Perhaps for Miss O'Neill as well," she said, trying hard not to sound dismissive of his feelings. "I can appreciate what you are all going through and, as I'm certain the Professor explained, I'm only here to help facilitate the process. My intentions are to speak with her, the DA, if possible, a few other people, and then I'm done. I should be gone by the weekend. I'm not here to interfere or to cause you or anyone else any additional pain."

He seemed relieved by her comments. "Mrs. Russo, I was born and raised in Keansbury, I live here with my family, so I hope you can appreciate how protective I am of this community. As the sheriff, my responsibility was to conduct an unbiased investigation of the crime, and based on all the evidence, I arrested Miss O'Neill. I believe I did my job professionally and without prejudice. It's now up to the DA to pursue the matter."

"I appreciate your words," Katie responded. "And, if I may, I'd like to ask you a few questions."

The sheriff nodded, confident in his ability to answer any and all.

"Sheriff, the Professor provided me with a copy of your

report and it was certainly very comprehensive. I'm curious as to how the police happened to be on the highway just as Miss O'Neill was exiting the path."

"Mrs. Russo," he said, "that stretch of highway is desolate and tends to be popular among the teenage couples, so it's routinely patrolled just to keep things safe and under control."

The sheriff clarified a few more points, and Katie then ended her queries with one final question regarding the victim.

"Sheriff, Miss O'Neill's contention is that Mr. Keans stated that he was a substance abuser; however, the coroner's report proves otherwise. Did your department explore the possibility that he may have been involved with drugs in some other manner, possibly as a producer or dealer?"

It was obvious by his expression that he didn't appreciate the implication. He took a breath and then responded in a very deliberate and professional manner.

"Mrs. Russo, we did our jobs. We investigated Miss O'Neill's story thoroughly, regardless of our personal involvement with the victim. Mr. Keans was not a user, producer, or dealer of drugs. That is not my opinion, that is a fact. Now, if you don't have any more questions, I'll have Deputy Wong escort you to the interview room."

Katie knew that the conversation was over. She thanked him and started for the door, then turned. "Sheriff, just one more thing. I assume you keep some type of visitor's log. I would appreciate if I could get a copy of the names of everyone who has visited Miss O'Neill since she's been incarcerated."

"That won't be possible," he said rather abruptly.

It was obvious to him that he was trying her patience. "I'm sorry, Counselor, I didn't mean to imply that I won't give it to you, but rather that it won't be necessary. With the exception of a couple attorneys, she hasn't had any other visitors."

Katie was quietly stunned. A lifetime in Keansbury, and not a single visitor—how could that be?

"Sheriff, in the three months or so that's she's been in prison, no family or friends have been to see her?"

"No one." He opened his office door and called out to the deputy.

Katie followed Deputy Wong dutifully through a few locked doors and down a long corridor. The station seemed fairly large, and she wondered to herself just how much use it got in a town such as this.

"In here, please," the deputy said as she unlocked another door that led into a small anteroom. Here, Katie was frisked and instructed to leave her purse and jacket. Finally, one more door that led into the interview room. As she entered, the deputy continued with some rules about pressing a buzzer when she was through, but Katie wasn't paying attention. She was distracted by the slumped figure already seated at the table. The door clicked behind her, but still no movement or indication that the prisoner knew someone was there. Katie walked slowly toward the table, not wanting to startle her. She noticed her left hand was cuffed to a hook in the table.

"Miss O'Neill, my name is Katherine Russo. I'm an attorney." Still no response.

"Miss O'Neill?"

She finally turned slightly toward Katie.

"Miss O'Neill, I'm a friend of Professor Kyle. He wants to help you, but he's ill, so he asked me to speak with you in his place. Do you understand?" Several seconds passed. "Miss O'Neill, would you prefer I leave?"

She turned in her chair. "No, I'm sorry, please stay." Her voice was weak and soft, almost as if she hadn't used it for some time. She slowly lifted her head and brushed her hair to the side with her free hand, exposing a strikingly beautiful face. Her blue eyes offset by her ashen shoulder-length hair portrayed her more as a prom queen than a murderess. But Katie knew full well that killers come in all types of packaging. They weren't always the shadowy figures of nightmares or the hardened faces splashed across news reports. Sometimes they wore soft cardigans and spoke in gentle tones. Sometimes they were neighbors who waved from across the street, or quiet loners who never raised their voices. Evil didn't always announce itself with menace; more often, it slipped in quietly, disguised as ordinary.

"How is he, the Professor?"

Katie thought it was interesting that her first question was to ask about the Professor.

"He's undergoing tests and, hopefully, the doctors will know soon. Miss O'Neill, the Professor is concerned about you as well. He's concerned that you may not be fully aware of the situation you're in and the possible consequences. I know you've been through this many times already, but I'd like you to take your time and tell me your version of what happened."

They spent about an hour together, reviewing Jennifer's statement and the conflicting evidence. When they concluded, Katie spoke to her about some of her options, including manslaughter.

"I appreciate your assistance, Mrs. Russo, but as I told the other attorneys, I cannot plead guilty to something I didn't do. I didn't kill him. *I didn't.*"

"All right, Miss O'Neill," Katie said with great disappointment. She knew how rare it was for the Professor to ask her for help; not being able to convince Jennifer to accept a plea deal felt like she was failing him. "I'll be in touch with you again."

She rang the buzzer to summon the deputy. Glancing back at Jennifer, she was surprised that she felt some modicum of compassion for this seemingly tragic figure. She wondered if this was just another cold-hearted liar, or someone really lost in a mental maze of despair and disenchantment. Katie gathered her belongings and thanked Deputy Wong for her assistance. As she was leaving, the clerk handed her a phone message. It was from Assistant District Attorney Ryan asking if she would be available to meet, "if convenient." He would see her at Grandpa Silverio's restaurant at 3:00. She didn't want to pass up the opportunity to discuss some aspects of the case, so she decided to accept his offer. Checking her watch, she was glad to see that she had sufficient time to take advantage of the picture-perfect day by walking the seven blocks or so to the restaurant. The fresh crisp air and brisk strides would be invigorating for both her body and mind.

CHAPTER 8

Katie stepped outside, took a few quick cleansing breaths, and began her journey eastward. This was the first time since arriving that she'd had the chance to be part of the town. Pausing occasionally, she admired a lovely seascape painting in Gianna's Art Gallery, inhaled the aroma of freshly baked bread from Dixie Lee's Bakery, and became tempted by a pair of slingback sandals in Carly's Shoe Emporium that she absolutely didn't need. Although enjoying the walk, it wasn't lost on Katie that these and all the other establishments still bore respectful black adornments. It also didn't escape her that the faces she encountered seemed somewhat somber, their smiles somewhat forced. Not wanting to be overly paranoid, she couldn't quite shake the feeling that everyone knew who she was and why she was there. She almost felt the need to explain to them that she was only doing the Professor a favor and that she was not representing the woman who so impacted their lives. Finally arriving at her destination, she maneuvered around the green, white, and red banner prominently displayed at the entranceway. She had barely stepped inside before she was greeted warmly by a robust man proclaiming to be the owner and chef. "*Buongiorno, Signora*, I am Lorenzo. Welcome to my restaurant."

He gently grabbed her elbow, escorting her to a table decorated with a red and white checkered tablecloth and matching napkins. Within moments, a young man placed a cup of espresso before her.

"Ah," Lorenzo said, "*per favore*, please enjoy while you wait for Signor Ryan. He will be just a little late, si?"

His accent was decidedly noticeable, but it only made him more endearing, authentic, and comfortable. It almost felt as if she was among Matt's family. She knew a little Italian and enjoyed responding in kind. Lorenzo was pleasantly surprised and continued in the language, explaining how his grandfather, Silverio, had built the restaurant, and now his own grandchildren helped him cook and serve. After several minutes, he excused himself to greet another patron who had just entered. She took the free time to savor the espresso while reviewing the enticing menu.

Since arriving, Katie hadn't taken notice of the other patrons. It was only now that she realized that they were quiet and often looking her way. Their eyes quickly moved from her to the front door. The door was to her back, so she wasn't certain who had entered. As Lorenzo moved forward, he motioned something to his grandson; young Pietro smiled at her as he removed the only other chair from her table. Her questioning look was soon answered as ADA Ryan arrived, positioning his wheelchair into the empty space. He maneuvered effortlessly, suggesting a long familiarity with his means of transportation. He reached over, extending his hand as he introduced himself.

"Mrs. Russo, I'm Assistant District Attorney Mark Ryan. I was unavoidably detained, but I'm certain Lorenzo has filled the time with countless stories and an outstanding cup of espresso. District Attorney Sia Basil is currently on assignment in the neighboring county, and as the assigned prosecutor on this case, I am happy to meet with you."

They shook hands and exchanged pleasantries. Before either had a chance to say anything further, Lorenzo excitedly placed a platter of antipasti on the table. Ryan reached for some cheese and olives, but Katie seemed somewhat distracted. She was admiring his good looks and the ease and confidence with which he presented himself. He ordered a glass of house wine for them both.

"Mr. Ryan, admittedly, I'm accustomed to being somewhat skeptical of a prosecutor's motives, so I am very interested in why you asked to meet with me."

"Shoot from the hip, I like that in a person. Well, to be equally candid, I know you are a well-respected defense attorney. I know you have visited Miss O'Neill. I know Professor Kyle has asked you to look into this case. But what I don't know is what exactly are *your* motives." He had planned to be a bit more subtle, but she asked so he answered.

"Motive? I haven't any motive. As you've already mentioned, I'm here on behalf of the Professor. His only concern is that justice is carried out, fairly and swiftly, and that's a direct quote. I also think that he may feel that as a woman and an outsider, I may be able to reach out to Miss O'Neill on a different level, perhaps allowing her to be more forthcoming. And, if she's agreeable, I will help her through the trial, should it even come to that."

"Should it even come to that," he repeated. "That's exactly what this town doesn't need. I was hoping that your meeting with her this morning would have produced a mutually acceptable outcome. So, without violating any client-attorney privilege, I'm asking... Did it? Is she now willing, as you've put it, to be forthcoming?" Any glimmer of hope would have been acceptable. He wanted desperately to spare the community any more pain.

This was a somewhat uneasy situation for Katie. She had taken up the cause for the accused, yet she wished she could have had more encouraging words for the prosecution. "Mr. Ryan, Miss O'Neill's contentions remain consistent with the statements already on the record. I truly have nothing else to contribute at this point." She wasn't sure why she added *at this point.*

He was understandably disappointed, but resigned to the fact that this case would be brought before a jury. The trial date had yet to be scheduled, however, he assured Katie that with their irrefutable evidence, a guilty verdict would be swift. Normally, she would have thought him to be overconfident. However, in this instance, she knew he most likely wasn't far from the truth.

Their continued conversation was pleasant enough and varied, ranging from choice of grad school to which dessert on the menu would offer the greatest amount of chocolate. But Katie was still curious and navigated the discussion back to the town. As she dug her fork into the chocolate-covered cannoli, she asked Ryan about the Keans family, its business, and why there didn't seem to be an influx of media covering this crime.

As his details filled in the gaps, Katie had a better understanding of the community dynamics. "Mr. Ryan, you've been so generous with your time and patience. Just one more thing I'm still not clear regarding the media. Pardon my choice of words, but all the elements of this crime appear perfect fodder for the tabloids. However, I haven't seen any indication that they or even the legitimate press are present. Am I wrong?"

He sipped his coffee and went on to explain. "No, not at all. At the onset, there was a sufficient amount of coverage. After all, as you've said, this story does have all the elements for sensationalism... Prestigious family, girl from the wrong side of the tracks, unrequited love. The fourth estate looked for skeletons in everyone's closet, but none were to be found. Interest soon waned. The consensus was that it was just another lonely, disillusioned, and very misguided young woman exacting vengeance when spurned. Admittedly, we all worked hard to keep this as low-key as possible, for everyone's sake. The act itself was unfathomable, and the last thing we needed was to be put under a microscope of ridicule." He took another sip and continued. "Look, Mrs. Russo, I still have the hope and belief that the quicker this is all over, the better chance there is for this town to heal."

"I'm getting the impression from you, the Professor, and the sheriff that there is a possibility that Keansbury may not survive this. Of course it's devastating, but—"

He responded before she could finish her question. "Aside from the obvious name connection, this town exists because of the Keans import/export business. It ceases, we cease. And, right now, no one is certain of its future. Mr. Keans Sr. is the owner and operator; essentially its heart and soul. Since the death of his son, I don't think he's been to the office more than one or two times. His right-hand man, Aaron VanAnt, has managed to keep things afloat. But make no mistake, the business is suffering, and so are we."

"And the boys' mother, Mrs. Keans. How is she dealing with all of this?" Katie asked.

"She's not. I've tried to see her several times, but she's been virtually bedridden with grief. Mrs. Russo, the entire Keans family has been a lifeforce here, not just in terms of business, but with their presence, their participation, their vivacity. That's gone. The question now is what remains."

Ryan took a breath. He could feel his face red with passion, realizing he hadn't spoken so easily and emotionally to anyone about all of this. Katie was an excellent orator, but she was also an excellent listener. "I'm sorry," he said, "I didn't mean to go on like that." He seemed a little embarrassed.

"Please don't apologize. Your feelings and passion are perfectly understandable." She was going to offer more, but the sound of his beeper concluded any further discussion.

"Ah, sorry, Mrs. Russo, but duty calls." He really was sorry to leave. A formidable colleague and a beautiful woman, a combination that was easy to enjoy. He pushed himself away from the table and motioned to Lorenzo to put the meal on his tab. He extended his hand. "It was a pleasure meeting you, Mrs. Russo. I hope we'll see each other again before you leave."

"It was my pleasure, Mr. Ryan, and thank you for the delicious bites." With that, he turned his wheelchair toward the door. As he started maneuvering forward, she called to him. "Mr. Ryan, the evidence against Miss O'Neill... Everything appears so overwhelming. Neatly packaged. You know what they say, if it looks too good to be true..."

He stopped and turned his head to her, glad for the opportunity for one more exchange. "I can understand your perspective as a defense attorney, but, Mrs. Russo, it's neatly packaged because it's the truth. However rationalized, the undeniable truth is that she ended that young man's life." He turned, gripped both wheels, and moved forward. She couldn't see his face, but with a grin he shouted back to her. "Besides, you know what they say, never look a gift horse in the mouth." And with that, he left.

Touche, she thought, and wondered just how formidable of an opponent he would be in the courtroom. She muttered to herself, "I guess I'll never know."

CHAPTER 9

She started back to the police station to retrieve her car. Avoiding redundancy, she crossed to the other side of the street, curious about the quaint-looking shops. Midway, Katie noticed the library prominently poised on the side street. She glanced, continued walking, then paused. It occurred to her that she had read a statement from the head librarian claiming to have overheard a lover's quarrel between Jennifer and the victim. A brief visit wouldn't take too much time. So, she spun around and made a right toward the library. Reminiscent of the New York Public Library, two scaled-down statues of lions stood guard at the entranceway to the three-story building. Walking inside the lobby, Katie noticed the dozen or so meticulously positioned signs detailing library rules and directions. One arrow pointed straight ahead to the first-floor help desk.

"Good afternoon, my name is Mrs. Gleaton. Welcome to the Keansbury Public Library. How may I help you?" She wore a smart blue jacket emblazoned with the library seal and, Katie observed, a black armband.

Katie thanked her for her help and, with the information at hand, she climbed the twenty or so steps to the second floor.

Straight ahead, another information desk, but this one was larger and more ornate, clearly befitting a person of authority. She stepped to the front of the desk and a prominently displayed nameplate signaled she was in the right place. *Mr. Ernest Adams.* Not being at his station, Katie glanced around, but didn't catch sight of him. Or anyone else, for that matter. The floor seemed deserted; tables were empty and book stacks neatly untouched. She waited a few more minutes, then decided to just try again in the morning. As she turned toward the stairs, she gasped, letting out a small scream as she literally crashed into someone. The sound of her voice and an armful of books hitting the floor echoed throughout.

"Excuse me, I'm so sorry," she stammered as she bent to collect the works of Agatha Christie scattered about her feet.

"Good afternoon, my name is Ernest Adams. Welcome to Keansbury Public Library. How may I help you?" He made no acknowledgement of their close encounter.

As she placed the last book on the desktop, she noted that his greeting and jacket were identical to that of the young woman on the first floor. *"He must run a tight ship,"* she thought. Managing to lower her heart rate and gain some composure, she introduced herself. "My name is Katherine Russo and I'm an attorney and a close friend of Professor Kyle." His perceived formality prompted her to use her given name, something she rarely did.

"Ah, how is the Professor fairing? I do hope he is mending properly. Please offer him my regards."

She nodded and continued. "He is getting the best care possible. Mr. Adams, despite his condition, the Professor had been trying to look into the unfortunate death of young Mr. Keans. As he is now physically unable to continue, has asked me for assistance." Katie was purposefully vague, not wanting him to feel challenged. "On his behalf, I was hoping I could ask you a few questions about your statement to the sheriff. I know the Professor would appreciate it."

His demeanor softened somewhat. "All right," he offered. "But I don't have much time. At precisely 4:45, I will be conducting our daily staff meeting."

"Tight ship." With that, Katie asked and he answered. They reviewed where the couple had been seated in proximity to his desk and precisely what he had heard and observed. Mr. Adams' recall of the events was nearly verbatim with his initial statement given several months prior.

"I saw and heard them argue," he explained matter-of-factly. "Then young Keans walked away, she begged him for another chance, he said no and left."

It was obvious Mr. Adams was a very detailed, regimented, prideful man. But he was also elderly, late seventies most likely, and she couldn't help but wonder if his adherence to his story was based on fact or his need to maintain the perception of competency.

It was 4:40, and Katie was politely dismissed. She thanked him and assured that his best wishes would be relayed to the Professor. Once again back on the street and heading to her car, she replayed their conversation. *"Even if his hearing isn't impaired,"* she thought, *"he still would not have been able to accurately hear their full conversation, not given the distance between their table and his desk."* This time, she uttered her thoughts aloud. "As for them arguing loudly, he would never have allowed that. Not in his library."

She finally reached her car, turned, and took one quick look back at the library. "Not in his library." With a deep sigh, she left town.

It was early evening when Katie finished the last of her phone calls. Her plan to stop and see the Professor had changed when Phyllis informed her that he was too exhausted from the "endless stream of well-intentioned visitors." The unexpected free time gave her the opportunity to speak with her partners, her mother-in-law, and, most certainly, Matt, saving his call for last.

Katie was still pleasantly full from the appetizers she had consumed and decided to forego dinner, although convincing Maria not to cook did challenge her persuasion skills. Still feeling surprisingly energetic, she threw on a pair of sweats and opted for a walk on the beach. The sun still lingered in the evening sky, leaving ample time for a pleasant stroll. A handful of people dotted the shore, but it was far less crowded than usual. With a sandal dangling from each hand, she playfully waded at the water's edge, conscious of the sensation of being both invigorated and calmed at the same time. Her thoughts turned to Matt, wishing he was with her now, hand in hand; wishing she had the same conviction and confidence as he did in her ability to be a good mother. A splash of water jolted her back to the here and now.

"Sorry," a teenage boy apologized as he went to rescue his football. "He threw it over my head."

Katie scooped it up and threw a perfect spiral to the boy's friend several yards away.

"Hey, good arm, lady," the young boy screamed in amazement.

She laughed and turned back toward the house. *"That's what young people should be doing,"* she thought. *"Playing and having fun, not being murdered or locked up in prison awaiting a death sentence."* Her pace quickened as she looked at her watch. She dusted off the sand and slipped on her sandals, quickly returning to the house.

"I'm back, Maria," she shouted as she reached for the phone. "Deputy Wong, this is Katie Russo, we met earlier this morning. I was wondering if I may ask a favor of you."

CHAPTER 10

Within minutes, Katie was back on the road. Her thoughts stirred with emotion—chief among them, a fierce determination to help the Professor in any way she could. Despite knowing the odds were very slim that Jennifer would revise her account, Katie felt compelled to try again. Perhaps it was loyalty to the Professor. Or perhaps something in Jennifer's story had resonated with her in a way she hadn't expected. Either way, Katie had promised her another visit before leaving.

Before she knew it, she pulled into the same parking space as that morning.

As she started to enter the sheriff's office, she took a quick glance up and down the street. It was void of any traffic or people. It seemed quiet. "*Eerily quiet*,", she thought.

"Thank you again, Deputy Wong. I know it's late and after visiting hours, so I really do appreciate this."

"No problem. I was working late anyway. I have about another 45 minutes of work to catch up on. Deputy Theo will be coming on duty then, but you'll need to leave when I do. I'll come by when I'm ready."

"Certainly," Katie said as she once again followed her down the hallway.

Jennifer was seated at the table, but unlike the morning, she responded immediately to Katie's presence. By the look in her eyes, it was obvious she was anticipating some good news.

"Thank you for seeing me, Miss O'Neill. I hope you don't mind me visiting so late."

"I'm always up at night reading. Between school and my two jobs, the night was the only time I had to read. Just a habit, I suppose..." Her voice trailed off, bereft of any further social interaction.

"Miss O'Neill, since this morning, I had the opportunity to speak to the assistant district attorney and even had a brief conversation with Mr. Adams at the library. Is there anything you can think of that you may not have mentioned to me earlier?"

Jennifer knew that the question meant no good news would be forthcoming. She shook her head no as she lowered it to avoid further eye contact with Katie.

"I'm sorry, Miss O'Neill. There is probably some evidence that could be challenged, but thus far, there is still so much critical evidence that just doesn't support anything you've said. I want to help you, but you must be truthful with me."

"*I have been.*"

Katie was startled by the force with which she uttered those words.

"I have been." This time she said it softer, embarrassed by her outburst. Sitting tall, she continued speaking, as if it were her last opportunity.

"One day, one fateful day, I was studying in the library. I was seated at the corner table, that's where I always sit. I heard someone say something, but I didn't look up. After all, no one would be speaking to me. Then I heard the chair opposite me move, and I did look up. It was Peter Keans Junior. He apologized for disturbing me, introduced himself, and then proceeded to sit. I was flustered, as if he needed to identify himself, and I didn't say a word."

Jennifer paused, looking directly at Katie, then continued. "In case you haven't noticed, my social skills are rather lacking," she said in a self-deprecating manner. "I can recite every volume of Shakespeare in old English, I can even calculate complex trig equations in seconds, but I can't manage to put two simple words together in a conversation."

She took a deep breath and continued. "He made some small talk about classes and then his demeanor changed. He became serious. He said he'd always admired me. Of course, I thought he was being facetious. But he said it again. He said that despite my uncle and other hardships I've had to face, that I always worked hard and never seemed to give up. He wanted to know how I managed to have such strength."

Not wanting to interrupt Jennifer's train of thought, Katie carefully removed a pad and jotted down some notes...*uncle, hardships*. Jennifer hadn't mentioned these prior.

"I mustered up some courage and asked if anything was wrong, if he needed some help. He smiled and said he just wished he had the courage that I had. I didn't know what he was talking about. So, I asked him again if there was something I could do to help. He seemed so lost, so sad. He told me it was too late, that I couldn't help him, no one could help him now. I'm not sure why I went on, but I said I could help if it involved schoolwork. He just shook his head. I mentioned gambling, alcohol, and then drugs. That's when he became visibly upset. So, I told him that if it was drug-related there were many treatments available, private, and confidential, and no one would need to know. He thanked me as he stood up. 'It's too late for me," he said. "The addiction has already taken hold, it's in my blood.'" He smiled and walked away.

"Two days later, I saw him again with some of his friends in the library. My concern for helping him must have overtaken my nervousness, because I stood and loudly called out his name. Mr. Adams motioned me to be quiet. Peter came over to my table. Before he could say anything, I showed him the brochures and information I had gathered on various drug rehabilitation clinics. He looked at me so solemnly and said it was too late for him. With that, he turned and walked away. I yelled to him to wait, to please give me another chance. I had more information I wanted to share with him. But he never looked back. I could see that my yelling upset Mr. Adams. He rushed toward me and told me to either be quiet or leave the library. I sat down again and returned to my studies, but I couldn't concentrate. I felt like I had let Peter down. There was so much help available, but he seemed to have lost hope. I didn't realize it then, but that was the last time I would see him alive."

Katie continued to take notes, but never interrupted. She had heard Jennifer's story earlier that morning, but not with the same specificity and certainly not with the same emotion. Something had shifted—her spine straighter, her voice steadier, her eyes locked on Katie's with a determination that hadn't been there previously.

Jennifer sighed, collected herself, and continued. "On that fateful day, my phone rang and it was Peter. He said he needed my help and to meet him at Pals Cabin at 8 that night. Tell no one. And then he hung up. I was surprised by the call, but somewhat relieved that he was open to receiving support. I remember looking at my watch and it was exactly 5:45. I was home and I had been working on a report for the Professor that I wanted to complete before leaving. The next time I checked my watch, it was 7:30, later than anticipated. I quickly grabbed my sweater and house key. Just as I was leaving, I realized that earlier I had discarded the drug literature. Not wanting to keep Peter waiting, I decided I would obtain additional materials the next day. I locked the door and left. I headed west along Main Street. A full moon provided sufficient lighting for my twenty-five-minute walk. When I got to the base of the patch leading to the cabin, I took the shortcut up the hill. Rahway Road. It's a bit rocky, but years of use has made it passable. I crossed over the small bridge, pushed through some overgrown shrubbery, and made my way to the cabin. The moonlight provided enough brightness for me to see a car and the outline of the cabin, but no light was visible inside. I called out Peter's name, but there wasn't any response. I moved to the front door, knocked, and called out his name again. As I hit the door, it pushed opened. I took one step in and instinctively ran my hand against the side wall, looking for a light switch. I recall finding the switch and nervously flicking it up and down, but no light came on. I took another step or two inside and then remained motionless for a few moments, not sure what to do. It was still and musty, but I could smell the cherry-like aroma from the Sirenacus plants. Quickly looking around the room, I noticed a stream of moonlight peering through the window on the far-right wall. I walked tentatively toward the light and noticed something on the floor near the table. As I moved closer, I could make out a shoe, then a leg, and then it finally registered I was looking at a man, probably Peter. I quickly knelt beside him and, to my horror, it *was* Peter. My heart was pounding as I touched his face. It was cold. I checked his wrist, but no pulse. All I could think of was that he had overdosed. I saw a telephone on the table, but it was out of order, so I stood up, raced out the door, and started back down the path."

Jennifer paused to take a sip of water, her hand shaking

slightly. Katie didn't speak. She simply waited, her silence a gentle invitation for Jennifer to continue when she was ready.

"I needed to get help, the police and an ambulance. I think I stumbled a few times, but I felt nothing. At that point, I was numb. As I approached the bridge on Rahway Road, I could see that there was something blocking its access. I think a large tree branch had fallen since I crossed just a short time earlier. I was frantic and didn't want to chance trying to move or climb over the object, so I retraced my steps toward the cabin and then proceeded down Lamberts Trail. This path is somewhat longer and it exits away from the town. But it's wider and easier to negotiate, particularly at night. I don't know how much time passed, but I finally reached the highway. I saw the taillights of a car traveling northbound, away from town. I remember flailing my arms and screaming for help, but apparently no one noticed. I was exhausted and out of breath from running. As I looked up and down the highway, I saw headlights approaching and within seconds the car pulled over. To my relief, I saw the sheriff's insignia on the door. At that point, my legs gave out and Deputy Wong grabbed me as I started to collapse and repeatedly asked me where I was hurt. I wasn't, I told her, it was Peter. She helped me into her car and we drove up to the cabin. I remained in the back seat as she entered the cabin. I saw the cabin light go on as she disappeared into the room. Moments later, she rushed out and radioed for assistance. Before long, the ambulance and other officers arrived."

Jennifer stopped again to catch her breath. Katie didn't need to ask—she could see that she wasn't just telling the story; she was feeling every moment of it, all over again.

"The next thing I realized, I was being escorted to the hospital. In all the commotion, I hadn't noticed my hands, knees, and clothing were stained with blood. They treated my cuts and gave me a sedative, which was a welcome relief. I think

I passed out for a short time, and when I awoke, Sheriff Michaels was in the room, very eager to speak with me. He confirmed that Peter was dead and he wanted to know what happened. I told him exactly what I'm telling you now. When he was finished, he said I could go home, but I was to remain there until his office concluded their investigation. One of the deputies drove me home and I spent the next day or so mostly sleeping. The next time I heard from the sheriff was when he came to my apartment to inform me that I was being charged with the death of Peter Keans Jr. I was brought here and read my rights, at which time, I foolishly declined the presence of an attorney. In my naiveté, I believed that I would reiterate my story and be released shortly thereafter. However, I was informed that the evidence did not coincide with my version of the events. Consequently, I was formally charged with murder, denied bail, and imprisoned for something I didn't do. Despite the attempts of two attorneys, the district attorney's office, and some overly anxious law enforcement officials, I have not and will not alter one word of what I told you."

And with that proclamation, she was finished.

"Miss O'Neill, you've mentioned several details that you hadn't mentioned earlier when we first met. I'm curious as to the omission."

"I'm...I'm sorry, I wasn't being evasive," Jennifer said apologetically. "I suppose I was just a bit worn out."

"It's okay, I can certainly understand."

Katie looked at her watch, having been unaware of how much time passed. *"If nothing else, her story was certainly engrossing,"* she thought. "Miss O'Neill, I've only had a day to make inquiries, on an unofficial basis, regarding your situation. And, everything that I've learned thus far differs dramatically from what you've had to say. The prevailing belief is that you were in love with the young Keans, but he was not with you.

You somehow lured him up to the cabin and committed murder."

"It's not true," Jennifer said, shaking her head. "It's not true."

Katie continued. "Then help me understand the evidence, Miss O'Neill. You claim that Mr. Keans was an admitted addict, yet the coroner's report indicates that he was not then or ever a drug abuser. There's no evidence that he was even connected in any way with drugs. What would be his motive for telling you such a lie?"

Katie paused to give Jennifer a moment to digest what she was saying.

"Regarding the night in question, you stated that the telephone was inoperative. However, Deputy Wong later confirmed it was functioning properly. You also claimed the cabin light was out, though you said you could see by the moonlight. Yet when officers inspected the room that same evening, the light was operational and the window shades were drawn—blocking any potential moonlight."

Jennifer was becoming agitated, but Katie knew she had to continue. "You say you took the alternate path because of the blockage at the bridge. Again, officers found the crossing to be accessible; no evidence of any fallen tree or debris. They contend that you took the alternate path because it led away from town. When they spotted you, you were running away, not looking for help. The deputy also noted that your hands and clothes were blood-soaked. Analysis indicated that it wasn't your blood, but that of Mr. Keans. And finally, the most damaging evidence of all: approximately ten yards from the path you took, the murder weapon was found. A knife, your kitchen knife, with your fingerprints and Mr. Keans' blood. Miss O'Neill, can you provide any plausible response to the evidence mounted against you?"

Jennifer exhaled and shook her head. "Mrs. Russo, I've gone

over this countless times. I honestly don't know what to say anymore—I have no logical reason why my statements appear unsubstantiated."

"Please, Miss O'Neill, I'm trying to help you. The district attorney's office is still willing to consider a lesser charge of manslaughter. You didn't intend on killing him; perhaps you did so in the heat of an argument?"

The knock on the door startled Katie. It was Deputy Wong informing her that she would be leaving in five minutes. Katie nodded and gathered her notes.

"Miss O'Neill, I'll see to it that you are provided with a competent attorney for the trial. I'll inform the Professor. I wish you well."

As Katie reached for the door, she heard the sound of a chair scraping against the floor. Turning, she saw Jennifer standing, her wrist still connected to the table.

"When the sheriff first told me to stay at home while he investigated, I wasn't worried. Surely, he would identify Peter's killer. Then, when I was brought here and accused of the crime, I was concerned, but still certain I would be exonerated. The days turned to weeks turned to months. Now, I'm awaiting my trial to begin, a trial that I've been told time and again, will render a verdict of guilty. If I'm fortunate, my sentence will be life imprisonment. Mrs. Russo, I'm *terrified*. I can't fathom any explanation as to why my truth has no substantiation. And, as frightened and terrified as I am, I'm holding onto the truth. It's all I have."

Jennifer instinctively started to move toward Katie, but was pulled back by the handcuff. She gripped the table with her free hand to steady herself. Gaining her composure, she stood as tall as possible, head up and eyes fixed on Katie.

"Mrs. Russo, in my entire life, everything I've ever had, I've earned. I've neither asked for any help nor has any help ever been given. This situation I'm in is beyond my control. I don't know what happened or why it happened. The only thing I know for certain is that I need help. Your help. Please, help me. If anyone can uncover the truth, you can. Please." With that, Jennifer sat down, assuming a defeated posture.

Katie said nothing. She had the sensation of being a juror, listening to the impassioned plea of a defense attorney. She closed the door behind her and left the building with Deputy Wong.

CHAPTER 11

"Mrs. Russo, good morning. It's nice to see you again."

"Doctor Christian, it's nice to see you too." She extended her hand as she rose to greet him.

"You looked a little lost in thought. I'm sorry, I didn't mean to interrupt."

"Oh no, not at all." Their meeting this time was much more cordial than the first. "I'm waiting to see the Professor. He has a few visitors, so I thought I'd give them some privacy. I've been going over all the things I need to do and I'm afraid my mind got a bit overloaded."

"I can relate to that," he said with a laugh. "I just came to the lounge to grab a cup of coffee. May I get you a refill?"

She nodded. "Doctor, I spoke with Phyllis this morning and she brought me up to date on the Professor's status. I inappropriately expressed my concern to you the first time we met; however, I'm afraid my trepidation has not abated."

He spun around the chair closest to her and sat, leaning forward as if casually engaging a dear friend. Realizing that his gesture was too revealing, he quickly conformed to a more professional posture. There was no denying he was attracted to her.

"The Professor has advised me that I may speak freely to you. His condition requires hip surgery, but we first must ensure his overall physical condition is stable. Right now, we are trying to get his diabetes and high blood pressure in check. Once that is taken care of, we can move forward with the surgery. It's taking much longer than I'd like, but he is progressing, and I am nevertheless optimistic about his prognosis."

She seemed to find some modicum of comfort in his words. "Thank you for your candidness." She reached into her purse to retrieve a business card and placed it in his hand. "I think by now you can tell that when it comes to the Professor, I'm pretty much Jello."

He smiled at the thought.

"Attempts at being cool, calm, and collected dissolve fairly quickly. All I want is for him to be healthy. If there's anything I can do to help facilitate that process, I would appreciate if you would contact me directly."

He placed the card in his pocket. "They're very fortunate to count you as a dear friend." He glanced at his watch and apologized for having to leave. As he placed the chair back to its original spot, she took the brief opportunity to ask him an unrelated question.

"Doctor Christian, as you may know, on behalf of the Professor, I've made a few inquiries regarding the death of Mr. Keans Jr. I was wondering if you were on duty the day he was brought to this hospital?"

"As a matter of fact, I was. All available doctors were rushed to the emergency room, but unfortunately, he was already dead on arrival. From what I understand, a very tragic situation. I'm sorry, I really must run. I hope to see you again."

Katie smiled as he turned and left. The Professor's visitors finally departed, but when Katie went into his room, she found him napping. Not wanting to be a disturbance, she returned to the lounge and spent the next hour or so speaking with her office. Phyllis arrived just as Katie finished her conversation. They waited together until the familiar aroma of lunch caught their attention. It was important to build up his strength, so Phyllis confiscated his tray from the young dawdling aide and brought it to his room. Ever so gently, she nudged him until he woke. She propped his pillows, positioned his tray, cut his food, and held his fingers as she guided each forkful. It was heartwarming to witness the subtle exchange of tenderness between the two of them. When he was finished eating, he motioned Katie to sit closer.

"Sorry, my dear, I didn't mean to ignore you, but my *caregiver* won't let anyone interrupt my daily ingestion of nutritional nourishment." He laughed as he spoke and Phyllis playfully slapped his shoulder. She bent down to give him a kiss on the forehead, then left with the dirty trays.

He turned his full attention to Katie, and a serious tone came to his voice. "I know you well enough to know you've worked hard these past two days, and I do appreciate it, Katie. So, tell me what you've learned."

She spent the next hour detailing her conversations and impressions. He interjected a few questions, but mostly just listened intently. Phyllis had returned midway through their discussion, bringing Katie yet another cup of coffee. She politely took a sip, then set the cup on the bedside table. The discussion was stimulating enough; more caffeine was definitely not what she needed.

"Professor, now that I've spent some time with Jennifer, she strikes me as deeply quiet—withdrawn, almost fragile. There's a kind of solitude that clings to her, and while that may be understandable given her history, I can't shake the feeling that there's more beneath the surface. There's something in her eyes —guarded, yes, but also haunted. I'd like to know more about her."

"Well, Katie, from what I know, her parents died in a car accident when she was just a child. Custody fell to her aunt and uncle—reclusive types, not much for community. The aunt seemed pleasant enough, but the uncle was notoriously difficult. The wife smoked heavily and eventually succumbed to lung disease, and after her death, the uncle grew increasingly volatile —drinking too much, arguing with anyone who crossed him. I've heard he kept Jennifer on a short leash: school, work, and little else. No friends, no outings. Some teachers tried to step in, but he wouldn't budge. After he passed, Jennifer kept to her routine—school and work, nothing more. She's been helping me recently, and when I asked about her future, all she said was that she wants to go to college. That's the extent of what she'll share. Around town, people label her as antisocial, even a bit odd, but if you ask me, I don't think she's ever been shown another way to be."

"That saddens me, Professor, but perhaps it does give credence to her inability to deal with the young boy's rejection. Given this information, I'm even more disappointed that I wasn't able to secure the outcome you hoped for."

He grabbed her hand. "Oh, Katie, you sound as if you let me down. I wanted to spare this town any further agony, but more importantly, I wanted to make certain that Jennifer had every opportunity to be heard. Heard by someone who I could trust to be objective and unbiased. I know, with all my heart, you are that person."

She was relieved. "I made some calls last night and a good friend of mine agreed to take on Jennifer's case, pro bono. He's a very strong attorney and a very compassionate man. I think he would be a good fit. If you think it's appropriate, I'll have him come up here to meet with her." Given the obvious circumstances of the case, Katie didn't feel it necessary to spend any additional time in Keansbury. She waited for the Professor's response, hoping he'd understand her anxiousness to return to her practice. He seemed reluctant.

"I wish it were you. I'm not necessarily comfortable with another attorney, however, Jennifer will need to have the final say. I suppose it's time for me to step back and let the system operate as it should." He didn't sound convinced. "Everyone has done their best to bring this to a swift, but just, conclusion. Regrettably, it will take longer than hoped, but we all must accept that."

He continued to hold her hand as he intentionally focused the conversation on what was going on in Katie's life. She purposefully kept the discussion superficial, talking mostly about her upcoming cases and Matt's burgeoning business. Although he had the capacity to listen like a priest, therapist, and best friend all rolled into one, this was not the time to burden him with the uncertainties she was feeling regarding motherhood. After a half-hour, she sensed his increasing tiredness. She kissed him goodbye and walked arm in arm with Phyllis to the elevator.

"I'm sorry of the circumstances, but it has been so good to see you again, Kate. I know it means a lot to him to know he can count on you. He's missed you and Matt."

"Oh, and we've missed both of you as well. I promise we'll be better at visiting. I'd like to stop by in the morning before I leave for home. Would that be all right?"

Phyllis gave Katie a warm embrace. "Of course, dear. Your visits do him a world of good."

Katie entered the elevator and gave a small wave as the doors closed. She glanced at her watch, not at all aware of the time. It was nearly 3 in the afternoon. The effects of the caffeine had yet to wear off, so she decided to expend that energy by doing some exploring before dinner. She needed to do something to shake the image in her mind. Not of the Professor, but of Jennifer. "If anyone could uncover the truth..." She wasn't aware that she was mumbling as she left the lobby. "I'm a damn good attorney, not a magician. There is no defense."

CHAPTER 12

The mid-afternoon sun and warmth were a welcome tonic. Katie instinctively drove toward the beach, slowly inhaling and exhaling the lingering salt air. As she approached the end of the road, she decided to head south, away from the Professor's home. The houses in this section of town were moderately sized and well kept, although there were signs of battle scars undoubtedly from the ocean's wrath. At first, the structures were clustered together, but the farther south she drove, they became fewer and farther between. Katie noticed the road itself appeared wider than its northern counterpart and was punctuated by dozens of filled-in potholes. As the area became more desolate, she decided she would return to town and do some shopping. A bend in the road lay just ahead. She would follow it to the other side and make a U-turn there. As she navigated the tip on the bend, she was taken aback by what she saw before her. A large sign signaled the gateway to *KEANSBURY INDUSTRIES*. It occurred to her that she had been so busy with the Professor, she hadn't given any thought to the Keans' business to which everyone had spoken so highly. And here it was!

Katie pulled the car to the side of the road and stepped out to get a better look. Buildings, one small ship, equipment. Although it had the appearance of a much scaled-down version of the Port of New York, she knew she was gazing at the very heart and soul of the community. *"Welcome to Oz,"* she thought. Sandwiched between the ocean and dunes, under different circumstances, it could seemingly double as a fortress. The entranceway was secured by a guard booth and a large barbed-wire fence. There appeared to be some activity on the property, but it occurred to Katie that it was more akin to a ghost town than a thriving international port.

Her curiosity warranted a closer inspection. Stepping back into her car, she drove toward the black-draped guard booth, stopped as indicated, but was surprised that it seemed to be left unattended. After impatiently waiting several minutes, she proceeded through the gate and private property sign and opted to take a self-guided tour. She moved slowly, passing the offices, warehouse, and loading dock. Here, she noted several young men skillfully maneuvering a forklift of pallets from a shipping container to the awaiting flatbed truck. A few of the men spotted her and smiled, but seemed unconcerned by her presence. From behind one of the crates appeared a larger man in a suit and hardhat. He walked over to the forklift operator, said something in Spanish, then turned his attention toward her. He waved, although Katie interpreted it more as a signal rather than a friendly greeting. She put the car in park and let down the window.

"Miss, I don't see an entrance pass on your windshield and this is private property. What's your business here?" As he drew near, she noticed the meticulous grooming, the tailored suit that suggested luxury, and the gleam of a silk tie. He exuded sophistication—yet there was something about him that remained quietly formidable, perhaps even a bit intimidating.

"I stopped at the guard station, but no one was there. My name is Katherine Russo and I—"

He interrupted, not letting her finish her sentence. "Ah, you're the friend of our Professor. I'm sorry to be so abrupt. We've had someone from the press snooping around and a few curiosity seekers, and I'm afraid I mistook you for one. My name is Aaron VanAnt. I'm Mr. Keans' partner."

She was relieved to have this imposing figure on her side. Katie turned off the ignition and stepped out of the car. She extended her hand and noticed how it seemed lost in his.

"I'm the one who's sorry. I didn't mean to cause you any concern. I can certainly understand your reaction."

"Nonsense. In fact, if you have some time, Mrs. Russo, I would be happy to show you around." She nodded in agreement. He gently put his hand on her elbow, guiding her toward the office building. "Why don't we start here. And how is our Professor doing today? He's such a lovely man..."

They walked for about a half-hour and he talked nearly the entire time, apparently enjoying a willing audience. Katie found him fascinating. His gentle demeanor contrasted with his large appearance; *a gentle giant,* she thought. The tour ended with a return to the office. He brought her to the all-but-empty cafeteria for a late afternoon cup of coffee. A few men were finishing their meals and stopped by the table to pay their respects. Although speaking Spanish, Katie understood enough to know they wished them both a good afternoon.

"Mr. VanAnt, the Professor tells me that your family has also been in this town for a couple of generations."

"Yes," he responded, "almost as long as the Keans family. Our families have been close for many years. In fact, Senior and I were childhood friends. It was so natural that we would become business associates."

"I don't wish to be insensitive, but would you mind if I asked you a few questions about Peter Jr.?" Her tone was intentionally calm and comforting.

He nodded and sighed; it was apparently difficult.

"What was his role here at the port?"

"He was, rightfully so, being groomed to take over one day. He worked in the yard and handled all the paperwork relating to the imports and exports. He was scheduled to one day start working on internal operations such as payroll, customer service, and things like that."

Katie didn't want to pry, but she was curious and didn't want to miss the opportunity to learn more about the Keans. "He sounds like a wonderful young man, and I do want to express my sincere sympathy over this town's loss."

He nodded, unable to speak. He took a sip of coffee and regained his composure. "Losing Junior was like losing my own son. My wife and I have been devastated by his death, especially the senseless way it occurred. As hard as it has been for us, you can well imagine the state his parents are in. Unbelievably tragic." His face was getting red, his anger clearly showing.

"Mr. VanAnt, as you may know, the Professor asked me to speak with Miss O'Neill. I did so only to be of help." She made certain her tone continued calm and reassuring, not wanting to give the misimpression that she was speaking as a defense attorney. "Miss O'Neill is unwavering in her claim of innocence."

He was quick to respond, the red deepening in color. "I'm not surprised by anything she says. She's always been a strange girl. Her uncle was strange. I guess it was just in the genes. However, that's not an excuse. Mrs. Russo, as far as myself and this community are concerned, she killed him. Whether by accident or intentional, she *killed* him. The sooner she's removed from here, the better. We have enough to deal with without her presence being a constant painful reminder."

He tried to take another sip of coffee, but his shaking hand made him unsteady. A small amount poured onto the table. Katie grabbed a few napkins to blot up the puddle. She worried that she may have pushed him too far, but as concerned as she felt for him, she was compelled to continue the discussion.

"I can only imagine the pressure you've been under. The Professor mentioned that Mr. Keans Sr. has had virtually no involvement with the business since his son's death."

He paused a moment, then looked directly at Katie. "One does what one needs to do to survive. I have a responsibility to our customers, our workers, our community, and our families. A lot of people have been affected by this tragedy, and I'll do everything and anything it takes to see that this business continues."

Katie felt a chill up her spine. His words almost sounded like a threat. Perhaps he wasn't quite the gentle giant she had thought. It was clear that the conversation had gone as far as it was going to go. "I'm certain you have everyone's support and appreciation."

Katie glanced at her watch and noted the lateness of the hour. "I've taken up enough of your time." She rose and extended her hand. "This was an unexpected pleasure meeting you, and I very much enjoyed the tour."

"Likewise." He held the chair for her, the way a gentleman did in an old black-and-white film, and then escorted her to the elevator. "I hope you don't mind if I say goodbye here. I have a few hours of paperwork ahead of me and I'd better get started."

"Not at all. Again, thank you."

He stood there looking at her until the doors closed. The chill she got earlier seemed to return. She tried to explain away her discomfort. After all, he had a right to feel such anger, and it wasn't directed toward her. More chills as she walked briskly to the car, only this time, they were caused by the late afternoon breeze off the water. She slid into the seat and turned on the engine and the heater and waited until she was sufficiently warmed. As she drove out the gate, she thought about his words. Other than Jennifer, everyone she'd spoken to since arriving were aligned in their sentiment, although none expressed it so succinctly as Mr. VanAnt. "*The sooner she's removed from here, the better.*" Katie rounded the bend, happy to be heading toward the comfort of the Professor's home.

As he lost sight of her car, VanAnt drew the blinds and returned to his paperwork.

CHAPTER 13

Katie rose early, hoping to beat the evening traffic back into the city. She finished packing her small valise and took one last of sip of tea before hurrying down the stairs. Not surprisingly, Maria was waiting with a bag in hand: two homemade blueberry muffins for the long drive home. The two women embraced and Maria walked her to the door. In just a short time, Katie came to care for Maria and her phenomenal meals.

As the women stepped outside, Katie saw an unfamiliar man waving to them from the greenhouse. "Señora, that's my husband, Carlos. He was visiting his brother in Ferryville, only returning last night."

Having a few minutes to spare, Katie walked over and extended her hand along with a pleasant, "Hola."

"Señora, my name is Carlos. My wife, she told me much about you and how nice you have been. I have been away and now I have much to do. Would you like to see the flowers I grow? Please come see the greenhouse."

She wanted to leave, but did not want to appear rude. "I have a few minutes, I would enjoy seeing them."

The flowers and plants were varied and beautiful; he was very animated as he explained each one. As she walked toward the rear of the greenhouse, she recognized a familiar aroma.

"Ah, this is a Sirenacus plant. It is a hearty plant brought over from Europe many decades ago. You are very lucky, señora, it only has a smell three weeks during the year. Only in June for three weeks."

Maria yelled at Carlos. "Carlos, leave the señora alone, she must get home." Katie laughed at Maria's booming voice.

"Sorry, señora, I just am so proud of my babies."

Katie thanked Carlos for the tour and put her bag and goodies in the car. She was anxious to leave, as she intended to stop and see the Professor before leaving for the city. One last wave goodbye and she was now on the road, heading toward the hospital. She called Phyllis to ensure the Professor was feeling strong enough for an early morning visit and, thankfully, he was.

The combination of familiarity and speed placed her in the parking lot in what seemed like only minutes. She walked briskly down the corridor, oblivious to Doctor Christian's, "Good morning." Finally realizing her unintentional snub, Katie slowed down long enough to extend a gracious response.

"I seem to catch you at the most inopportune moments," he said with a laugh.

"And, I always seem to be saying I'm sorry. And, once again, I am. By the way, don't you ever leave here?"

"As a matter of fact, I'm just finishing up my shift. Any chance you have time to join me for some breakfast? My treat." He felt like a young boy asking out a girl for the first time.

"Oh, I appreciate the offer, but I'm here to say goodbye to the Professor and then I'll be leaving for home."

Disappointed, he wished her well and uttered something about hoping to see her again. He watched until she entered the

Professor's room. "*Under different circumstances,*" he thought as he, too, left for home.

The Professor was sitting up and seemed rather robust, although Katie wasn't sure if she had just become accustomed to his appearance or if he was indeed showing improvement. She sat on the edge of the bed and began, without prompting, reviewing the events of the week up to and including her unplanned meeting with Mr. VanAnt. When she finished, she offered her apologies. "I'm sorry, Professor. I'm sorry this didn't end the way you had hoped. I wish I could have done more."

"Nonsense, my dear. I'm so grateful for all you've done. One phone call and you're here, helping me, without a moment's hesitation. I absolutely don't want to appear as if I'm pressuring you, but if you find that you have some available time, you are the person I would like to work with Jennifer. But, as I said, no pressure."

Katie grasped his hand and smiled. "Wow, that was no pressure? That was a pretty thick layer of guilt."

"Oh, you know me, I say what I think, no filter." Although he said it with a smile, it was an accurate statement.

"Professor, I will admit, I'm intrigued and I've been thinking of Miss O'Neill's story. Do you think it's *possible* that there's a morsel of truth to any of it?"

"Honestly, Katie, at the beginning I had hoped so, but now, as far as I can tell, there doesn't seem to be any viable option other than the obvious one."

"Unless..." Katie said.

"Is there something you've uncovered?" His response almost sounded desperate.

"No, Professor, it was more of a feeling than anything else. Besides, we both know all too well that *feelings* don't make for good closing arguments." She bent down and gave him a hug as tight as he could tolerate. She didn't want to let go. He kissed her on the forehead and she slowly pulled away.

"I'll be checking in daily with Phyllis. And promise me, Professor, if there's anything you need from me or Matt, you'll tell her. Promise me."

"I promise. Now get going. You have a long ride ahead of you and there's a very special person who is probably pacing waiting for your return."

She looked at him again and became misty. She hated leaving him in such a state. Smiling, she reluctantly turned and left the room.

CHAPTER 14

She welcomed the sight of the George Washington Bridge, congestion and all. It was good to be home. She was exhilarated with anticipation at seeing Matt and loved that he still made her heart pound. Before long, Katie had crossed the bridge, returned the car, and waited impatiently for the elevator to arrive to take her to their 12th-floor apartment. She flung open the door to find Matt standing there with a bouquet of sunflowers. Katie dropped her bags and wrapped her arms around him, crushing some petals between them.

"I've missed you so much." It had only been a few days, yet seeing him again sent Katie's heart fluttering.

He said nothing. Just squeezed her a bit harder, kissed her a bit longer. Reluctantly, they parted. He closed the door and picked up her bags as she stooped to gather some of the fallen stems.

"I've made dinner, if you're hungry." He hung up her coat in the hall closet and carried the bags to their bedroom. She followed closely behind.

"Dinner can wait," she whispered.

They never did get to eat that night, and wound up throwing

most of it out in the morning. The remainder of the weekend was spent leisurely, just enjoying each other's company and a few of the more delectable sights and sounds the city had to offer. They talked endlessly, although Katie purposefully avoided revisiting the past week's events. Selfishly, she didn't want to think about the Professor, Jennifer's last words to her, or even the poor young murder victim. In fact, she didn't want to think at all. She just wanted to savor every moment of their time together before the realities of Monday morning re-entered their lives.

CHAPTER 15

After an emotional few days with the Professor, returning to her usual work routine was a welcome relief. Her law firm, and its reputation, was burgeoning at a pace far more aggressive than they could have hoped. As a group, they worked diligently at trying to ensure a balance between high-profile and low-profile cases. More to the point, the rich and poor were represented. Katie, in particular, garnered the most satisfaction from taking on the latter. Although her upbringing would suggest that she wanted for nothing, she much more easily identified with the underdog. Those were the people she wanted most to protect and, very often, those were the cases that offered her the greatest challenges as an attorney. She never second-guessed herself about going into private practice with Thomas and Zoe. The ability to choose her own clients and her volunteer work for the Legal Aid Society enabled her to reach into the community of humanness that was of such importance to her.

The work week was packed with meetings, court, and paperwork. Before she knew it, it was late Friday, and rather than staying well into the night, Katie hoisted a stack of files into her briefcase—or, more accurately, briefcases. She didn't mind the seemingly endless reading and writing as long as she could do some of it at home with Matt nearby. She, and Matt for that matter, had careers where the phrase "9 to 5" just didn't apply.

It was early Saturday morning and Katie lay in bed, quietly dreaming, until she was startled by the sound of the phone. She heard Matt answer and remark that he'd be there as soon as possible. "*Not the Professor*," she prayed. Her heart stopped for a moment.

"Sorry, honey, that was Margaret at Paulie Industries. They're experiencing problems with the mainframe and I need to get out there as quickly as possible. It may take the day. I *told* them to upgrade." He was so annoyed by their frantic phone call, he completely overlooked the distressed expression that enveloped her face. She exhaled and dropped her head back onto the pillow.

Within minutes, Matt was showered and dressed. He gave her a gentle kiss on the forehead, said he would call later, and left.

It wasn't quite how she expected to spend the day. They had prepared a long list of errands, but those good intentions would remain on the refrigerator door for the time being. Deciding not to let the unexpected turn of events render her mood or day unproductive, Katie opted to curl up with a good file. She donned her comfy sweats, made a cup of tea, and grabbed the larger of her two briefcases.

Heading toward her office in the corner of their apartment, it seemed apparent that the day dictated a change of scenery. With the movement of a few chairs here and there, a makeshift office was soon set up on the living room floor. Pulling the curtains fully apart, she only then noticed it was raining. "*Perfect*," she thought. Although not wanting to ruin the day for others, at least the rain made her being inside much more tolerable.

Attacking file after file, the hours passed easily. Matt called a few times, the last confirming his worst fear about his client's antiquated system. "Don't wait up," he said.

As evening approached and her stomach growled, dinner seemed most prudent. She opened the refrigerator door and smiled at the dozen or so Tupperware containers, each housing a small portion of unused cuisine. Food shopping was number one on their to-do list. Ever the survivor, Katie managed to put together a plate of palatable munchies accompanied by a handful of Ritz crackers and a much-needed glass of white wine. She thought she'd eat and work, but her concentration was soon waning, as was the intermittent light of the day. When she finished eating, Katie poured herself another glass of wine. She snuggled into the corner of the sofa with her legs tucked underneath and the comforter over her lap. The long day and the sweetness of the wine were starting to influence her thoughts. Since returning home, she was determined to keep focused on Matt and her work. It was only now, however, that her defenses were weakening. Avoidance was not her usual modus operandi, so it was especially unsettling to recognize that it had infiltrated her life since returning. Her parents, children, the Professor, Jennifer—they all swirled around and around. They were unrelated pieces, yet they were all connected. Somehow, seeing the Professor seemed to stir the pot of emotions. However, tonight it was becoming too much to think about. Nothing made sense. She rested her head on her arm and, with no effort whatsoever, fell asleep.

"Katie, wake up." He nudged her gently. She looked peaceful, but contorted. A few months ago, she'd had a pinched nerve in her neck, and he was concerned that her present positioning might give rise to a flare-up. She stirred, then opened her eyes.

"Oh, Matt, you're home early."

He gave a small laugh. "It's 2:30 in the morning. Come on, let's go to bed."

It took her a moment to release the kinks in her legs and neck. She grabbed his arm and walked somewhat unsteadily down the hallway. Too tired to even change, she thankfully stretched out on the bed and fell immediately back to sleep. Matt put a blanket over her and quietly slipped into bed.

Katie awoke first. It took her a moment to recall why and how she was in her bedroom. She turned and realized Matt was in bed too. She smiled. He wasn't just sleeping; he seemed almost unconscious. She grabbed her slippers and robe, closed the door, and went to one of the two spare rooms to take a shower. They were scheduled to go to his parents for Sunday dinner, but there was plenty of time.

She was sitting at the kitchen table, reading the paper, when he walked in. "Good morning, or is it good afternoon?" he mumbled as he grabbed a cup of coffee. "I hope I look a little better than I feel."

"You look wonderful. A wee bit tired, but wonderful." She gave him a peck on the cheek. "You know, we don't have to go to your parents' if you're not up to it. I'm sure they'll understand."

"Katherine, exactly how long have you known my mother?" he said in a very mocking tone. "Not go to Sunday dinner, they'll understand? Exactly who are you talking about?"

"You've got a point," Katie said, laughing. "I'll get dressed while you shower."

As always, it was a wonderfully bubbly visit with his family, but she was glad they were finally returning home by taxi. Katie had her arm through Matt's and rested her head on his shoulder.

"Katie, is everything all right?" he asked. "You seemed a bit preoccupied this afternoon." Before she even responded, he continued. "Actually, you've seemed that way for a while, but I've been hesitant to bring it up."

She squeezed his arm, wishing they weren't having this conversation now, in a taxi.

"Matt, I'm sorry. I had a lovely time today. I didn't mean to give you cause for concern."

He finally mustered up the courage to ask her the question that he'd been successfully avoiding for weeks. "Are you having any doubts? Doubts about us?"

She quickly released his arm and sat up straight. "Listen to me. I should have spoken to you about this sooner, but I'm really not certain what I'm feeling. It's nothing, it's everything. I've worked hard, for so long, to overcome insecurities about myself, my capabilities as a professional, as a wife, and as a woman. But recently, I've felt these insecurities slowly creeping back in. I'm not certain why. Perhaps it's all the talk we've had about starting a family. That may have been the catalyst, but it isn't the only reason. Then I saw the Professor, and it stirred up everything—those joyful moments we shared, and the painful ones from home. It unsettled me all over again. Matt, I've been keeping up with everything I'm supposed to—at work, at home—but it's like I'm moving through life on autopilot. There's no spark in anything I do."

The look on his face as she was talking was disheartening. He asked for the truth, but his expression indicated he wasn't quite as ready as he may have thought. Regardless, she needed to continue. He broke the dam, and there was no holding back the water. She knew this certainly wasn't the ideal locale for such a conversation, nor was the situation helped by the driver's obvious efforts to eavesdrop.

"And, inexplicably, meeting Jennifer was especially troubling. I can't seem to shake that experience. Matt, she was invisible. I don't know how to explain it any more clearly.

Looking into her eyes, I knew exactly how she felt. She believed herself to be invisible. I've seen that look before, as a child, looking into my own mirror." Katie started to cry, but continued. "With all that being said, with all the doubts that I feel, there is one thing I am most assuredly certain of. I fell in love with you the moment I saw you in the Professor's office, and every day since then I've loved you a little more." She grabbed his hands. "My life started with you and, God willing, it will end with you."

They embraced, not noticing the broad smile on the driver's face. He finally pulled the taxi in front of their apartment building.

"No, this one's on me," said the driver, but Matt handed him a $100 bill and told him to keep it.

"Thank you, my friend," the driver said with much surprise.

Matt nodded. It hadn't escaped him that the driver intentionally drove around the block several times to give them time to finish their conversation.

Katie waited by the elevator, brushing away a few tears with her sleeve.

"Are you okay?" he asked.

"Only if you are," she whispered.

He held her close to him.

"Matt, I *need* to go back. I need to go back and help that young woman."

He held her tighter.

"There's something about her that's gotten to me. Against all odds, just suppose for one moment there's a shred of truth to her story. Can you fathom the despair, the loneliness, the panic she must be experiencing? I can. I've lived those feelings over and over again. This all sounds insane to me, so I can only imagine what you must be thinking."

"Listen, I love you and trust you. If that's what you need to do, then go with my blessing. Just promise me that you'll take care of yourself, of us. Promise that you'll talk to me. Promise that you'll ask for my help. Promise you'll come home to me..." His words trailed off.

She kissed him passionately. "I promise, especially the part about coming home to you."

No need for any more talking that night. They went straight to bed.

CHAPTER 16

Katie took about two weeks to get everything in order before leaving for Keansbury. Her partners were understanding, but nevertheless disappointed in her decision to take on this case, especially given their heavy workload. She assured them that there would be no financial burden on the partnership and that her departure would be brief. As for rationalizing her decision, she focused on her obligation to the Professor rather than bringing up any conversation about how she was feeling. At least that was something concrete they could understand and it didn't sound challenging to her mental health.

"While I'm away, I assure you that I will be available for conference calls and any other requirements you may have. You know that I have put people in place to lessen the caseload burden, so please don't worry." She was sincere, but Katie couldn't help but feel somewhat guilty.

As for the Professor, he was extremely appreciative to have Katie return. Although selfishly excited at the prospect, he was nevertheless concerned that he was responsible for disrupting her home and career. He spoke with Matt before agreeing to let her return. Katie found it a bit amusing that even as a grown woman, the Professor still acted in a fatherly manner. Phyllis was also relieved to have Katie there, knowing that her visits were actually therapeutic. So, with everything in order, Katie decided to leave early on Monday morning so as to give her and Matt alone time over the weekend. He was nothing if not a tower of strength and support. Since their taxi ride, their communication, verbal and physical, had become more intimate. The time apart would be difficult, but she knew she'd made the right decision. After a long and tearful kiss, she was on her way, yet again. This time she knew what to expect. Or did she?

CHAPTER 17

Before long, Katie realized she was passing the still-draped Keansbury welcome sign. As she drove nearer the beach, she lowered the window, anxious to get her much-needed dose of the salty air, but was disappointed by the lack of the bold and captivating aroma of the Sirenacus plant. Her disappointment faded as soon as she reached the Professor's driveway and was greeted by Maria, who nearly lifted Katie off her feet. Excitedly interspersing both Spanish and English, Maria practically carried her directly to the kitchen for a late morning snack that was grand in both appearance and taste. Katie felt somewhat awkward about the attention, but imagined that it was Maria's way of expressing her relief of having someone close by that cared for the Professor as much as she did. Regardless, she adored Maria and, shamelessly, her cooking.

After unpacking and settling in, she decided to make a brief stop to see the Professor before heading over to the police station. She made her way to his room and was met by the familiar sight of Phyllis keeping vigil by his side. The Professor seemed to be napping while Phyllis poured over what appeared to be an endless pile of new reading material.

Phyllis had heard the room door open and was finally rewarded with the sight of the person she had been waiting for all morning. A feeling of déjà vu came over Katie as the two women slipped out into the hallway and embraced with so much love and support. Phyllis held tightly to Katie's hand and began walking her toward the window at the end of the corridor.

"I feel so guilty that you're here again, but I am so thankfully reassured. He seems to respond to you most of all."

Katie mustered a weak smile, but clearly her face screamed concern. "Phyllis, we've spoken about this over the weeks, but I'm still not understanding why the Professor hasn't had his operation. It seems like a month or so ago you said he was finally scheduled. There's clearly something you're not telling me. Please, what's going on?"

"I'm truly not trying to hide anything from you. Please believe me. He really *was* doing so much better, and then about two weeks ago, he took a turn for the worse. Doctor Christian was very disappointed, but more concerning to me was the fact that he was somewhat perplexed by it all. Then, I told Sean that you were coming back and he began to improve. That's why I said earlier that you being here is so good for him. I know that's a huge burden to put on your shoulders."

Katie squeezed Phyllis' hand and pledged to her that as long as the Professor needed her, she'd be there for him. It was exactly what Phyllis required; her expression changed from panic to relief with every word Katie uttered. They chatted for a while longer and then went back to the room to see if the Professor showed any signs of awakening. Disappointingly, he did not, so Katie offered another reassuring hug and promised to check in on him later in the day. "If the Professor wakes before I get back, please tell him that I'm meeting with Miss O'Neill and I'll update him this evening."

"I will, and be careful, my dear," Phyllis whispered. Katie left without hearing Phyllis' final word of caution.

Arriving at the sheriff's office seemed very familiar by now, and Katie was especially pleased to see that Deputy Wong was on duty. They greeted each other warmly, demonstrating that some type of tentative bonding had been established. Their conversation was politely interrupted by the sheriff, who apologized for his hasty departure and pledged full cooperation of his department. His pace didn't allow for Katie to say anything beyond a "Hello."

"We're very busy today," the deputy noted, making Katie wonder if she was stating a fact or offering an excuse for the sheriff. In any event, she was there to see Jennifer, and distractions of any kind were not going to be permitted. Unlike her previous visits, Jennifer was not in the room when Katie entered. Her wait was only about ten minutes, and she used the time to get her notes and paperwork in order. In all the hubbub of the past several weeks, it only now occurred to Katie that she wasn't even certain if Jennifer knew of her visit. That question was answered as the deputy escorted Jennifer to the table. She looked stunned and disbelieving, which made Katie feel terrible for the inexcusable oversight.

"Miss O'Neill, I'm so sorry for showing up unannounced like this. I can only imagine by your expression that I'm the last person you expected to see." Before Katie could say another word, Jennifer interrupted.

"What are you doing here? Why are you here? What's happened?" Jennifer held her breath, awaiting a response that she was too afraid to even hope for; a response she had no right to hope for. Katie had previously made it clear that she would not represent her, so why should she believe that her presence this afternoon was anything more than another favor for the Professor.

"Miss O'Neill, I know I said at our last visit that I would not be able to represent you. However, my schedule has changed and, if you still want me to, I will take your case. Would you like me to represent you?"

It took a moment for Jennifer to process what had just been said. Hope had abandoned her, and yet here it was, presenting itself in the form of a celebrated attorney. Her thoughts raced; in an instant she felt caught in a fragile balance between the possibility of rescue and the fear of being misled. She had pleaded with Katie, clinging to the hope of support. But after being told it wasn't an option, this unexpected shift left her wary. It was hard not to question the change.

Repeating her question, Katie asked, "Shall I represent you?"

She wanted to scream "Yes" for the entire town to hear, but reality quickly set in. "Mrs. Russo, I can't... I haven't..." Jennifer stuttered uncontrollably, then tried again. "I don't have any money. There's my apartment, but I don't fully own it, and..." Katie put her hand over Jennifer's and tried to calm her down.

"Miss O'Neill. Jennifer. This isn't about the money. We'll work something out. I'm here because you are entitled to a defense and I'd like to be the one that provides you with that defense. I'll be honest, the facts are against you and it would be nothing short of a miracle for you to walk away from a very long prison term. However, if you'll allow me, I will give you the best defense I'm able. So, what do you say? Shall I tell the ADA that I'm your legal representation?"

"Yes, yes please."

"Good. I'll be by first thing tomorrow morning and we'll get started." She gathered her untouched papers together and placed them back into her briefcase. "I'd like you to be well rested because, from here on out, it's going to be hard work." Katie rang the bell for one of the guards. "Oh, and there is one thing that I insist on. You have got to be honest with me. No lies.

Is that understood?" Jennifer nodded, still a bit in shock over what just transpired.

The door opened, and as Katie prepared to leave, Jennifer managed to compose herself enough to speak a few words. "Mrs. Russo." Katie turned. Jennifer paused a moment to steady herself. She was about to speak two words that she had never spoken before. Nothing had ever occurred in her life that necessitated their use. "Thank you."

Katie smiled and left.

CHAPTER 18

"Hard work" was an understatement for what Katie knew was ahead of her, so she wasted no time in getting settled at the Professor's home. With Maria's help, she reestablished herself in the oversized guest room and reorganized his den to mimic her office, or at least a moderate facsimile thereof. She then spent much of the afternoon on the phone, setting up appointments with ADA Ryan, Sheriff Michaels, and the medical examiner. Her last call was to the person she relied on the most for difficult cases such as this: Private Investigator Ali Randall...named by his mother after the greatest boxer of all time, Muhammad Ali. Katie awed at how he approached every assignment with tenacity and dogmatism. She often joked that the look he got on his face when chasing down a clue was akin to that of a hungry pit-bull savoring the leg of an approaching mailman. He also had a caustic wit which kept her on her toes... at least she thought it was wit. In any event, Katie reviewed the case with him briefly.

"Al, it's a small town established by a family that still resides there. Unfortunately, the founder's grandson was murdered and a young woman has been accused. Her story is pretty unbelievable, and it will be near impossible to prove otherwise. Oh, and by the way, your compensation will be limited."

"So what else is new?" he muttered and promised he'd be there by the end of the week.

Satisfied by what she had accomplished in this one day, Katie grabbed a quick bite and headed back to the hospital to spend the rest of the time with the Professor. After visiting hours, Katie bid Phyllis good night and returned to the house. She embraced the promise of sleep, but not before hearing Matt's voice. Their conversation, though short, was filled with warmth. With his words still echoing in her mind, it took only moments for Katie to drift into the hush of night.

CHAPTER 19

The morning sun peered through the curtains, catching Katie's eye; clearly a signal it was time to rise and shine. A welcoming shower was followed by the anticipation of a Maria breakfast. As she approached the kitchen, Katie was surprised to hear Maria conversing with Phyllis. The two woman were cheerfully communicating in both English and Spanish. While neither were entirely fluent, she doubted that they even realized it. It was clear that both women had transcended the employer/employee relationship and had become friends.

"Good morning, ladies," Katie announced as she entered the kitchen. Before she could utter another syllable, a cup of coffee and scrambled eggs were placed before her in a manner fit for queen.

Although Katie had a busy schedule, she knew it was important to share this time with them. The Professor's improvement last night clearly lifted Phyllis' spirits, and she didn't want to deprive her of those all-too-infrequent moments of encouragement.

"Phyllis, what a wonderful and unexpected surprise to see

you here." She corrected herself immediately. "How ridiculous of me, this is your home, why wouldn't you be here?"

She laughed. "Kate, you're absolutely correct. Although I have been staying with my sister, I missed Maria, so I stopped over before seeing Sean later."

After her second cup of coffee, Katie excused herself, retrieved her briefcase, and headed out for her morning schedule. She had offered Phyllis a ride to the hospital, but she preferred to spend a little more time with Maria and then had some errands to do. She said she and her sister would see Sean later.

As promised, Katie's first visit was to see Jennifer. The two spoke at length, at which time Katie thought she detected a very slight change in her demeanor, almost a bit of hope. It was unfamiliar ground for Jennifer, but something in her began to ease. Against her instincts, she allowed a sliver of trust to surface. Katie certainly did not want to give Jennifer any false sense of optimism; however, she did prefer having her client more human-like than robotic. Besides, at least at this juncture, there really was no benefit in continually reminding Jennifer that her only chance at walking away from this sordid mess was a large dose of divine intervention.

A few beeps of her watch reminded Katie of her appointment with ADA Ryan. She gently patted Jennifer's hand, smiled weakly, and left, intent on not being late for their meeting.

There were several critical issues to discuss with ADA Ryan, so it was important for Katie to be confident and assertive without seeming egotistical or aggressive. "Ah, the old balancing act," her partner Thomas would say.

Katie arrived in plenty of time, even stopping first to freshen up. Although the two had met previously, she knew a shared lunch was not the same as today's meeting. At that time, she was exchanging friendly information; now, she was trying to keep a young woman from being executed.

Ryan was waiting for Katie, a bit too anxiously for his liking. He wasn't some love-struck teenager, yet something about Katie stirred that same breathless, wide-eyed wonder in him.

A soft knock at the door, and his secretary, Stacey, informed him of Mrs. Russo's arrival.

"Please show her in," he said as he wheeled his chair away from behind his desk. "It's so nice to see you again, Mrs. Russo. Please sit down." He motioned to an adequately sized oval conference table. "Coffee, tea?"

"Nothing, thank you. It's nice of you to make yourself available on such short notice."

As she began emptying the contents of her briefcase, he asked how the Professor was doing. By now, that was the first question posed by nearly everyone she encountered. She was beginning to feel like his medical representative. She acknowledged the Professor's steady progress, and before pleasantries could gain any traction, Katie launched into her intentions...postponement, change of venue, bail.

As she continued, he realized it was going to be a challenge; not just this first official meeting, but the entire process. For the community's sake, he would have preferred a different outcome. However, the reality of the trial and all that it would entail began to energize him in a way that he hadn't felt in a very long time. No matter how weak he perceived her case, he knew she would be a fierce combatant that would force him to redefine his limits. Each word she uttered, each gesture she made, only served to make him more resolute in finding Jennifer O'Neill guilty of murder. It wasn't revenge; it was justice. He lifted his head from the dozens of papers strewn across the table and looked at Katie.

It was symbolic, but he finally took off the rose-colored glasses and put on his bifocals. He interrupted her dozens of requests. "No, absolutely not…"

Their meeting lasted another hour.

CHAPTER 20

Ali would be arriving this afternoon, and Katie was amazed how an entire week had flown by so quickly since meeting with the ADA on Monday. The entire process of working with the prosecutor's department was handled in a very professional manner, much quicker than the pace to which she had become accustomed in New York. Consequently, Katie found herself working all week at a frenetic pace, getting motions filed, completing paperwork, and efficiently dealing with general issues.

Given the situation, Katie was, for the most part, satisfied with the outcome of the meeting, especially with the agreement of a change in venue to Clarkston. However, she had hoped for a community farther away than a mere 45 minutes. She knew the Keans name would have influence there, but at least it wouldn't be as immediate or prevalent as it was currently. Katie was also pleased to learn that Judge Christopher Grayson would be presiding. Although never appearing before his court, she knew him to be strict, but fair and approachable. Her major disappointment was in not getting a lengthier postponement. She had argued for a three-month continuance to properly put forth a defense, but six weeks was considered more than adequate. The court was not going to tolerate any further delay. However, the court was more lenient when it came to incarceration. Katie successfully petitioned Judge Grayson to permit Jennifer to wear an ankle bracelet and, thanks to the Professor, to be confined to his home. In coordination with the parole officers, Sheriff Michaels would oversee the monitoring and management of the arrangement.

In preparation for Ali's arrival, Katie had also spent time during the week organizing all the data. She had a reputation as a fanatical list maker, so the Professor's den was now filled with sticky notes neatly arranged by past, present, and future issues. She wanted everything in order for when she reviewed the case with him.

Katie took a deep breath, sunk back in the Professor's chair, and took one more glance around the den. Notes, pictures, books. Yes, this was for Ali, but more importantly, it was her battle plan. How they proceeded from this point forward would be based on all the hard work she laid out in this room. She was more a dove than a hawk and wasn't accustomed to using military jargon as a point of reference. However, in this case, there was no mistake about it; this was going to be a war. And like any good general, a battle plan had to be developed, implemented, and revised as the conflict evolved.

"I see you have the art gallery all set up for me."

"Al!" she screamed, having been so deep in thought she hadn't even heard him come in. Katie always called him Al; it had an air of familiarity, and the name reminded her of her favorite uncle. She jumped up and embraced him with all the love and tenderness of a dear friend. "It is so wonderful to see you again. How is your mother? Did you meet Maria? Well, of course you did, she let you in."

He enjoyed being so appreciated and found it amusing to

hear the usually poised attorney reduced to blubbering. The enthusiasm continued as they both caught up on all the need-to-know personal issues. In between bouts of gossip, they devoured another one of Maria's gourmet lunches.

"Have you been eating like this since you've been here?" Ali asked, somewhat disbelieving of what Maria considered a lunch. "I'm not sure I can move!"

"Welcome to my world," Katie said with a grin. "I'm embarrassed to say I am now addicted. She puts a spell over you...you're full, you're immobilized, yet you can't help wondering what the next meal will be like. It's a good thing she's on our side."

Ali helped Maria clear the trays from the den to the kitchen and he returned with a new tray of coffee and chocolate cake. "I tried to say no to the dessert, but it was as if she didn't hear me."

Katie laughed, having already learned the futility of arguing with Maria. As Ali made space on the desk for the tray, Katie promptly slid the doors closed. The sound the two oak doors made when touching was akin to that of a judge's gavel, symbolically signaling that a serious discussion was now in session. Katie motioned for Ali to sit in the Professor's chair as she headed over to the first set of notes. With coffee in hand, he, too, melted into the comfort of the leather as he listened intently to detail after detail.

"Al, Peter Keans Junior was a respected and, by all accounts, well-liked young man—his killing was brutal and senseless. That loss alone is devastating, but as the grandson of Keansbury's founder, the ripple effects have been profound. Now, a young woman, Jennifer O'Neill, stands accused, and the intensity of the blame directed at her has been nothing short of vicious."

Katie continued with her update. Ali interjected a question or two, but Katie's overviews were always so thorough that nearly all potential questions had already been anticipated. She got that from the Professor.

After an hour, she was through. She felt certain that she had presented the situation completely and now waited for Ali's response. He took a moment, wanting to be supportive, but honest. He stood up and walked around the room, desperately trying to regain strength in his legs. Finally, he turned to her. "That's one remarkable story." He hesitated.

"*And*?" she demanded.

"*And*, that's one remarkable story that seems about as open and shut of a case as we've ever worked on together. Look, I know you're doing this to help the Professor, and I can clearly see that you've pointed out a few places where one can possibly poke a hole or two, but..." Again, he hesitated.

"Come on, just say it. Tell me what you think. You've never been one to mince words with me, so please, just tell me what you think." This time she was demanding.

"Okay, *but*, I think this is wrong." He really wanted to say insane, but didn't see the need to be so cruel. "I know you, sometimes better than you know yourself. And I see that you're giving up your professional time and your personal time with Matt. I see that you would do anything in the world to help the Professor, even at the risk of your own reputation. I see that this girl is guilty; planned or unplanned, she is guilty. And most of all, when this is all said and done, I see you getting hurt. That's the part I hate the most. You'll give of yourself to everyone, and in the end, you will be hurt."

She was taken aback by his words. She wanted his honestly, but that wasn't what she expected. He somehow hit a nerve that she didn't even realize was exposed.

"Wow," was all she could muster.

He took a few minutes and then continued in an intentionally upbeat manner. "Hey, it's me. Whatever you need,

I've got your back. Point me in the direction and I'm there. We've been in bad situations before. All I ask is that you be careful, physically and emotionally. Deal?"

She smiled at him. She really loved this dear man, a friend she was so fortunate to have in her life. "Deal."

"Okay then. Let's take a fifteen-minute break and I'll go get us a fresh pot of coffee. Besides, I want to see if I can get a peek at what Maria has on the dinner menu. When we reconvene, let's go over what I can do to help, starting tomorrow morning. People, places...whatever you need." With that, he picked up the tray, slid the doors open, and headed toward the kitchen.

"We've got this," she whispered to herself. "I've got this. No more frayed nerves. This is about Jennifer—about her defense. Nothing else."

The sound of lighthearted chatter drifted from the kitchen, so she decided to join them. After all, she'd only been granted a fifteen-minute break, and—she chuckled inwardly—she wasn't about to waste it. Katie knew that once they returned to the den, the real work would begin.

She followed the laughter, head held high, shoulders squared. "I've got this," she repeated, steady and sure.

CHAPTER 21

They had forged a plan of action and Ali was already in town attempting to meet with a laundry list of names. Katie had hoped that at the top of the list would be Junior's parents, at least Mrs. Keans. However, she already knew that would most likely be fruitless. Several weeks after the funeral, Senior had a breakdown and was admitted to Oakwood Sanitarium, where he remains. Any attempt to collect information from Mrs. Keans, who became reclusive and barely audible, would be futile. Katie had hoped one of Junior's parents might offer a deeper, more personal glimpse into his character, so their unavailability left her disappointed. Still, this setback didn't shake her confidence in the list she'd compiled.

While Ali was in town interviewing various members of the community, Katie remained at the house awaiting the arrival of the sheriff and Jennifer. She noticed Maria bustling about nervously, obviously still uneasy about the living arrangements. Although they all did their best to reassure Maria, the Professor was adamant about having Jennifer staying at the house. Frankly, if it came down between the two of them, the Professor was willing to lose Maria. This was a matter of life and death, and he would not change his mind regardless of his affection for her.

A little after 1pm, the sheriff and Jennifer arrived, along with Agent Tracy, whose job was to affix the ankle bracelet. Other than a brief introduction, no pleasantries were even attempted. They hurriedly gathered in the den, and within a few minutes the bracelet was activated. The sheriff reiterated the ground rules and cautioned that any deviation would result in an immediate return to jail. He reminded everyone that he was utterly opposed to "this set up" and that he and his deputies were following a strict "no tolerance policy." That being said, he turned on his heels, motioned to Agent Tracy, and left. He was abrupt, but at least he had agreed to send a squad car to patrol the area on a regular basis. It wasn't so much to ensure Jennifer didn't get out as it was to make certain no unwelcomed persons got in. All parties had agreed to keep Jennifer's whereabouts as quiet as possible, but with the accuracy and speed of the informal network of communication in this community, that was an unrealistic expectation.

Katie took a deep breath. "How about we get you settled. You'll be staying in the upstairs spare room, next to mine. I stopped by your apartment yesterday and took whatever clothes and toiletries I thought you might want. And if you need something else, we'll get it for you." Katie made every attempt at trying to sound upbeat despite the circumstances. She gently put her arm under Jennifer's to help her to her feet. She looked shell-shocked. As they reached the bottom of the stairs, Maria appeared.

"Whenever you are ready, I have something for you to eat in the kitchen," Maria managed to say in a slightly nervous tone. Katie grabbed the woman's hand and squeezed it with appreciation.

"Gracias, Maria. We will be down soon. Gracias."

Not surprisingly, the next few days seemed to disappear with great velocity. Work was interrupted only by meals and a few cherished hours of sleep. Otherwise, it was interview after interview, followed by a lengthy debriefing and more strategizing. Katie and Ali were able to come up with a few holes in the prosecutor's case, but certainly not enough at this point to secure an acquittal. Exploring every detail was imperative, but painstakingly slow and, more often than not, unproductive. "Excellence is in the details," the Professor would often lecture. And Katie knew that if she was to believe Jennifer, then somewhere in those seemingly endless details was the answer to her freedom.

Despite the exhaustive work process, at least the living arrangements had finally settled into a more acceptable situation. No doubt, they were an eclectic group amassed under one roof, but at least the initial tension that permeated the household had finally abated. Maria had been the most guarded and apprehensive regarding Jennifer, but that eventually transformed into motherly concern. It certainly didn't hurt that Jennifer was virtually maintenance-free and spoke, among other languages, fluent Spanish. Fortunately, Ali also had a good command of the language, which was a huge asset not only in the household, but in communicating with a good-sized portion of the town's population.

CHAPTER 22

There was an air of promise in the morning, and Ali was anxious to get started with another day's investigation. One glance in the mirror and he was certain that his jeans, white shirt, and sports jacket were comfortable and respectful. He grabbed his favorite and essential "tools of the trade": notepad, pen, and tape recorder. He shoved them in his jacket pocket, grabbed his car keys, and hurried down the stairs. He poked his head into the den to tell Katie he was leaving and she nodded, but said nothing. She was so relieved to have him on this case. She needed help, desperately, and she could think of no one she would rather have at her side. He had the uncanny ability to be sponge-like, absorbing a lot and fitting in anywhere. As the sound of his car engine became fainter, Katie refocused on the pile of papers before her.

With guidance from Maria, Ali started his investigation on the west side of Keansbury, known as Espana. Decades of Spanish immigrants transformed this section into a thriving community of proud citizens, nearly all of whom were affiliated with Keansbury Industries. Maria had said that the area had always been filled with music and very satisfied patrons, particularly with the opening of the new tapas bar. But, since the murder, Espana, like the rest of Keansbury, had become a mere shadow of its former self.

Maria suggested several locations where he would be able to find the most residents during the late morning—the bodega on Ocean View Avenue, the bakery shop on Atlantic Drive, and the auto garage on Carr Avenue. She recommended that he wait until noon to visit the two more popular restaurants on 3rd Street.

Ali was concerned about finding a convenient parking space, but his worry was unfounded as the streets seemed oddly vacant. He spent the morning walking and talking. Thanks to Maria's clear directions, he was able to navigate the town efficiently, stopping at every shop that remained open. Each location yielded a sufficient number of residents willing to speak, with only a handful declining outright. He asked about their roles in the community, their ties to Junior and the Keans family, and how the tragedy had affected their lives. Despite the sensitive nature of his questions, people were warm and candid —his fluency in the language helped ease the exchanges. Yet, the responses proved disappointingly uniform: most were content with life in the town and held the Keans family in high regard. Still, the looming closure of the port had stirred deep concern about the town's future. The loss of young Keans had sparked considerable anger, all of it directed squarely at Jennifer.

The sun directly overhead reminded Ali to check his watch. It was 12:15, and he didn't want to miss the opportunity to meet with a lunchtime gathering. He stopped at the first recommended restaurant only to be met with a large *"Closed"* sign. He rushed to the other a few blocks away, hoping it had not suffered the same fate. As he approached his destination, he was relieved to inhale familiar and delectable aromas escaping from two slightly opened front windows at Iberia Tavern. He pulled hard on the baroque-style front door and entered to a large, but surprisingly subdued, group of young men. After a quick surveillance of the room, he gravitated to a table of five men and introduced himself as a friend of the Professor and Maria. He wanted information, and he knew any mention of Jennifer would result in a wall of silence. The men were cordial and willing to answer his probing questions while consuming a lunch of garlic shrimp, chorizo, and a warm loaf of bread. The conversation was seemingly pleasant and fluid, so Ali was a bit taken aback when the three younger men abruptly stood up and announced they were leaving. He wasn't certain if he had said something to offend them, and he was relieved to hear that they were merely returning to their jobs at the port. The other two men remained. There were still some unanswered questions, so Ali continued the conversation, speaking in Spanish. He was surprised when they both responded in perfect English.

"Presumptuous on my part, I just assumed you only spoke Spanish," Ali said, hoping that he didn't appear rude.

"Oh, not a problem," said Santiago. "In Espana, there are only a few of us still here that speak English. We worked at Keansbury Industries, which offered English classes, and Antonio and I," he pointed to his companion, "took advantage of the opportunity."

Ali was curious about the other three men. "Did your friends also take classes?"

"No, about a year or two ago, they stopped offering them, so most of the fellows here just pick up words and phrases the best they can."

Ali wasn't certain if any of the conversation was relevant to the case, but he did find the dynamics interesting. Young men that had gone to the local high school tended to work at jobs in town; others tended to work at the port.

"Mr. Keans was very generous in ensuring our community was able to work and provide for our families," Santiago offered.

Ali was curious. "And what work do you both do at the port?"

"Ah, unfortunately, we both were laid off last year."

"I can see how his son's death has impacted the business," Ali said.

Antonio spoke up after finishing his coffee. "Actually, we were laid off before the tragedy, but it's working out. I'll be starting a new job in the city next month."

"And I will be going to Fairfield University, finishing my degree in education," Santiago interjected. "So, you see, sometimes things have a way of working out."

Neither Antonio nor Santiago were in a rush, so Ali ordered another sangria and continued to gather as much information as possible. Nothing at the moment appeared unique or unusual, given the circumstances, but he would share it all with Katie and together they would sift through each piece with a fine-tooth comb.

CHAPTER 23

It was a long day, so Ali was relieved to be back at the house. Maria heard him come in, so she hurried over to greet him with her usual lovely smile and the inevitable reassurance that she would prepare food for him in the kitchen.

He gave her a hug. "Oh, I love you, Maria, but I can't possibly eat another bite. I spent the afternoon at Iberia Tavern and I am stuffed," he said, trying not to sound unappreciative.

"Okay, then I make you a small plate," she said affirmatively.

As he walked to the Professor's den, he knew he had lost the battle. "I'm gonna die," he muttered under his breath.

Ali slid open the doors to see Katie sitting at the Professor's desk pouring over a pile of papers. She looked slightly disheveled, pencil behind her ear, eyeglasses perched on top of her head. She managed a quick "Hi" as she looked frantic, lifting paper after paper. "I can't find my glasses." She sounded overwhelmed.

He pointed to the top of her head. She grabbed them with a sigh of disgust and threw them on the desk.

Ali wasn't accustomed to seeing her looking so defeated. "I guess I don't need to ask you how your day has been."

"I'm sorry, it's just…" She didn't finish. "Al, how did you make out today? Anything helpful? *Please* let there be something."

He took a seat near the window. "I met with about ten fellows that worked or still work at the port. They all say pretty much the same thing…daily but limited interaction with Junior, but they liked him and, similar to everyone else in town that we've spoken to, no one can recall anyone having a beef with him. The overall work environment is good, some took advantage of classes they offered. Needless to say, those that still are employed are very worried about their jobs. Business has plummeted drastically since the murder. Senior hasn't been back, and VanAnt is looked upon as second best. I'm sorry there isn't more."

"Don't be silly. You did fine, as you always do." She rested her elbows on the desk and rubbed her temples. She paused for a minute, then stood up and walked to the middle of the room. "Here's the problem," she said as she waved her outstretched arms. "If we believe that Jennifer is innocent, as incredulous as it might seem, then somewhere in these stacks of papers and dozens of photos is our killer. And the problem is, I can't see it, I can't feel it, and I'm as troubled as I've ever been about a case. I am her last line of defense, her last bit of hope, and failure is not an option."

"Okay, then, what's next?" he said calmly.

"I'm going to freshen up and then go to the hospital to see the Professor. Although I give him daily updates, I haven't been with him in person for two days. I want to check on his progress personally, and I think it will be helpful to talk to him about the case face to face."

"By the way," Ali asked, "where is Jennifer?"

"She's in the spare room. She hardly ever leaves. I've tried to engage her in general conversation, but she's fairly uncommunicative. She does read; in fact, she's a voracious reader. Maria has been going to the library for her and the list of requested books is impressive. For now, all I need is for her to be calm and safe."

"Would it be okay if I tried to talk to her this afternoon?" Ali asked.

"Absolutely!" Katie nodded.

"So, in the meantime, what would you like me to do?" he asked.

Just then, Maria knocked on the door, announcing, " Señor Ali, your food is ready in the kitchen."

Katie laughed as she answered Ali. "Go and eat!!"

"I wonder if the Professor has a pair of large sweatpants I can borrow," he moaned.

CHAPTER 24

Katie knocked lightly on the door and walked gingerly into the Professor's room, not wanting to possibly wake him. To her surprise, she saw him playing cards with a nurse. She had expected to see Phyllis.

"This is Nurse Cathy, you met her before. And she's off duty, so it's all legitimate," he said playfully.

"And why is there a large pile of pretzels in front of Nurse Cathy and only two or three in front of you, Professor?" Katie teased.

Nurse Cathy answered, "Because he's a wonderful patient but an awful card player!"

After introductions, the nurse announced her departure. "Nice to formally meet you, Mrs. Russo. And I will see you on Friday, Mr. Card Shark." She grabbed a napkin and filled it with the pile of pretzels. "I won them fair and square," she boasted as she kissed the Professor on the forehead and left.

Katie waited till the door closed and then sat at the edge of the hospital bed. "I'm worried, Professor. The trial starts soon and I'm worried. We've talked about this constantly, that young man is just squeaky clean. Jennifer insisted he talked to her about being a drug addict, and there just isn't a shred of evidence that points in that direction."

The Professor measured his words. "Honey…" He very rarely called her that, but when he did, she knew it was going to be followed by a seriously unpleasant conversation. "Honey, you've worked tirelessly on this case and I feel responsible for getting you involved. I wanted desperately for you to find a hole in the prosecutor's case, but I think we're all at that juncture where the road clearly leads to guilty. The drug angle is not plausible. In fact, almost everything she's said isn't plausible. At this point, if I were her attorney, I would try yet again to have her face the inevitable outcome and agree to a lesser charge of manslaughter. I think ADA Ryan would agree to that. Crime of passion."

Katie was taken aback by his words, having anticipated that the Professor would provide some overlooked insight. Instead, he was suggesting throwing in the towel, a notion that surprised her. Though mildly disappointed, she reminded herself that she was still new to the case—unlike the Professor, who had been immersed in it for quite a while. Not wanting to further engage, Katie stood up and walked to the window, gathering her thoughts as she gazed out. With her back to him, she said, "Professor, each time I visit, you look stronger and stronger. I spoke with Phyllis this morning, and she said she's counting the days until you get paroled."

The Professor grinned. "Spoken like a true lawyer's wife, but overly optimistic. Doctor Christian hopes it won't be too much longer, but first the operation followed by physical therapy. Good news, if I remain stable the next few days, then the operation will be scheduled shortly."

She turned around to face him. "That's wonderful news. You've been here for such a long time, so it will be great to have you back home and seated at your desk where you belong. And don't worry about us, we'll make other arrangements."

He quickly responded adamantly, "First, I don't have a timeline yet for my discharge, and second, even if it's sooner rather than later, I would absolutely not entertain you leaving. There is more than enough room to accommodate everyone. And quite frankly, I don't anticipate a lengthy trial. Your stay will most likely be shorter than we would all hope for."

Katie knew his feelings about the case, but since she had agreed to represent Jennifer, she had hoped he would show a modicum of support. She gave him a light hug. "I better get back to work. Al was going to try to spend a little time with Jennifer and hopefully he might surprise us with some new information. I'll give it a try tonight. Rest up and I'll talk to you tomorrow."

He smiled and nodded.

Katie entered the elevator along with Nurse Cathy. The nurse took the opportunity to speak with Katie.

"I've been working here a short time, but I can tell what a wonderful man Professor Kyle is and how important he is to the community. Some days his room looks like half the town is in there!"

The perfect segue for Katie. "Cathy, did anyone visit the Professor before I arrived?"

"My shift was extra busy today, so I'm not certain of all his visitors. However, I did see someone that's visited before. I think his name is Van something or other."

"Have a good rest of the day," Cathy said as she hurriedly exited the elevator. "I have a first date tonight and I intend to look spectacular!"

Nurse Cathy's exuberance was lost on Katie. She remained in the elevator, trying to process what had transpired. She wasn't certain if she was just grasping at straws or if her feeling was valid. VanAnt visits, and the Professor advises surrender, despite some of her findings. Coincidence? Or something more? Katie didn't buy into coincidences—they were like a grain of sand in the eye: minor, yet irritating enough to demand attention.

The entrance of several people onto the elevator startled Katie back to the present. She apologized as she unintentionally pushed a young man in an effort to quickly exit. As she drove back to the house, she just could not shake that feeling. Something about that man she didn't like, didn't trust. She made a mental note to delve deeper into VanAnt's background.

CHAPTER 25

With a different perspective, Katie was anxious to revisit the information that was wallpapering the den. She was headed there when she heard some chatter in the kitchen. Walking in, she was extremely surprised and very pleased to see Jennifer sitting at the table with Ali and Maria. In front of each was a plate holding only a few crumbs remaining from what was once a full apple pie that Maria had made in the morning.

"And where is my slice of pie?" Katie asked jokingly.

Three smiling faces looked downward. Katie realized that in all the months she had been with Jennifer, this was the first time she saw her genuinely smile. Clearly, Ali had performed a miracle.

The four housemates spent an hour together mostly talking about books, with Jennifer clearly dominating the conversation. Her knowledge of Shakespeare was beyond impressive. Early on, the Professor had told Katie that Jennifer was brilliant, and now she witnessed it firsthand. Another 15 minutes and Jennifer's stamina was starting to wane, so she excused herself and went back to her room.

"Thank you both," Katie said. "This was just what I hoped

for. Al, your personality brought her down, and, Maria, your apple pie kept her here. When the trial starts, it's going to be rough on her, so, Maria anything you can do to help will be very much appreciated."

"Of course, señora, I will make a hundred pies!" Maria said sincerely.

Katie gave her a big hug of thanks. It was gratifying to feel the support from everyone here.

There was so much to do, and Katie wanted to talk to Ali about what transpired earlier at the hospital. However, she convinced herself to just sit and take a longer break and, against her better judgement, it was impossible to deny the slice of blueberry pie that magically appeared in front of her. Each sip of coffee was a cozy hug.

"Good news, the Professor should be operated on very soon, and then it will just be a matter of time before he'll be back home."

Ali and Maria responded in unison, "Wonderful."

"Maria," Ali asked, "how long have you and your husband worked for the Professor?"

"We come here when my Miguel he was 13 years old, he is now 24. We stayed with a family friend one hour away. Carlos worked hard starting a landscaping business and the Professor was kind enough to hire him. I would often come too, and one day the Professor asked if I could help Señora Phyllis because he was away so much of the time working in the city. Of course, I help, and the next thing I know, I am hired full-time. Our life was complete when he said we could live here. A wonderful man."

Katie took a final sip and asked Maria, "I see Miguel's picture on the counter. He's a very handsome young man. I haven't had the chance to meet him, does he visit?"

"Señora, like his father, my Miguel works very hard. He is a big shot at his company, so he doesn't have much free time to come here. However, many times he sends a car to bring me and my husband to New York and we stay in a fancy hotel. We are blessed to have such a wonderful son."

Katie noticed Maria seemed to glow each time she mentioned his name.

"You know, señora, when we arrived, we only spoke very little English and together we did our best. Señora Phyllis helped whenever she was here. Miguel learned more in school, and when he worked at the port, he took the English class, then his English was perfect."

Ali interjected that he had spoken with several young men earlier and they, too, had learned English through the port. "What made him leave Keansbury?"

"About two years ago, he lost his job at the port. Oh, not because he not a good worker, but because his job no longer there," Maria said. "So, he went to school in New York and now he a big shot!" She said it with such pride and a lot of bragging.

Katie pushed away from the table and motioned to Ali that it was time they get back to work. "Maria, thank you again for the pie and the conversation. I look forward to someday meeting Miguel. We will be in the den if you need us."

"Okay, señora, I will call you when dinner is ready, and maybe the señorita will join too."

Katie and Ali just looked at one another with a glance that said, *Don't even bother saying anything.* She whispered to Ali, asking him if he could also get her a pair of large sweatpants.

CHAPTER 26

Ali took his usual seat by the window, but Katie was pacing across the room.

"Are you ok?" he asked concerned.

"Yes, of course," she responded, unconvincingly.

"Look, Katie, I know when you're yessing me! These past several weeks in particular have been overwhelming...driving back and forth to Clarkson, selecting a jury panel, interviewing and reinterviewing everyone in town, worrying about the Professor, and most definitely missing Matt. You've been a one-man band."

"That's not true. I couldn't do any of this without the support from you and the Professor. But I definitely agree, I miss Matt terribly. He's clearing his schedule and plans on being here at least for the first week of the trial." Trying to lighten the mood, she said, "And really, the biggest issue is I'm having a hard time breathing. This morning, I went to buckle my belt and had to move it over a notch. If I didn't know better, I would swear that Maria was trying to do this to us deliberately."

He nodded and chuckled. "Okay then, let's get back to business."

They talked for several hours, particularly with Katie expressing her uneasiness with the day's happenings at the hospital. She told Ali that something about VanAnt was a little disturbing. "I just can't seem to shake it. I just can't shake the feeling," she said. "I know backing Jennifer might seem irrational, but I expected the Professor to at least offer *some* support, or a lead to follow. He's always been honest, transparent. But now I'm wondering if VanAnt's presence has clouded his judgment. He's vulnerable right now."

She paused, then added, "Let's shift our attention to the port—especially Junior's role and how closely he's tied to VanAnt."

Ali did most of the talking, and Katie listened and processed every word. He revisited every bit of information they had already gathered but tried to look at it from a different angle. He read aloud some of the notes: Junior worked primarily on the docks with the crew when shipping containers were unloaded. Paperwork was transferred, and it was his job to review and pass them along to VanAnt.

"Katie, I've spoken with virtually every worker during the four months prior to the murder."

"And VanAnt?" she asked.

"I spoke with him and, again, he was viewed as second-in-command, tough but fair. He told me that he and Senior offered all workers a free breakfast and dinner, but he took credit for implementing the free English classes. I recall he mentioned discontinuing the classes, but was a bit vague as to why. He said something about budget, but the meal plan still remains in place. He also told me that his relationship with Junior was like an uncle and nephew; he cared about him as much as his own children."

"Yes," she said, "he told me the same. The two families are very close."

Ali continued, "You know, a good thing about the classes is

that Santiago, for example, was able to procure a good job after being laid off."

"Miguel," she said.

"What?" he asked.

"You said Santiago. His name is Miguel."

"No, I do mean Santiago. I spoke with him, Antonio, and several others this morning. I thought I mentioned that some of the men had been laid off and found other employment."

"Wait a sec, go back to your meetings," she said. "The men that were laid off, had they all taken the English classes?" She was anxious; she didn't know what, if anything, she had, but it felt like a potential development.

He quickly thumbed through his notepad. "Antonio, Santiago, Diego, two, three more, yes," he said.

"Al, it's the same story Maria just shared about Miguel." She was cautiously optimistic.

"Are we on to something? Is there a connection to Junior?" he asked excitedly. "Katie, what does this mean?"

"It means we are going back to the port tomorrow. I want you to talk to the dock crew again, see if there's anything more you can find out about these English classes."

"And you?" he asked.

"I'm going to pay a visit to the second-in-command, whether he likes it or not."

They shared a look that said they were done for the day.

"I'm going to go to my room, call Matt, and then, as they say, crash! Al, would you do me a favor please? Jennifer seems to take to you, would you see if you could get her to come down for some dinner. The more at ease she is, the better she'll be for the trial."

"Absolutely, I will. And don't be surprised if Maria barges into your room with a full tray!"

"Good night," she said cheekily.

CHAPTER 27

Morning came fast, a surprisingly sound sleep before being awakened by a symphony of waves crashing on the rocks. Katie readied quickly; she had much to do today, and wasting time was never one of her faults. The smell of freshly brewed coffee drew her immediately to the kitchen.

"Good morning, Maria. And please, just coffee. I am still so full from yesterday's cornucopia of delights. I haven't seen Al, has he been down yet?"

"Si, señora," Maria said, clearly disappointed that food was not requested. "I made breakfast for he and the señorita; he brings the tray to her room."

Katie finished her second cup of coffee and returned upstairs to Jennifer's room. Tapping on the door, she waited for a reply before entering. She was pleased to see them both seated at the table eating breakfast and talking.

"Good morning, you two."

"And good morning to you," Ali said cheerfully. "We've been discussing Shakespeare, to which Jennifer has offered a very unique perspective on his writing."

Jennifer said nothing, but managed a nod and a weak smile. To Katie, these were minor miracles.

"Jennifer, would you mind if I borrowed Ali for a while? There's much to do today, and I could certainly use his assistance." With that, Ali got up from the table and promised Jennifer he would return later to continue the discussion.

To the delight of Katie, Jennifer seemed to come alive at the prospect of sharing insight regarding Shakespeare. She looked directly at Ali and proclaimed, "I'm intrigued by the idea that Macbeth can be read as a psychological study of ambition unraveling in isolation, rather than a purely political tragedy—it's a lens that shifts the entire emotional weight of the play."

Ali nodded, seemingly in agreement, then he and Katie left.

As they started their drive to the port, Katie turned to Ali and asked curiously, "By the way, what was that Macbeth comment all about?"

"I have absolutely *no* idea," Ali said. somewhat deflated. "That girl belongs in Mensa!"

Katie chuckled.

By the time they arrived at the entranceway to the port, their strategy had been put in place. At this point it was only a hunch, but Katie had a feeling that something was amiss with the English classes. Ali was charged with speaking to the day crew again, with a focus on the classes and any possible connection to Junior. Katie was going to attempt to meet with VanAnt again. She hoped her unplanned visit would catch him off guard.

In anticipation of being stopped at the gate, Katie was prepared with a plausible rationale for their visit. However, like the first time she came, no one was nearby to question their presence, so she continued straight to the dock.

A cluster of men—albeit a very small cluster—were loading a truck, so Ali believed that would be a good place for him to start. It was apparent that they remembered him as they greeted him warmly with handshakes and pats on the back. He motioned for Katie to continue on. She reversed, then turned to the right and drove directly to the main office, parking in front of the building's entranceway. As she exited the car and looked around, it saddened her to see that there were so few cars occupying the hundreds of available spaces.

She approached the front door and was again surprised to find it unlocked and no one stationed behind the guard desk. Fortunately, she recalled VanAnt's office was on the second floor, accessible by the first elevator bank. A loud ring of the elevator announced her arrival to his floor, so she waited patiently, expecting someone to heed the call. No one came. Hesitancy was never an issue with Katie, so she slowly made her way through the maze of empty cubicles until she saw a light peering from the end office. The door was ajar, and looking in she saw VanAnt seated at his desk. She knocked on the door. Although certainly not her intent, she found it slightly amusing to see him jump, as they say, out of his skin.

"I am so sorry. I am so sorry, Mr. VanAnt!" she said, not wanting to alienate him. "I called out, but obviously you didn't hear me," she lied.

It took a few seconds for him to compose himself, at which point he very quickly slammed closed the two office books on his desk and turned over what appeared to be a legal document.

"You clearly startled me, Mrs. Russo. I didn't hear you nor was I was expecting you. Did we have an appointment?" he said, visibly annoyed.

"No, we didn't, and I can only apologize again. I had a few questions and I was told you would be the best source to provide the answers." Although sounding trite, she once again lied.

He sat for a moment, collecting his composure, then, like a flick of a switch, he became remarkably cordial. "I will help with your questions, but why don't we walk over to the cafeteria. I'm sure I can rustle up a coffee."

Katie was impressed with the way he turned from tiger to pussycat in just a few seconds. *"He's smooth,"* she thought. *"No, he's slick. Very slick."* A flicker of unease crept in as she wondered who, exactly, she was dealing with.

They walked over to the cafeteria located on other side of the floor. It was eerily quiet, remnants of a ghost town. "Would you like medium or dark coffee?" he asked, standing by the Keurig machine.

"Dark is fine, and no milk or sugar please."

"That's perfect," he said. "We seem to be out of both."

Gently placing the cup in front of her, he asked, "Now, what questions do you have that I may be of help?"

"When we met for the first time, despite the horrific tragedy, you were adamant about keeping the business afloat in support of the community. I'm sad to say, from the outside looking in, I have observed a dramatic decline overall. What happened?"

"It's very true. Unfortunately, as hard as I've tried, without Senior at the helm, our overseas clients began looking for other areas along the coast to dock. A ripple effect, a snowball that turned into an avalanche."

She wasn't sure about his words, but she did believe he was disheartened about the situation.

"And the men and women that worked here, are they still all employed?" she asked, feigning ignorance.

"That's been the hardest part for me," he said. "As you can see, today is a typical day. I've had to let go of 90% of the employees, we only have a skeleton crew. Perhaps you saw them as you drove in, they comprise the full staff. They come in the morning and do whatever is left to do. Only one or two work late afternoon or evenings."

Katie continued, "My colleague and I have spoken to many

of your employees, and they all were so appreciative of what you did for them, the free meals and the English classes."

He nodded with a smile. "Yes, it was a privilege to share. Our business prospered and we wanted to share. Our workers lived here in Keansbury or in neighboring towns. We did well, they did well, the communities did well. Everyone benefited."

Katie felt like he was being sincere.

"Mr. VanAnt, as I mentioned, my colleague spoke with some of your workers. The other day he happened to meet a few at Iberia Tavern."

He quickly interrupted, "One of my favorites. The garlic shrimp is excellent."

"I'm sure it is," she said, and quickly continued. "They spoke perfect English, having benefited from your generous classes. Unfortunately, they had all been laid off during, as you put it, a prosperous time." She noticed a slight uneasiness in his body language. "Was there a reason for these layoffs?"

Shifting twice in his chair, he replied, "I don't know exactly to whom your colleague spoke, but I know we parted ways with several workers whose jobs had become redundant."

"Did you refill those positions?"

His tone changed. "No, we did not. I just told you the positions were redundant. We took no pleasure from releasing workers, but we did ensure they were well compensated. That I recall for certain."

"You had discontinued the English classes at some point, but kept the food plan. May I ask why?"

"Our wonderful instructor retired, and it just became chaotic trying to find a replacement. We had intended to restart, but..." He didn't finish. He was already on the defensive and clearly getting wary of her questions, so she tried to sound calm and not accusatory.

"One last question, if I may. Was Junior involved with any of the free meal or class programs? Did he handle any of the purchasing, scheduling, or administration?"

From years of interviews, Katie knew when someone had reached their boiling point. His tone and demeanor clearly suggested their meeting was nearing its conclusion.

VanAnt responded in no uncertain terms. "No, he did not, and what exactly are you suggesting? Do you think meals or classes were the cause of his demise? That's ridiculous, and I resent the implication."

"Of course not. When we first met, you were kind enough to tell me about Junior's work here, and I'm only trying to learn a bit more. I am not suggesting anything, just asking."

Thankfully, his cell phone rang, breaking the tension at least for the moment. She could only hear his end of the conversation, but clearly someone needed his presence, to which he replied he would be down momentarily. He stood up, expecting Katie to do the same.

"Mr. VanAnt, I'd like to use the restroom. And please, don't let me hold you up. I know the way out and will leave promptly."

"Of course, and please accept my apology for sounding harsh. My feeling about your client hasn't changed. In fact, it's only intensified. However, if you need anything from me, please don't hesitate to ask." He reached out his hand and she obliged.

"No apologies necessary. I know my questions may have sounded intrusive."

He turned and walked hurriedly toward the elevator. As he waited, she could feel his eyes on her. She pretended not to notice as she cleaned the table and put the dirty cups in the kitchen. As soon as she heard the elevator bell, she turned and made certain he entered. She heard the doors close. Gathering up her nerve, she raced to the other side of the floor, back to his office. With rapid speed, she turned over the document and read as much as she could before flipping it back. She then opened the two books, doing the same. And then she heard the elevator bell.

He was back, and she needed an escape plan. She had seconds before he would be in sight of his office. She darted out and ran in the opposite direction, virtually circling the entire floor to get back to the cafeteria. With nerves of steel or sheer stupidity, she peered around the corner of the cubicle wall to see him walk into his office. She prayed she remembered to close the books. It occurred to Katie that he may have noticed that she did not exit the building, so she ran into the restroom. Her heart was pounding as she heard his footsteps coming her way. She wet her hands and then grabbed some paper towels. Just as he approached the door, she flung it open and walked out, pretending to be drying her hands with the towels. "I'm sorry it took me so long. I'm embarrassed to say, but Maria has been force-feeding me for days and it finally caught up with me." With a great deal of relief, he seemed to believe yet another lie.

"Let me escort you out." He held her elbow and walked back to the elevator. As they approached the front entrance, he pointed to Ali, leaning against the car. "By the way, you neglected to mention that *he* was here talking to my employees."

"No ulterior motive, I assure you. He is friendly with some of the men, so I'm sure he was just passing time waiting for me." The final lie. Katie could still feel the effects of her escapade; her heart was pounding. However, she gave her best performance of being calm, cordial, and in control.

"Mrs. Russo, as I said earlier, I am available if you need anything further. However, next time, if there is a next time, please make an appointment!"

He stayed at the entrance until he was certain they were off the property. A tiny bead of sweat formed on his brow. He reached in his pocket for his cell phone. "We have a bit of a situation," were his only words before disconnecting.

Once out of sight of the port, Ali started to tell Katie what had occurred. "VanAnt was very surprised to see me speaking with the men and became quite upset. I'm not certain, but I think he made a threat."

"Al, I'm sorry I put you in that situation, and I want to hear everything, but please, let's just drive back in silence. We can debrief at the house."

He wasn't offended. He knew her well enough to recognize when something was brewing inside. What he didn't realize was that her heart was still pounding in her ears!

CHAPTER 28

"Al, give me a little time to record my notes, I'll be in the den."

"Okay, I'll go check on Jennifer and then I'll be down."

Katie's recall was excellent, but she nevertheless wanted to ensure that her mental notes were accurately recorded. She was a stickler for details, so her typical procedure was to type her notes and then catalogue them according to topic. These notes were to be added to the thin folder titled *VanAnt*. She was so engrossed in her work, she barely heard a light tap on the door. Assuming it was Al, she yelled for him to come in.

As the sliding doors opened, she heard a soft voice, "Am I interrupting?"

She looked up and was pleasantly surprised to see the Professor's wife. "Phyllis!" she exclaimed with great enthusiasm. "Seeing you is never an interruption." Jumping out of the chair, she greeted Phyllis with a genuinely warm hug. She had often told the Professor that one of the things she liked best about him was Phyllis.

"Wonderful news, Kate. Please don't be cross with me, but

Sean had his surgery today. It all happened so quickly, I didn't have time to let you or anyone else know. I'm really sorry, but it's done and all went well. It's amazing what they do nowadays, they already have him walking. If all continues in the right direction, he should be discharged soon."

"Phyllis, of course I'm not upset. In fact, that's the best news I've heard. I am so happy for you both and I promise to see him soon. Are you leaving now, or do you have time to sit for a few minutes?" She didn't wait for a response. "I realized that in all the time I've been here, you and I have hardly spoken about anything other than the Professor." Katie grabbed Phyllis' hand and escorted her to the sofa.

"Can I get you a coffee or something else to drink?" "Oh, I'm being ridiculous," Katie said. "This is your house and I'm treating you like a guest."

Phyllis gave a slight laugh. "I'm happy you feel comfortable enough here to think of this as your home."

"Now that the Professor is doing so well, will you be returning to the house?" Katie couldn't help but wonder.

"I just came for a few items, some clothes and papers, but I'll be returning to stay with my sister. She's been wonderful support and company."

Katie interjected, "And you and the Professor have been wonderful support to me. Actually, considering his health, I was concerned I was overwhelming him with this trial, but he's been adamant that I keep him in the loop."

With a look of resignation, Phyllis agreed. "I've tried reminding him that he's retired, but he hasn't quite grasped that concept."

"Phyllis, I know I've said this before, but it's worth repeating. I so appreciate you letting us stay here. I don't know how we would have managed otherwise."

Noticing the slight change in Phyllis' demeanor, Katie asked, "Oh, I'm sorry, Phyllis. Perhaps we've overstayed our welcome?" Katie was unsure what prompted the shift and worried she may have inadvertently offended Phyllis.

"No, not at all. However, to be honest, I'm uneasy with that girl staying here. I was opposed to it and surprised by Sean's insistence. Kate, believe me, having lived with a defense attorney for so long, I understand the work you do. But the Keans are our dear friends and I'm concerned that I have been giving sanctuary to their son's killer."

Katie was a little taken aback by what she just heard. "I'm really sorry for causing you such distress, and if you want us to make other arrangements, I absolutely understand."

Again, Phyllis repeated, "No, I want you to stay, but I also wanted you to know how I feel. Sean has asked me to stop talking about it, and I have, but I felt I could be honest with you."

Katie was relieved to be staying because at this point, there weren't any possible "other arrangements."

"I'm glad you feel you can be honest with me, and, Phyllis, if there's *anything* you're not on board with, please let me know. You can bypass the Professor and come directly to me!"

Phyllis smiled and nodded at the thought, but Katie knew there were no secrets between her and the Professor, so bypassing him would be inconceivable. A short pause in the conversation gave way to a change of subject.

"Phyllis, I know you're friends with the Keans, but I'm curious, are you and the Professor friendly with the VanAnts?"

"We are, but not as close as the Keans. I like his wife, Corrie, but Aaron reminds me of a car salesman, a little deceptive, a little manipulative. I really shouldn't say that. He and Sean have become closer; he visits regularly. Why do you ask?"

Interestingly, Katie had begun to describe him similarly. "Oh, I spent a little time with him this morning. An interesting man." She was intentionally vague. "I will say it is very commendable the way he implemented the food and English classes for the employees, although he mentioned that the classes had to be discontinued."

"Kate, my relationship with the Keans and VanAnts was on a personal level. I don't really know much about the business side, although I do know that Maria's son Miguel learned to speak English there."

Katie was a little uneasy questioning Phyllis in this manner, but she was hoping to get useful information without having to explain her reasoning.

"Yes, Maria told me about Miguel, and Ali said that several of the workers he had spoken with were very appreciative of the English classes. What a wonderful opportunity given to them. Mr. VanAnt expressed disappointment in having to discontinue the classes. He said that the instructor had retired and they were unable to find a replacement. Are you and the Professor acquaintances with the instructor?"

"Not really, I think we may have met him once or twice at a town function."

Katie wasn't sure how much further she could press Phyllis before she would seriously question her motive.

"Do you happen to remember his name?"

"Possibly Mason or Chase, last name Park or Palmer. As I said, we barely knew him, but I do seem to remember that he moved to Florida. Maybe a health issue? Why don't you ask Sean, I'm sure he would know."

A bit underhanded, but Katie obtained the info she needed. "Oh, I was just curious, not a Professor issue." She hoped Phyllis wouldn't mention any of their conversation to him. Katie was just about to change the subject when Ali walked in. Perfect timing.

"Ali, it's so good to see you," she said warmly.

"What a nice surprise," he said. "It's so good to see you too, Mrs. Kyle." Turning to Katie, "Am I interrupting?"

It was Phyllis who responded. "That was my opening line, and no, you are not interrupting. As a matter of fact, I need to get on my way. You two have work to do, and I have a husband that needs hand holding." She gave Katie a hug. "I'll see you soon, and please take care of yourself. Take good care." It sounded like a warning. She gave Ali a quick hug and left.

"It was nice to see Phyllis, did you know she was coming here today?"

"No. In fact, when she knocked on the door, I thought it was you. She shared some good news, the Professor finally had his operation and he's doing well."

"Oh, that's wonderful, Katie. That poor fellow seems to have been in that hospital forever. I'm sure it's a relief to you."

"It certainly is. But after Phyllis told me about the Professor, I took the opportunity to ask her a few questions. I feel a little guilty. I wanted to get information on VanAnt, so I tried to be blasé about the questions I asked. I care about her, so I just didn't want to be direct and then get her knowingly involved in the issues of the case."

"So, did you get your answers?" he asked.

"I got answers leading to more questions." Changing direction, she asked, "You were with Jennifer for a time, how is she doing?"

"I think the realization that the trial starts soon has sunk in. She wasn't even up for a Shakespeare discussion." Her despair was unsettling to him, so he promised Katie he'd try again later.

"Do what you can, because soon I'll need to have the hard

conversation with her about trial expectations. Anyway, this afternoon we need to concentrate on the findings from this morning, but first let's take a half-hour break. I can't believe I'm saying this, but I need sustenance. I can't wait to see the expression on Maria's face when we walk into the kitchen and ask for food. It may just be the happiest face we see today."

CHAPTER 29

It was late afternoon when they finally got back to work. Katie grabbed her notes and a marker and stood in front of the information board; Ali repositioned his favorite chair to get a better view. As she detailed her conversation with VanAnt, she began rearranging the sticky notes to reflect a different perspective. She drew a line down the middle of one of the boards, thereby creating a new section. "I'm labeling this side *BUSINESS*." Turning to Ali, she said, "Much of this time I have been focusing on the relationship between Jennifer and Junior. I don't yet know what it means, if anything, but I now think I need to look at the relationship between the port and Junior." She quickly filled the board with old and new notes, reflecting conversations with VanAnt and Phyllis. When Ali contributed his information from the morning, it was clear that the English classes may possibly be an important piece of the puzzle.

"Al, I'd like you to look into the retired instructor. Phyllis isn't certain, but this was the best she could recall." She handed him a piece of paper with the names. "Do you have an operative in Florida?"

"Yes, a good man, Derek Nessa. I'll reach out as soon as we're done."

"You know what to tell him. I want absolutely anything he can discover."

Katie often used paid services online, but she always wanted the kitchen sink of information, right down to what someone ate for breakfast. The dialogue between the two was fast and steady, with Katie having to pause a few times to catch up with the note writing. There was so much to share that another board became necessary.

Ali continued as Katie prepared more notes. "You know, it's a shame what's happening to these fellows. They're hard workers and they're worried about their jobs. Because they don't speak English, they're concerned that there are very limited local opportunities for them. Most of this crew had signed up for classes just a week before they were cancelled." She was so deep in thought, he wasn't sure she even heard him.

"Anything regarding the layoffs?" Katie hoped.

Ali, too, had a good memory, but he preferred to refer to his notepad just in case. "All that these fellows knew was that some men from the day and afternoon shifts were let go. The party line is that they were let go because the positions were no longer needed. However, the rumor mill says they were let go because they made too much money. Several were replaced by cheaper workers. That's not unusual for a business to do," he said. "They also repeated what we already knew; they didn't have very much contact with Junior—" Ali didn't get to finish his findings, as Katie interrupted.

"Wait a minute, what did you say? Go back a few thoughts." Katie felt a flicker of doubt—had she just heard something that didn't quite align with previous information?

He wasn't certain what he had said that made her jump.

"Let's see, men were laid off from both shifts, made too much money. Katie, I'm not sure what you heard."

"Did I hear you correctly that the men that were laid off were replaced by cheaper workers?"

"Yes, I don't know if that's true, but that's the scuttlebutt. In fact, one of the men in today's crew is one of those replacements. How is this significant?"

"When I spoke with VanAnt, I said that the men that were laid off happened to speak English and I asked why. He seemed a little irritated by the question and said those positions were redundant. I asked if they were replaced, and he snapped and said no, I just told you they were redundant."

"That's right, you did say that. But what does it mean?"

"I'm just not sure yet, but I'm getting a stronger feeling that something is going on down at Keans Industries and somehow, the business, Junior, and Jennifer are connected!"

She saved this last bit of news till the end, knowing that Ali would be upset with her. "And there's more, Al. I was a bit of a Miss Marple just before I came down to the parking lot."

"Go on." He was reserving his anger until he heard exactly what she had done. Ever since they met and started working together, he always told her to leave the private investigating to him. From his years of experience, he knew all too well how quickly things could escalate, and he never wanted to see her in a potentially harmful situation.

Katie continued, giving a blow-by-blow account, and she even sounded a bit too excited when she got to the part about cleverly exiting the restroom. Ali, however, remained grim-faced and admonished her, as she had expected. She promised to leave all future snooping to him. "Al, I get it. Now let me tell you the product of my sleuthing. I turned over the papers first and it was a legal document indicating the sale of his house." She added all the information onto sticky notes. "I didn't have time to read any further, so the question remains, is he moving to a less expensive house or is he possibly leaving Keansbury for good, and why?" Katie found herself increasingly questioning VanAnt's role in Junior's murder. If he was indeed headed out of town, could that be a sign he was trying to evade scrutiny?

"What about the notebooks?" he asked.

"There were two ledgers, each containing a hand-written list of names followed by a dollar amount."

"Hand-written? Who keeps a paper ledger these days? Everything is computerized. I'm going to answer my own question," Ali said. "Someone who has something to hide and knows that once it's on the computer, it's accessible forever!"

"My thought exactly," she concurred.

"Katie, I know you didn't have much time, but did you happen to recognize any of the names?"

"I recall the first two names listed, but I don't know who they are. Yusuf and Franz. I'm guessing that these are first names; last names were not listed."

She finished affixing the last of the notes onto the board. Taking a step back, she scanned all the information that had been gathered since day one.

"Al, it's here. Somewhere on these boards is our answer, I can feel it. I'm positive that it has to do with the business, with VanAnt, with Junior, and somehow with Jennifer."

He questioned if she would discuss all this with the Professor.

"I don't think I will at this time. I'm not sure he would be up for it so soon after the operation. Besides, VanAnt has been visiting the Professor more regularly and I don't know if it's social or business. At this point, I'm not sure I would even know what to say. I feel like we have a 1,000-piece puzzle and several important pieces are missing from the box." Katie turned toward Ali. "I need you to follow up on two things. We already spoke about the instructor. The other—I'd like you to see if you can meet up with some of the workers again, perhaps at that restaurant you went to the other day. I would prefer you did not go back to the port. I want to know if they're familiar with Yusuf and Franz. And see if they ever noticed an altercation between VanAnt and Junior."

Ali pushed the chair back to the window. "I'll head over to Iberia Tavern now, maybe I'll get lucky and catch one of the crew members there. On the ride over, I'll call my Florida colleague."

Katie was pleased that things were in motion.

As he reached the sliding doors, he turned around and asked, "What will you be doing?"

"I'm going to finish up here and then try to spend some time with Jennifer. Al, if you uncover anything at all, please come find me, I don't care how late."

He nodded and, like the Flash, he was gone.

CHAPTER 30

It was early evening when Katie realized she was talking to herself and absent-mindedly rubbing her temples, both clear signs that it was time for a break. As important as it was to continue working, she knew it was also important to spend some time with Jennifer. She first needed a few moments to collect her thoughts and to refresh with a cold splash of water on her face. Ascending the staircase, she felt confident of her speech, but less confident of its reception.

Rapping lightly on the bedroom door, she waited for a response that did not come, so she entered quietly. She saw Jennifer seated in front of the open window. The ocean breeze moved the curtains like a choregraphed dance, with each panel gently brushing her cheeks. Katie expected to see her with a book, but instead, she was just staring motionless. Regardless of her deportment, Katie knew it was the right time to talk. She grabbed a chair, slid it across the floor, and placed it next to Jennifer. She had intentionally made noise in the hopes of snapping Jennifer out of her trance.

"Jennifer, I'd like to talk to you about the trial expectations." Her voice was calm. A strong gust of wind blew the curtains against them both, so she got up and lowered the window. She proceeded, now with a more forceful tone, "Jennifer, look at me, please, look at me." She turned her head to face Katie, but kept her eyes turned downward.

"Jennifer, many months ago you asked me to help you. No, you begged me to help you. Quite frankly, your story was rather unbelievable. However, the Professor was concerned and asked for my help. I wasn't sure at first, but I never say no to the Professor. And then I got to know you. Look at me, please."

Jennifer finally made eye contact. Katie placed each of her hands in hers and said slowly and with much feeling, "Jennifer, I came here for the Professor, but I've stayed here for *you*. As crazy, wild, and implausible as your story is, I believe you." She repeated herself. "I believe you."

Jennifer's eyes became watery as Katie continued. "All this time I've trusted you, trusted that you have told me the truth, trusted that you're willing to see this through regardless of the plea offerings that have been made. And now, I'm asking you to trust me. The Professor, Ali, me, we've all worked tirelessly on your behalf, and when the trial starts, I need you to trust that I am doing everything in my power to expose the lies and uncover the truth. Your truth."

"I do trust you," Jennifer said weakly.

"Thank you," Katie replied. "Now, here's what I want to you to do. I need you to be present. I need you to be composed, no matter how difficult. The prosecution will be interviewing witness after witness, all testifying contra to what you know, what we know, to be the truth. The jury will be looking at you, your expressions, your reactions. I want you to stay calm and to listen to what's being said and take note of any inconsistencies. Can you do that for me?"

She nodded affirmatively.

"Each day of the trial, a sheriff's officer will be taking you to and from the court. I will follow behind. Under no circumstances should you speak with anyone unless I'm with you. Okay?"

Another nod.

"Tomorrow, we'll go over more details and we'll put together an appropriate wardrobe. Lastly, I'd like you to leave this room more often. I realize you can't go outdoors, but the house is huge, and it would be good for you to move around, stretch your legs. And I'd like you to take your meals in the kitchen. Maria will love your company."

"All right, I'll do as you ask," she said softly. It was a lot for Jennifer to absorb, but she willingly complied. Bit by bit, she started to lower the defenses she had been forced to build around herself. She wasn't certain what she was beginning to feel, she just knew it felt welcoming.

Katie stood up to leave. "Jennifer, you have been through so much in your life and I can't even imagine the toll this has taken on you. But through it all, you've persevered, and despite the hardships, you haven't given up. I'm very proud of you. Get some rest and I'll see you in the morning."

Jennifer waited for the door to close before she let the tears flow. No one had ever told her they were proud of her.

CHAPTER 31

It was late when Ali returned to the house. He wasn't surprised to see the light shining from the Professor's den, but he was surprised to see Katie fast asleep with her head resting on a pile of papers.

"Katie," he whispered as he touched her shoulder.

She opened her eyes and wondered why Ali was in her bedroom. It took a moment for her to catch her bearings.

"Katie, you asked me to find you no matter how late. It's 1:30. I have some news."

She stood up to stretch and get the feeling back in her hand, which had the misfortune of acting as her pillow. "Tell me something good, Al, please."

"Well, we got lucky. Some of the fellows were at the restaurant and they were happy to have me join them." He grabbed his notebook. "Let me just give you the overall workings. The ships arrive at the port and they remove the containers. Before the death of Junior, there would be several ships at the port on any given day. Since then, one, rarely two. Once they're unloaded, Junior would come down from the office and handle the paperwork, checking that the cargo matched the forms, and then he would return to the office. Katie, they didn't know for certain, but it is assumed that Junior collaborated with VanAnt. He used to do that job, but once Junior joined it was made his responsibility. I'm guessing he was in training. Anyway, here's the interesting part. A dedicated set of drivers would show up to collect their cargo, they recall about seven or eight. Yusuf and Franz were two of those drivers. The drivers would arrive and Junior would return to let the workers know which cargo was to be loaded onto the trucks. Once the work was completed, the drivers left."

Katie wanted to know if the workers recalled any of the company names on the trucks.

"I did ask them that question and, as far as they could recall, they believed that a phone number may have been listed, but no names."

All those trucks and no names; very odd, she thought.

"Oh, one last thing, Katie. The old-time workers remembered an incident between Junior and VanAnt. Junior began checking some of the contents of the boxes against the paperwork. He opened a crate, and soon VanAnt came rushing down. They didn't understand what was said between them, but they noticed that Junior stopped checking and never looked inside another crate again."

Katie took a moment to process. "Al, we are uncovering some very shady dealings at Keans Industries, possibly something important to our case. But even if VanAnt is engaging in criminal activities, I have yet to connect this to Jennifer. By her own account, she's never stepped foot at the port and she isn't personally acquainted with VanAnt."

She was tired and she could tell Ali was too. "Let's get some sleep. We can start up fresh in the morning. By the way, did they recall any of the names of the other drivers?"

"Ah, yes," he said as he reached for his notepad.

"No, not tonight. We'll review them in the morning." Leaving the den, she turned to take one more look at the wall of information. "In the morning," she said, and with that she switched off the lights and closed the sliding doors.

CHAPTER 32

orning came quickly, and Katie was moving at a rapid
pace. Time was now at a premium. At the Professor's
insistence, she intended to see him to do a final review of old
and new information. Not surprisingly, he had phoned Katie
wanting an update; a minor thing like an operation wasn't going
to curtail his interest. With no time for breakfast, Katie stopped
by the kitchen for a quick sip of coffee and was very happy to see
Jennifer seated at the table talking with Maria.

"Good morning, ladies. It's nice to see you both."

Jennifer smiled while Maria jumped up, expecting to make
another banquet breakfast. Katie politely waved her arms,
signaling no food this morning. She took one last sip of coffee
and told Jennifer she was going to see the Professor and would
be back sometime in the afternoon. Katie walked over to
Jennifer, placing her hand on her shoulder. "Maria, look after
my associate here."

"Of course, señora. I will be showing the señorita how to
prepare paella."

"I look forward to dinner," Katie said excitedly, then gave a
wink to Maria and left. She felt a quiet joy watching Jennifer

emerge from her room and engage. Maria, much like Ali, offered a steady and welcome presence.

The drive to the hospital felt like déjà vu; she'd taken this trip countless times since living at the house. Before she knew it, she was entering the Professor's room and was pleasantly surprised to see he was well enough to be playing cards with Nurse Cathy. As usual, all the pretzels were piled neatly in front of her.

"Professor, wouldn't it be less humiliating if you just bought Nurse Cathy a bag of pretzels?" Katie laughed as she wrapped her arms around him. "I'm so glad you're doing so well. Clearly the operation was successful."

"Please, Mrs. Russo, it's the only joy I get each day," Nurse Cathy said with a grin as she gathered up her winnings. She continued proudly, "Did you notice the Professor is sitting in a regular chair at the table? He walked here on his own."

"Professor, that is amazing!" Turning to Nurse Cathy, Katie asked if he would be discharged soon.

"It's not for me to say, that will be up to Doctor Christian, but I know he is genuinely pleased with all the progress he's made. I'm sure he'll be talking to the Professor soon. I better get going, I have rounds to do and pretzels to share. Good to see you again, Mrs. Russo."

Katie nodded and smiled, then turned to the Professor. "Professor, are you up for a long conversation? I'd like to go over the entire case before we start next week, but I don't want to tire you, so please be honest."

"Of course, I want to hear everything," he said. "Grab that comfortable chair and let's get started."

Katie started by rehearsing her opening statement to the jury, then began to detail all the information that she had collected. "Professor, Ali and I have spoken to almost everyone in this town countless times. We've met with the sheriff and the prosecutor and reviewed all the available data. It won't be much, but I know I can poke a few holes here and there. In my opening statement, I intend to highlight the misinterpretation by Mr. Adams of the conversations between Jennifer and Junior. I will draw attention to the forensic inconsistencies with regards to the knife and, based on the configuration of the trail's direction, I will point out that it naturally leads away from town, casting doubt on the assumption that Jennifer was running away. I will suggest that someone else orchestrated the murder and deliberately implicated my client—a quiet, solitary individual with no history of violence. The evidence will show that my client was not the architect of this crime, but its scapegoat."

The Professor listened intently, nodded several times, and took a few notes, although his impeccable memory was legendary. She paused, taking a sip of water and waiting for some verbal comment from the Professor.

"I know you very well," he said. "What aren't you telling me?"

She had fully intended to tell him of her suspicions about VanAnt, but her hesitation was based on their relationship. Katie didn't want to put the Professor in an awkward situation, possibly having to divulge some private conversations between him and VanAnt. However, Jennifer's life was in the balance, so she knew she needed to pursue all roads, regardless where they led. Not wanting to face him, Katie walked over to stare out the window and continued.

"Professor, I've come into some information that strongly suggests there is something unlawful happening at Keans Industries and VanAnt is involved." She detailed her conversations with him, particularly his demeanor and inconsistencies. She also mentioned about the English classes, the handwritten ledgers, and most importantly, his interactions with Junior. "I've also found out that he is selling his house, not at all certain if he's downsizing or leaving the area altogether." She turned to face him and was taken aback by his facial expression.

"Katie, I've never minced words with you before and I won't start now. I'm quite stunned and, quite frankly, perplexed."

She was deflated; this was not what she had expected or hoped for.

"I've known the Keans for years, and I can assure you everything they've done has been above board. Although I'm not as close with VanAnt, I can assure you that he, too, is above reproach. To think he is responsible for Junior's death is unimaginable. He cared for that boy as if he was his own. Katie, I am getting a little tired, would you please help me back into bed?"

She wrapped her arms around him and lifted, surprised by how little effort it took. All these months in the hospital had transformed his hefty frame into a shadow of its former self. Once he was comfortably positioned, he continued.

"Everything you just told me is purely circumstantial. And more importantly, I see absolutely no connection between Keans Industries and Jennifer. At no time had she ever mentioned them to me. Quite frankly, I'm totally surprised by your approach. I had gotten you involved in the hopes of convincing her to plead to a lesser charge; it never occurred to me that you would be going to trial with the expectation of an acquittal." His tone carried a hint of firmness, but it wasn't aggressive or angry. He simply wanted to make his point without sounding harsh.

Katie temporarily found herself without words. After composing herself, she responded, "Professor, I believe VanAnt is responsible for Junior's death." It was the first time she had said that out loud. "I know it's still just a bunch of puzzle pieces, but if I can put them together, then I can next look for a connection to Jennifer."

She could see he was getting tired, and his tone softened. "Katie, I'm trying to be helpful, not hurtful. I know you're not forgetting Jennifer's account of that day... He was a drug user, he invited her to meet him, her fingerprints on the knife. This has all been discounted, and she has not rescinded one single word. If you go into court with this tale, you will be discredited and she will be convicted."

The mood—or the tension—was interrupted by the ring of Katie's cell phone. Grabbing the phone, she saw it was Ali. "Professor, would you excuse me for a moment? I need to take this call. I'll step outside." She didn't wait for a response.

In the hallway, she answered his call. "Hi, Katie, how's it going with the Professor?" he asked innocently. She could only respond that she would discuss it with him later in the day.

"Al, please tell me you have something." It sounded as if she was pleading, and she was.

"Katie, I heard back from my Florida colleague. He found out that the instructor's name is Mason Parkence. The short version is that he and his wife, Emily, have indeed retired to Florida. Fort Myers, to be exact. However, he did not leave his position willingly. He was dismissed. VanAnt did the deed and informed him that the business was going in a different direction, so his services were no longer needed. It was VanAnt that mentioned retiring to Florida. He even gave him a sizeable severance package seemingly to encourage the move. Another thing, Katie, Parkence recalled the names of all his students and was disappointed when some of them were laid off."

"More lies," Katie thought. "Al, do you have those names?"

"Yes. He even keeps in touch with a few. Does this help?"

"Absolutely, another puzzle piece. Al, listen, I stepped away from the Professor to take this call and I want to get back to him. Let's get together this afternoon. And, Al, good work!"

She walked back into the room and the Professor asked if everything was okay.

"Yes," she responded. "It was Al, just checking in." Based on the Professor's reaction to VanAnt, she decided not to tell him of Al's findings. "Professor, I see you're tired, but may I ask you just one last thing? As a legal representative, did you ever have any personal or business association with Senior or VanAnt?" She wasn't certain how he would respond, but he answered immediately.

"Nothing personal, but on a limited basis I did some work for the business. I prepared contracts, reviewed forms, and gave them some legal direction. It wasn't much, but I never saw anything out of line. And because of our relationship, I did it gratis."

She nodded and walked over to the table to grab her purse and briefcase.

"Katie," he started to say, but she interrupted him.

"It's fine, Professor. I wanted your input and you gave it to me. I appreciate all that you had to say." She bent down to give him a peck on his cheek.

"Katie, one last thing. Try again with Jennifer. See if you can convince her to accept a lesser charge. I would hate to see her convicted of first-degree murder."

Katie gave a weak smile and left the room. As she walked down the hallway, she tried to process what had transpired. She wanted him to be honest, but she never expected such a definitive response to her assertions. There didn't seem to be any wiggle room; he was convinced she was trying to make a viable story out of inconsequential pieces of data. In all the years she had known the Professor, she had never questioned or challenged his viewpoint. Until now.

CHAPTER 33

Katie sat in the hospital car park for a moment, unable to move. She was worried. She knew the Professor was only trying to help, but if she couldn't convince him of Jennifer's innocence, how could she possibly convince a jury? At the very least, she needed to put doubt in the minds of the panel of men and women; sitting still was not an option. She mentally regrouped and made a call. "May I speak with Officer Wong? This is Katie Russo." Several minutes passed.

"Mrs. Russo, this is Officer Wong."

"Officer Wong, I need your help. May I buy you a cup of coffee?" Katie tried not to sound desperate.

"I'm rather busy today, Mrs. Russo. May I ask what this is about?"

"It's about the trial, and I really could use your assistance. I know it's asking a lot, but I would appreciate if you could spare me 15 minutes away from the office. Please." This time, Katie did sound desperate.

Reluctantly, the officer agreed. She told Katie a time and location to meet.

"Thank you so much, I will see you there shortly." Katie let out a sigh of relief.

"Black," Office Wong said before disconnecting.

Confused, Katie asked, "I'm sorry, what did you say?"

"Black," the officer repeated. "I take my coffee black and no sugar."

"Got it," Katie said with a smile. She started the car and exited the parking lot.

Driving into town, she first stopped at Annie's Diner to pick up the coffees. As she entered, she realized she was the only customer. She stood at the end of the counter waiting for someone to acknowledge her presence. The owner, Mr. Vick Fern, walked over with a hostile expression.

"Good morning. I'd like to order two coffees to go, please."

His tone matched his expression. "We're out of coffee." He leaned in and was just about to say more when his wife grabbed his arm.

"Vick, go in the kitchen. I'll take care of this." Her calm tone was reassuring as he stepped back and walked away. "I'm sorry," she continued. "With the lack of customers, we're all just a bit on edge. He didn't mean any harm."

"I understand, Annie. No apologies necessary."

"I'll get you those coffees. Sugar, milk?" she asked.

"Just black." Katie reached into her wallet when Annie waved her hand.

"It's fine, on the house."

Katie thanked her, but left $20 on the counter before she left. She wasn't sure if they would feel insulted, but she knew even this small amount would be of help.

It was only a few minutes' drive to the agreed-upon meeting spot at the edge of town. It was a small park with a few benches and one picnic table. Arriving, Katie could see that Officer Wong was already waiting. She made some pleasantries as she handed her the coffee. Behind them was a sizeable ditch roped off with yellow tape. Katie was curious. "What is happening here?"

The officer explained that the town had intended on building a new playground. Construction had started, but everything came to a halt after the incident. She called it an incident.

"I can tell that many things have changed since I first arrived. For instance, I stopped by the café to buy the coffees and Mr. Fern demonstrated a threatening posture."

Office Wong felt the need to respond. "Mrs. Russo, when you first arrived, people were cordial because you were a friend of the beloved Professor and they believed your role was to represent Jennifer in pleading to a lesser crime, thus avoiding a trial. Also, this town had yet to feel the full financial impact of what had happened. Now, they realize they will have to endure the burden of a trial while their town has literally deflated. Now, you said you needed my help. What do you need?" She was cordial but professional.

"First, may I ask you what you know about Mr. VanAnt?"

A little baffled by the question, the officer responded, "I know he's very well-liked and respected by the community. He is a prominent member of Keans Industries. I know him to say hello, but we certainly don't travel in the same social circle. Why do you ask?"

This wasn't the occasion to hold back, so Katie dove right in. "I've uncovered some evidence that suggests there may be some illegalities occurring at Keans Industries, and I think, I repeat, I *think*, that Mr. VanAnt is involved."

The officer's expression was not unlike that of the Professor's. Without interruption, she let Katie continue.

"It is my belief that whatever occurred there may have contributed to the death of Junior." Katie paused, waiting for the officer to say something...anything. The silence, as they say, was deafening.

Officer Wong finally responded. "Mrs. Russo, let me get this straight. You used a few hedging expressions...*may, I think, suggests*. Bottom line, tell me straight, are you saying that you believe Mr. VanAnt is personally responsible for Junior's death?"

"Yes, I am," Katie said firmly and with conviction. The deputy's eyes widened. "Officer Wong, I realize I'm a majority of one, which is why I need your help. I've read and reread your report, and there is no mention at all about Keans Industries. There was no investigation of the business as a possible link to the murder."

The officer was clearly taken aback. "Mrs. Russo, we explored all logical roads and none of them led to the business. We were fair and impartial, but this crime was so clearly black and white. There is no other suspect and no other motive other than a lover's quarrel."

Katie took out her notebook and placed it on the table. "Deputy, please let me take you through what I've uncovered, and then let me know if you think there is a possibility that Miss O'Neill is innocent." Methodically, she went through all the information as if she was presenting to the jury. When she finished, she looked directly into the officer's eyes. "Well, what do you think?"

Deputy Wong banged her hand on the table, stood up, and paced back and forth. "This is just crazy." She banged her hand on the table once again. "If there is even a shred of truth to what you've just showed me, oh goodness, Mrs. Russo, you have poked a hornet's nest of unimaginable proportions!"

Katie was exhilarated. Finally, someone had a sliver of doubt.

"Mrs. Russo, why are you telling me and not the sheriff? Have you gone to the prosecutor with this?"

"Because I trust you and I know the sheriff isn't interested in anything I have to say. No, I have not spoken with Mr. Ryan, and I don't intend to. I still need the glue that binds this all together, and that's why I asked to speak with you first."

"What is it you want from me?" The deputy was confused.

"I would like you to do some digging on VanAnt. My colleague and I have gone as far as we can legally go. I'm hoping to talk to the sheriff and ask for a warrant for the business' financial records, but I just need a bit more compelling reasoning. I know if I can get my hands on those numbers and their client list, I'll be that much closer to putting this puzzle together."

The deputy did another spin around. "And what exactly am I to tell the sheriff?"

Katie took a deep breath. "We both know he would never believe a word I'm saying, which is why I've come to you. I know it's asking a lot, but this is someone's life we're talking about. I'm asking you to do this on your own, just one day's worth of investigating. I need to save this girl's life, and I'm asking, no pleading, for your help."

The deputy was quite disturbed at this point. "Well, let me ask you this. What if by some chance there is something suspicious going on? What does that have to do with your client?"

"*That's the six million-dollar question,*" Katie thought. "I don't know that yet. However, if I can prove VanAnt was responsible for Junior's death, then I can at least clear her of the murder. And before you ask, I do not believe she is involved in this murder in any fashion. I truly believe she is a victim as well."

The deputy grabbed her hat and squad car keys from the table. She was calm when she responded. "So, to sum up, at the risk of my job, you want me to do some digging on a revered member of this community to determine if he is a murderer, and you want me to do this without the knowledge or permission of the sheriff or prosecutor? Is that accurate?"

Katie looked up at the deputy and with a sheepish grin. "Yes."

Deputy Wong made some kind of audible moan and left. Katie tossed the coffee cups into the garbage and walked back to her car, praying that she'd come through.

CHAPTER 34

K atie walked into the house, hungry and mentally exhausted. She heard talking in the kitchen, so she headed there immediately, hoping the paella Maria had promised was ready for the taking. Entering, she screamed with delight, "Matt!"

She ran into his arms with a bear hug so tight, a minute longer and he would have turned blue. She was so excited. "What are you doing here? I mean, you weren't coming until Friday."

"I wanted to be here, so I managed to rearrange appointments."

Maria and Jennifer were laughing at how this professional woman had just turned into a giddy teenager.

"Señora, would you like to eat now?"

"In a little while, Maria." She turned to Matt. "Are you up for a beach walk?"

Jennifer gathered up her books and retreated to her room as the couple took to the beach. The afternoon sun and the ocean breeze made their stroll at the water's edge feel like a romantic date. Katie asked him about his work, but he was quick to let her know that all that could wait; he was here for her. She squeezed his hand.

"All right, you asked for it." And with that, she recounted every detail of the case, including her morning conversation with the Professor. When she finished, she nervously asked, "Hon, tell me honestly, what do you think?" She needed a fresh and unbiased viewpoint.

"Honestly, I think you're definitely on to something, and I'm somewhat confused at the Professor's reaction."

Katie breathed a sigh of relief, a relief that someone uninvolved was validating her perception. "You have no idea how much I needed to hear that."

They walked back to the house in silence; no more words were necessary. Maria had two plates already prepared. Katie ate slowly, wanting to spend as much time with Matt as possible before returning to the den.

"Hey, Matt, good to see you." Ali was equally surprised as he entered the kitchen.

"Good to see you too, my friend. I hear you're working too hard."

The two men chatted while Katie helped clear the table. Without asking, Maria placed a heaping plate in front of Ali. He caught the flicker of confusion in Matt's eyes, as if questioning why Maria had handed him food unprompted.

Turning to Matt, "Don't ask," Ali said with a grin. "Soon you will understand."

As the two were discussing the recent Manchester United vs Liverpool match, Katie heard the doorbell. "I'll get it, Maria." She opened the door to find Deputy Wong.

"I'm sorry to stop by unannounced. I was on my way home so I took the chance that you would be here."

Katie invited her in, but she declined.

"Mrs. Russo, I have some information for you, but you did not hear this from me."

Katie nodded. "Of course."

"About a year and a half ago, Mr. VanAnt was arrested for assault and battery. The altercation occurred in Lucca County, at an unnamed club. There was some disagreement with another customer. Anyway, through some high-level influence, the charge was dismissed and all the paperwork was swept under the table. I think there was a payoff to the victim. That's all I know."

Katie felt vindicated; the uncomfortable feeling she felt around him was real.

"Deputy, if the paperwork was concealed, who or what is your source?"

"No names. I spoke with a retired officer from Lucca who was involved with the incident. And, Mrs. Russo, I am told by several people that Mr. VanAnt has a temper. I need to go now." She turned and started to walk away.

"Deputy, it isn't lost on me the risk you've taken, and I am extremely grateful." She closed the door and hurried to the den.

"Is everything okay?" Ali asked as he and Matt came into the foyer.

Katie was so excited about what she just heard that she forgot Matt and Ali were waiting for her. "Matt, I'm so sorry, but I need to do some work now. I really am sorry. Al, I need you with me."

Matt gave her a kiss and reassured her that he understood. "I'll see you later, just do what you have to do."

He went up to the bedroom while Ali followed her into the den. She updated him on her conversations with the Professor and Deputy Wong. "That was the deputy at the door with some interesting news." They spent the next two hours pulling the pieces together and identifying weak spots in the prosecution's case.

"As we've discussed," Katie continued, "I'm confident we can undermine Mr. Adams's testimony and cast doubt on the knife and trail evidence—enough, I believe, to cast jury doubt. The prosecution has locked in on Jennifer as the sole suspect, but the deeper we dig into the port's underhanded operations, the stronger our case becomes for linking them to Junior's death. I'm convinced VanAnt is entangled in this, and I want him on the stand. But we'll need more concrete evidence to establish his culpability." She paused and took a deep breath. "We're close, Al."

She sent him off for the night as she put the finishing touches on their work. They both agreed that they had enough evidence to ask that a warrant be served; Katie was fully prepared to present probable cause to the sheriff in the hopes that he'd cooperate. She was certain that criminal activity was being committed by Keans Industries, and a review of their financial records would be invaluable to her case. And she was even more certain that Junior was involved, willingly or not, and that these activities resulted in his death. What she had not yet been able to do was to tie Jennifer to the murder. She and Ali developed several theories, but she knew at this point it was only conjecture. With a quick phone call to the sheriff, a meeting was set for early in the morning.

Finally, another workday was completed, and Katie was anxious to spend the rest of the evening with Matt. First, however, she stopped in to see Jennifer. Although not wanting to give her false hope, Katie felt it important to keep her spirits up by sharing some positive news. She was vague in its content, but she could see by her expression that it was favorably received. Goodnights were exchanged, and Katie left.

Entering her room, she could feel the coolness of night air

and the warmth of the fireplace. She found Matt lying cozily on the sofa with a glass of wine in hand. Kicking off her shoes, she snuggled next to him. He offered her his wine.

"Nothing for me, I just want to sit like this for a moment and enjoy the fire, the ocean breeze, and you." Within minutes, she was sound asleep.

CHAPTER 35

S he opened her eyes and for a moment wasn't certain if it was night or day.

Sitting up with some effort, still in her dress clothes, she realized it was morning. Katie called out for Matt.

"Morning," he said softly. "You were out in an instant and I just didn't want to wake you." He gave her a gentle kiss.

"You can still walk, so I'm guessing you haven't had a Maria breakfast yet," Katie said half-jokingly. "Let me shower and I'll meet you down there. Tread lightly." She glanced at the clock and was relieved to see it was early; plenty of time before going to see the sheriff. She joined Matt and Maria in the kitchen and smiled when she saw the size of Matt's breakfast plate. He gave her a *Help-me* glance; he was eating for a while and there was still no sight of the actual plate.

"Matt, has Ali been down?"

"He had a fast breakfast and went for a run on the beach. He said he won't be long."

Just then, Ali walked in from the patio. "Morning, Katie." He grabbed a protein shake from the fridge.

The only person missing was Jennifer. "Has anyone seen Jennifer this morning?"

"Señora, she has not been here. I knocked on the door, but she no answer."

Katie asked Ali if he would spend some time with her.

"I had planned on a visit, so of course."

"Katie, if you don't need my help, I thought I'd visit the Professor." Matt hadn't seen the Professor in many months.

"We can go into town together," she said. "I'll drop you off, go to the sheriff's office, and then come back to the hospital. It would be nice for the three of us to be together and talk about anything other than this case."

"Sounds like a good plan," he agreed.

Katie hurriedly went back to her room to gather her purse and jacket. On the way out, she stopped to see Jennifer. She didn't bother knocking, but called out as she opened the door. Jennifer was pacing.

"Jennifer, can you stop and sit with me, please?"

Jennifer sat with her head down, struggling to compose herself. Katie noticed her mood had been see-sawing the past week, so she tried once again to keep her spirits elevated. "Jenn, talk to me. What's going through your mind?" Her voice was calm and soothing, like a mother speaking to her child.

"I'm trying, Mrs. Russo. I really am. But I'm scared. And honestly, I don't know what to do with all these new feelings— trust, vulnerability, caring. They're unfamiliar, and they're hitting me all at once. They don't come easy. I want to do what you ask, I really do. But it's like standing in a storm without shelter. I don't know how to handle it all."

Katie gently brushed a strand of hair from Jennifer's face. "You're scared about the trial and you're dealing with new feelings. These aren't weaknesses. Actually, you're growing. You're facing fear and you're opening yourself up and letting people in. This takes courage, Jennifer, real courage. And I'll remind you, time and time again, you are not going through this alone. I'm here; we all are."

Katie leaned in and gave Jennifer a hug. "I'll see you later today."

Jennifer, for the first time, did something she had never done. She wrapped her arms around Katie and hugged back.

Matt and Ali were waiting in the foyer. Katie turned to Ali. "Al, Jennifer's having a hard time, please do what you can."

"I will," Ali said sincerely.

Kate and Matt left for town, stopping off at the hospital first, as planned, then to the sheriff's office. After a productive meeting with Sheriff Michaels, Katie was back at the hospital in minutes. As she pressed the elevator button, she was somewhat apprehensive, not wanting a repeat of yesterday's disappointing conversation. Her fears were unfounded as she entered the Professor's room. "I don't believe it. I just don't believe it." At the table sat the Professor and Matt playing cards. After brushing the cards and pretzels aside, the three musketeers, as the Processor had dubbed them many years ago, sat comfortably around the table and reminisced about old times. A short time later, Phyllis arrived, and the circle felt complete. A couple of hours had passed unnoticed when the Professor expressed tiredness. Matt assisted him into bed, and Katie announced it was time for them to take leave.

Matt was pleased with his visit. "The Professor looked good and sounded strong."

Katie agreed. "Matt, before I arrived, did the Professor make any mention of the trial?"

"The only thing he said was that he was sorry he got you involved and that he wished it hadn't come this far. I told him I have complete confidence in you and then I deftly changed the subject."

It was early afternoon, and Katie suggested they stop for a drink before returning to the house. "There's a charming town about a half-hour away. I've pretty much worn out my welcome here. And, we can celebrate a bit. The sheriff agreed, albeit half-heartedly, to prepare an affidavit to present to Judge Grayson. It took a lot of convincing on my part, but he finally acquiesced. He did ask me how I knew about the incident involving VanAnt, and I just told him it was through solid investigation. You know, Matt, the only chance I have is to get a warrant served and get those financials. I'm confident the answer, the last piece to the puzzle, lies somewhere in those books."

"That's great news, hon. Do you think you'll have the documentation that you need prior to the start of the trial?"

Katie knew it would be a long shot. "I don't know, but even if we do, I'll need help pouring over the financials. I have a call into my office to see who I can corral."

They continued reviewing the meeting details on the drive to the restaurant, but agreed there would be no more work talk upon arrival. Finally, Katie pulled into the parking lot and gave a big sigh as she exited the car. She knew there was a long road ahead, but for the first time she felt some relief. As they entered La Mare Café, they were greeted warmly by an adorable young lady named Peggy. Katie remarked it was such a welcoming contrast to her diner visit. They were escorted to the cafe's patio, where they shared a bottle of wine and enjoyed the ocean view.

"Hon, I've been meaning to ask you, have you spoken with your parents?" He knew their relationship was strained, but he still hoped for a reconciliation, for Katie's sake.

"Mom was busy, as usual, but I did talk with my dad. We were fine for the first two minutes until he questioned why I was handling such a low-level and unwinnable case."

"I'm sorry. You don't deserve that."

"You're right, I don't. After all these years, they still don't accept me for who I am. Matt, it's so frustrating, and you know what I've said all along. It has to do with money. To them, money means power—and power demands control and conformity. Growing up, I accepted coming in second to their social priorities, but even second place should have been worthy of support. All I ever got was disappointment at not being first. Even today, can you believe it? Even today, after everything I've accomplished, I could still hear it, that same old disappointment in my father's voice."

Katie, determined to let it go, changed the subject. "Well, on a much brighter note, I spoke with your mom and we laughed for an hour. I'm not even sure I know what we talked about; she kept switching between English and Italian. And I loved every second."

After finishing the wine, they headed back. Katie finally felt relaxed, refreshed, and reinvigorated. "Matt, I'm sorry, but I have a bit more work to do before we turn in for the night. How about I finish up, then we bring dinner up to the room. After that, we can have dessert."

"Katie, after another Maria meal, I don't think I could possibly have another one of her desserts!"

"I wasn't talking about food," Katie said with a sly grin.

"Now that's my favorite kind of dessert," Matt said, laughing.

By the time they arrived at the house, it was late afternoon. Matt sat on the deck with a book while Katie met Ali in the den.

"You look different, less stressed," Ali said. "Having Matt here has been good for you."

"Agreed!"

Ali continued, "I wish I could say the same about Jennifer. Katie, she seemed a little better, but I could tell she's stressed, worried. I don't think she's opened any of her books. I wish we could get her out of this house for a few hours."

"I've already made that request of the sheriff and received a resounding no. Let's just keep spending time with her." Katie was worried, knowing it may only get worse once the trial starts.

They finished up work and set a time to meet in the morning. Katie stopped in the kitchen and told Maria they would be retiring for the evening. She packed a small tray with dinner and said goodnight.

"Matt, I have dinner, are you ready to go?"

"Let me carry the tray." He dropped his book on the lounge chair and took the tray from Katie. Once in the room, they looked at the tray and then each other.

Neither had any interest in eating.

Katie said it first. "If you don't tell her, I won't."

Matt laughingly agreed. "Let's shower and then get right to dessert."

CHAPTER 36

It was very early Monday morning and Katie was already in the den putting the finishing touches on her opening statement to the jury. She was never satisfied until every detail was presented logically and in an order that was easily comprehended by the jurists, something the Professor had instilled in her from her early college days. She was so deep in thought that a rap on the door went unheard. It took two good morning greetings from Ali to finally get her attention

"Good morning, Al. Please come in. I'd like you to listen to this. Oh, sorry, would you like to get breakfast first?"

"Let me just grab a cup of coffee and then I'm all yours." He returned quickly and positioned his chair in front of the desk. He brought her a fresh cup as well.

Katie thankfully took a sip and smiled at him. He was not only a colleague, but a good friend. His kindness and thoughtfulness were unequaled. After one more sip, she began her statement. With Ali's help, she made a few adjustments and, when finished, she was satisfied that it met her objectives.

He was always honest with her. "I think it's solid, Katie."

"Al, it's good, but we both know I need some solid evidence to back it up. I've got to have those financials! I'm going to grab some breakfast and then go into town to see the sheriff. I need to know where he is on the warrant. And, Al, I have a few jobs for you this morning."

After an hour together going over all that still needed to be done, Ali finally admitted he needed sustenance.

"I'm a little hungry too," she admitted, so they called it a morning and headed to the kitchen.

Katie was happy to see Matt was already seated at the table, chatting with Maria. She gave him a hug around the neck and a peck on the cheek.

"Good morning to you both. Maria, if you wouldn't mind, I would love some scrambled eggs and toast."

"Gladly, señora, and I will get Señor Ali some too."

Ali just accepted his fate with a nod.

"Hon, I saw you two working, so I didn't want to interrupt."

"Matt, my love, you are never an interruption," she said with a slight grin.

The three sat and chatted for a while, talking about anything but the trial. Maria made a plate for Jennifer, but was disappointed when she returned with it untouched.

"Señora, the señorita is not doing good, she was just sitting at the window."

"Thank you, Maria, for trying. I'll go see her." Katie turned to Matt. "I have to go into town this morning, I hate leaving you alone."

"I forgot to tell you, I'm going into town too. I have a job," Matt explained. "Yesterday, I stopped at that diner you mentioned and coincidentally they were having a big problem with their internet connections. Everything that was wired and integrated was down. I mentioned that I might be of some help, so that's what I'm going to do today. They seemed very desperate."

Katie was surprised. "Do they know who you are? It sounds like a somewhat expensive operation, and my impression is that they don't have that kind of money."

"Yes, they know I'm your husband, but their desperation exceeded their disdain for our relationship. Besides, I made it very affordable. I'm doing it gratis."

Katie was pleased. "I think that's a wonderful gesture, and if, by association, it gets me some good-will points, then I'm even more for it."

Ali interjected, "Matt, I have some work in town as well, how about I drop you off? Actually, the diner is one of the places I planned on going."

"Perfect," Matt said. "Give me fifteen minutes."

They all got up from the table ready to take on the morning.

"Al, I'm going to spend some time with Jennifer, then I'll be at the sheriff's office. Please be sure to keep me posted on your findings."

He nodded.

After the two men left, Katie met with Jennifer. Once again, she tried to lift her spirits. Without being specific, she told her that there were solid leads and things were not as dire as Jennifer imagined. She wasn't sure if she made any headway. "And I don't want you to spend the day in this bedroom. This house is grand, walk around as much as possible, stretch your legs and clear your mind of all negative thoughts. Now, young lady, freshen up, and I'll tell Maria you'll be down for breakfast. I'll be in town for a while, so if you need anything, let Maria know."

Once Katie drove off, Jennifer reluctantly left the safety of her room and went to the kitchen. Maria, ever her cheerleader, tried to lift her sprits with a meal and lively conversation. Unfortunately, she noticed barely a morsel was eaten and an air of despondency filled the room. In an effort to be helpful, she suggested a change of location.

"Señorita, let's go into the conservatory. It's a beautiful day and you can feel the warmth of the sun on your face. I will make you a cup of tea."

Jennifer dutifully followed Maria.

The room was beautifully decorated; plants and flowers lined the glass walls. They were situated to provide privacy, but still allowed a panoramic view of the day and evening sky. Maria pushed the cushioned recliner in front of the television and helped a seemingly fragile Jennifer to get comfortably seated. She left to make the promised tea. Upon returning, she placed the tea on the small side table and turned on the television to the morning news. Maria encouraged Jennifer to try the herbal tea, hoping this particular blend would prove to be soothing. Jennifer took a sip and then rested the cup and saucer on her lap.

Maria was pleased. "Señorita, if you need me, I will be in the bedrooms, straightening up. I will check on you later."

Jennifer continued to sit emotionless, staring at the screen but virtually oblivious to the station's content. The anchors rambled on about the usual political and financial news, but ended the half-hour program with a feel-good story. The lead anchor, Daniella, related the story about two brothers in North Dakota that, despite warnings, went ice skating on their local pond. The ice broke and the younger brother fell into the freezing water. The older brother yelled for help while inching his way toward the cracked ice. Heroically, nearby hikers joined in and formed a long human chain with the elder brother leading the way. Within minutes, the youngster was pulled safely from the pond and immediately tended to by the nearby emergency care. The anchor spoke live to the mother, who said with great relief, "My two boys are active boys and they are always fighting with one another, but today they showed how much they really care. I am very proud of them both." Daniella thanked the mother for her time and turned and faced the camera, "Well, this is a story that truly proves the saying that 'blood is thicker than water!' May your day be a pleasant one, and we will see you all tomorrow."

It only took a moment for the words to sink in. Jennifer's heart began to pound and the blood seemed to drain from her face. She was shaking as she stood up. The teacup and saucer fell to the floor seemingly in slow motion. The realization of what she heard sent her into a frenzy. She ran out of the room screaming for Maria, who heard her cries from the upper floor. As she hurried down the stairs, Maria could see Jennifer in the foyer quickly pacing and muttering. She gently grabbed the young woman's shoulders and repeatedly pleaded to know what was wrong.

Jennifer screamed, "I need to see Mrs. Russo now. Now! Get the car keys, we're going into town." Maria tried to tell her that her ankle bracelet prevented her from leaving the house, but Jennifer was undeterred. "Please, please, we need to go now."

Maria reluctantly grabbed the keys and headed down the driveway. Carlos was landscaping in the front garden and looked on in bewilderment as the car passed. Maria gave him a quick worried glance which Carlos recognized as trouble. A long marriage rendered words unnecessary.

As they entered the avenue, Maria asked with extreme concern, "Where are we going? Jennifer, what has happened?"

Jennifer repeated, "I need to see Mrs. Russo now, she's somewhere in town. I need to see her now. They will hurt her."

Maria's heart was pounding as she tried desperately to keep the car from swerving. Events happened so quickly that she didn't have time to reconsider her actions. Should she have been coerced into breaking the law? Was she putting both of them in harm's way? Her mouth became dry and her body began to tremble; she wondered who was trembling more, she or Jennifer. As the town loomed nearer, she could barely make out what Jennifer was quietly muttering, something about water.

CHAPTER 37

The ride into town was a blur and seemed to take only seconds. Maria had no idea how to find Katie and, in her frantic rush, she had left her cell phone on the kitchen counter. Clearly unable to continue, she pulled over at the edge of town near the old children's park. She turned toward Jennifer, but before she could even speak, Jennifer bolted from the car and headed south toward the center. Maria was unsure what to do— remain parked or follow behind? She quickly looked around for the authorities, expecting them to respond to the ankle bracelet, but there was no obvious sign of their presence.

She decided to follow on foot, but as she exited, she could see a couple approaching Jennifer. She recognized them as the older couple that owns the tailor shop. Although unable to understand what they were saying, Maria could hear them shouting and waving their arms in an apparent hostile manner. A moment later, a car with two men stopped near the couple. It was the Cruz brothers, owners of the unique clothing store. They, too, began shouting at Jennifer. This time Maria heard them yell *"Killer."* Within minutes, several other residents happened on the scene, curious about the commotion. It didn't take long before the ever-growing group resembled a mob from an old Western, noose in hand. Their lives were upended, if not ruined, and before them was the very source. They continued forward, and with each step they took, Jennifer took several steps backward. She tried to defend herself, but her words were drowned out by the ever-increasing screaming and shouting.

Maria was frozen, leaning on the car for support. She watched helplessly as a terrified Jennifer retreated into the park. She yelled for her to come back to the car, but just then she saw her fall backwards over the yellow warning tape and then she was gone from sight! Everyone rushed to the crater to see Jennifer rolling helplessly over a landslide of debris, finally coming to a stop at the very bottom. She lay there motionless, covered with dirt and blood from the broken glass and jagged rocks. With a burst of adrenaline, Maria ran to the edge and dropped to her knees, sobbing, not sure if Jennifer was dead or alive.

Katie was at the sheriff's office, anxious to know if the warrant had been served. "I'm sorry, Sheriff, that you find me an inconvenience," she said, "but it's my client's life we're talking about, and I need those financials."

"Mrs. Russo, I know you see me as an obstruction of some kind, but I feel confident that the warrant will be approved and served tomorrow. Look, I know you're doing your job, so no, I don't find you an inconvenience. However, I do think you're wasting your time. Your client is guilty, but you have every right to be wrong."

Banging on the office door was Deputy Wong. "Sheriff, emergency." She didn't wait for a response; she flung open the door. "Sheriff, we have an alert that Miss O'Neill has stepped outside the designated boundary. The GPS has located her inside Keansbury, edge of town. And, Sheriff, someone called in for an ambulance at that site."

Katie was stunned. "What? That can't be, it's a mistake."

The sheriff grabbed his hat and jacket. Turning to Katie, he said, "Come on, ride with me." With sirens blaring, they made it to the park within minutes and were shocked to see the scene before them. The sheriff and deputies pushed through the crowd, making their way to the rim of the cavity. Katie followed behind. There at the bottom were Matt and Ali trying to comfort Jennifer. While both were at the diner, someone had run in to tell them of the situation and they raced over. They had made their way down to the bottom after calling for an ambulance.

Katie waved frantically to Matt while attempting to get to Jennifer. Deputy Wong grabbed her arm to hold her back. "It's too dangerous, stay here."

Just then, Katie looked to her right and saw Maria. She was contorted into a ball- like shape. "Maria, it's Katie. Maria, can you hear me?" There was no response; she was just rocking back and forth, sobbing uncontrollably. Katie knew she was in shock; she took off her jacket and placed it over Maria's shoulders. Just then the ambulances arrived. Holding her breath, Katie watched as the ambulance crew and the authorities worked together to safely bring Jennifer up. She was placed in the first ambulance, Maria in the second. Katie then looked frantically for Matt and Ali, both making their way back unscathed. She ran to them.

"What the hell happened? My God, what the hell happened?"

Neither had an answer. "We don't know. We were told there was a serious incident here with Jennifer, so we ran right over. When we got here, we saw her at the bottom, called the ambulance, and raced down to see if we could help." Matt held her closely. She could barely catch her breath.

"Matt, did she say anything? Was she able to say anything?"

"No, nothing. She's been unconscious."

Ali volunteered to go back to the house to inform Maria's

husband. "Katie, I'll see if he knows what happened, and if he's not able to drive, I'll bring him to the hospital."

"Al, *please*, call me immediately when you know anything."

The sheriff made his way through the crowd to speak with Katie. "Me and my deputies will get statements from everyone, and as soon as we have an idea of what has happened here, I'll let you know."

"Sheriff, I can't imagine what made her leave the house, but clearly she was not trying to escape."

"I know, Mrs. Russo. Why don't you get to the hospital, and when we have all the facts, we'll know how to proceed. I'll let the prosecutor know what's transpired and we'll go from there. I'm going to have Deputy Wong meet you at the hospital, she'll need to be there in case Miss O'Neill or Maria can shed some light. Do you need a ride?"

Katie noticed he seemed genuinely caring. All her dealings with the sheriff had been formal, so she appreciated the more concerning side he displayed.

"No, my husband is here, we'll go together."

It was all a blur, but soon they all sat impatiently in the waiting room, Katie, Matt, and Deputy Wong. Ali had returned with Carlos, but he was unable to shed any light on what occurred. Katie's mind was racing with random thoughts; she had been to this hospital so many times to see the Professor, but this area was unfamiliar. Finally, Doctor Christian came in with an update.

"Hello, Mrs. Russo. Sorry to see you under these circumstances." He turned to Carlos, whom he had known for many years. "Carlos, we were able to quiet Maria. She is sedated and will be sleeping for at least 12 hours. We will be moving her shortly to the second floor. You can certainly sit with her for as long as you like. If you stay over, just let one of the nurses know and they'll make sure you're comfortable."

Carlos shook the doctor's hand. "Thank you, señor, thank you."

"Doctor Christian, was Maria able to tell you anything about what happened?" Katie was anxiously hoping.

"Sorry, no, and she won't be saying anything for at least another day."

Carlos rushed to be by Maria's side.

Katie turned back to Doctor Christian. She didn't need any words, he could see the uneasiness in her eyes. "Mrs. Russo, all things considered, Jennifer is doing well. Things could have been much much worse. There are no broken bones and no internal injuries. However, if you saw her earlier, you know she has a multitude of cuts and bruises. Nothing life-threatening, but something we need to keep an eye on to make certain no infections occur."

Matt gave her a reassuring hug.

"May I see her, please?"

"Sure, but only for a moment. She, too, has been sedated so don't be concerned if she may be unresponsive."

Katie turned to Deputy Wong, who nodded her head with approval. It was highly doubtful that in her condition Jennifer would be revealing any details.

"She'll remain in emergency until tonight; I'll show you where she is. This way." The doctor pointed.

She followed the doctor to the small room at the end of the corridor.

"Mrs. Russo, you are listed as her emergency contact, so if there's any change in her condition, I will personally let you know."

She made a weak smile, nodded, and then turned toward the room. Taking a deep breath, she entered. Katie wasn't quite prepared for the site of Jennifer hooked up to an IV and an assortment of monitors. Her eyes began to well. She walked softly to the side of her bed and gently held her hand and stroked her forehead. Leaning over, she whispered, "Honey, it's Katie. I'm here with you. You've been hurt and you're in the hospital, but you're going to be okay." She was startled to feel Jennifer give a slight squeeze to her hand. Then, slowly, she turned her head and opened her eyes. "Jenn, it's Katie. I'm here and you're going to be okay."

With enormous determination and every ounce of her energy, Jennifer responded. Her voice was weak, soft, and she paused breathlessly between each word, but Katie was able to understand. "Go home, Mrs. Russo. You can't help me. You can't beat them." Then, surrendering to the medication, she closed her eyes and drifted off.

Katie stood up, stunned and bewildered. Looking up, seemingly to the heavens, she screamed, "Would someone please tell me what has happened, what is going on?!" She looked down at Jennifer with great despair. "How much more can you bare? Who is *them* that has so frightened you? Jennifer, I promise you, I am not going home and I am not giving up."

Katie walked angrily out of the room. "God help anyone that gets in my way!"

CHAPTER 38

Something sinister was in motion, and Katie was determined to find out just what that was. They regrouped in the waiting room to decide next steps. It was clear that both Maria and Jennifer would be unavailable for questioning, so Deputy Wong informed them of her return to the station. Ali decided he would go back to the house in the hopes of finding any indication as to what led to this law-breaking action. Matt was staying with Katie; she needed his support. Before leaving the hospital to meet with the sheriff, Katie and Matt stopped by the Professor's room to give him an update. He was shocked and just as puzzled as everyone else. Their stay was brief, and only when leaving did Katie notice the Professor's condition.

"Professor, you're walking, you're standing. That's wonderful."

He placed his hands together as in a prayer of thanks.

She hugged him tightly. "A blessing on such a horrendous day!"

"Please keep me updated."

"Of course, Professor. Hopefully I'll know more by

tomorrow." She and Matt walked down the corridor hand in hand.

"I'll drive," Matt said. "I can see you're overwhelmed with thoughts." They entered the elevator.

"Matt, I was so close to finding the answer to this puzzle, I could feel it. But, after what's just happened, I feel so very far away."

Trying to be of comfort and support, Matt put his arm around her shoulder. "Let's see what the sheriff has to say. Hopefully, he'll have something tangible."

As Katie and Matt stepped into the sheriff's station, the room was crowded with townspeople—faces she recognized. They occupied every available seat; each one engaged in quiet conversation with a deputy. A few heads lifted at the sight of Katie and Matt, but just as quickly their eyes dropped and gazes shifted, as though guilt had stirred and needed hiding. In the rear of the station was Deputy Wong, who motioned to them. She escorted Katie and Matt into the small conference room where the sheriff and prosecutor were waiting. Katie introduced Matt, and they both took a seat at the oval table.

The sheriff began, reading in part from his report. "Okay, let's get right to it. We still don't know why your client came into town. I can only tell you what purportedly happened when she did. She entered at the north end, by the old children's park, and began walking south, toward the center. As she approached, several residents noticed her and began a verbal exchange. Understandably, they were shocked to see your client, knowing that she was under house arrest. Anyway, there were some heated words said and said loudly. Soon, more and more residents joined in, and your client became concerned. She retreated toward the park, which she may not have noticed was under construction. Your client stumbled over the warning tape which was clearly arranged around the perimeter of that area. In her attempt to get up, she slipped and fell into the pit, sliding down to the bottom. At no time, was there any physical interaction between your client and the citizens. You were here, Mrs. Russo, when we were alerted that the ankle bracelet had been activated. The sheriff's department rushed over to find a crowd of residents and you, Mr. Russo, and Mr. Randall, attending to Miss O'Neill. The ambulances quickly arrived to treat both your client and Maria. I assume one of our citizens had called for the ambulance."

Matt interjected, "No, Sheriff, one of your citizens did not call for an ambulance. I did. And no one offered any help to Ali and me."

Katie sat there listening, looking calm on the outside, but seething on the inside.

The sheriff continued. "Mrs. Russo, your client violated house arrest, so when we discover the reasoning, we will take the appropriate action."

Katie stood up and banged her hands on the table. "My client has been under house arrest for months and months. She has barely left her bedroom, let alone stepped outside. None of us know why she risked leaving, but something or someone terrified her and possibly Maria. Clearly, she was not trying to escape. For God's sake, she came into town." She turned toward the prosecutor. "When she's released from the hospital, I am asking you, please, let her return to the house. I give you my word that she will be watched 24/7 and nothing like this will happen again. Please!"

He looked at Katie, requesting that she be seated. Being in a wheelchair, he didn't like to be towered over, feeling at a disadvantage. He preferred eye to eye interaction.

"Mrs. Russo, the sheriff and I have discussed options, and while we must follow the letter of the law, we are not heartless. I have spoken to the judge and, if agreeable, we will postpone the trial date for three weeks from today. This should give your client sufficient time to heal and be present. But just three weeks. Regardless of any other occurrence, the trial will not be postponed for even a second. Understood?"

Katie nodded.

The prosecutor continued. "When your client is released from the hospital, she will be allowed to return to the Professor's house. We're deferring any action until after hearing from her and Maria. I will hold you personally responsible should there be any more episodes. Understood?"

Again, another nod from Katie.

"The sheriff will continue with the remaining interviews and review any CCTV footage that's available. If we find that anyone physically harmed your client, we will take the necessary action. When your client is able to speak, the sheriff's office will take a statement; obviously, you will be present. However, as Mrs. Torres is not your client, we will take a statement from her without you."

Katie was relieved and surprisingly in agreement with what she heard from Ryan; not always a clear path between the defense and prosecution.

"I'm sorry of the circumstances, but it was nice meeting you, Mr. Russo," the prosecutor said as he wheeled himself toward the door. "Oh, and, Mrs. Russo, I happen to know your warrant request was approved." Turning toward the sheriff, he said, "I'm assuming you will be serving it tomorrow?"

The sheriff nodded. "As soon as I get the formal okay, it will be served."

The prosecutor continued. "Once I receive and process the evidence you are seeking, I will make it available to you. I don't agree with your argument and I'm not clear where you're going with all of this, but I look forward to being entertained."

Entertained. Katie didn't appreciate the sarcasm, but she was in no mood for word play. After all that had unfolded, the remark felt not only misplaced, but irritatingly flippant in light of the situation's seriousness.

"He'll be more than entertained," she thought to herself. *"It will be a blockbuster."*

Katie addressed the sheriff directly, her tone reserved. "Sheriff, I'm going back to the hospital for a while. If there's anything I find out that I can share, I will, of course, let you know immediately. I came here expecting an argument, but you and Mr. Ryan were surprisingly agreeable."

His expression was serious. "We are all confident that your client is guilty and will be convicted. That being said, she is entitled to be treated fairly and we believe we've done that. There should be no room for an appeal on a technicality."

Matt and Katie pushed away from the table and stood up to leave. "Sheriff, I'll see you tomorrow," Katie said. "Hopefully you'll have all the information I need." Matt nodded a goodbye and they left.

The station was noticeably empty; interviews were completed.

"Matt, would you drop me off at the hospital and I'll take a taxi back when I'm ready?"

"Not a chance," Matt said. "I'm staying with you."

She was hoping he'd say that. They drove back to the hospital, Katie feeling a little less pressured given the trial delay. Turning to Matt, she said, "This is one of the most complicated cases I've worked on, but, Matt, I will figure this out. I will."

Smiling, he agreed. "Never a doubt!"

CHAPTER 39

They were back at the hospital, in Jennifer's room. Matt was seated uncomfortably in the corner chair reading a sports magazine he found in the lobby. He glanced over to see Katie still sleeping, her head resting on one hand while holding Jennifer's with the other. He gently tapped her on the shoulder. "Hon, it's late. We should go."

She stirred, momentarily hoping it was Jennifer's voice she'd heard. "Oh, I closed my eyes for a moment."

Matt made a slight laughing sound. "Yes, that was two hours ago!"

She gave a long stretch, trying to right herself after being bent over for so long. "You're right, let me just check on Maria before we leave."

"While you were resting, I looked in on her. She was still sleeping. Carlos said the doctor told him that all the tests were good and she will be released tomorrow."

"Hopefully, Jennifer will be too." Before leaving, she rearranged Jennifer's pillows and tidied her blanket. She turned to Matt and put her arm through his. "I'm ready for a good night's sleep." And they left.

They arrived back at the house, which seemed somewhat empty without Maria and Jennifer. Ali heard the car and excitedly met them at the door.

"Let me show you this," he said, leading them to the conservatory.

The television was on, and resting on the carpet in front of the lounge chair was a used teacup and saucer. "I looked everywhere in the house, and this is the only thing I could find that was out of place. Perhaps she was seated here watching TV and someone startled her? Although, I didn't find anything to support that. I even checked the surrounding grounds and saw nothing. No footprints, no shrubbery disturbed."

"Good work, Al," Katie said. "Well, clearly something happened. Something so serious that Jennifer was willing to risk her freedom, her life, by leaving the house. We can surmise all evening, but what we need is for them both to relate today's events. Al, please shut off the TV, but we'll leave the cup and saucer as is. Are either of you hungry? I'm sure Maria has an ample supply of food in the fridge."

Ali was exhausted. "I grabbed a bite earlier, so if you don't need me anymore this evening, I'll head to bed."

"That's an excellent idea, Al. Let's all get some much-needed rest and hopefully things will make more sense in the morning. Okay with you, Matt?"

"Bed!" Matt responded definitively.

They secured the house and said their goodnights.

Matt was already in bed when Katie slipped in. She pulled his arm over her and tried desperately to relax. He knew her so well.

"Shh, quiet your mind, let it go for tonight. It will all be there in the morning."

CHAPTER 40

Morning came quickly. Matt stirred and realized Katie wasn't in bed. He quickly showered, dressed, and headed down to the kitchen. He could smell the welcoming aroma of coffee and was pleasantly surprised to see that Katie had prepared a full breakfast for them all. Ali came soon after, and the three ate while replaying the previous day's events. They were discussing options for the morning when the phone rang. Katie jumped to answer. There was a brief exchange, and then she hung up.

"That was Carlos. Maria is being discharged now and they'll be back within the hour. He said she's calm and able to speak, but she's feeling guilty for driving Jennifer into town. She is blaming herself for what happened."

Katie no sooner sat down than the phone rang again. It was the sheriff, another brief conversation. "That was the sheriff, and the warrant is being served this morning. Things are in motion, but before I do anything else I need to speak with Maria. Matt, I'd like your help. I need to be here when Maria arrives, but I'd like someone to be with Jennifer. Would you go see her and let me know if there's any change? If she wakes up, I'd like one of us to be there."

"Of course. Whatever you need me to do, I'm here for you!" He grabbed her hand and squeezed tightly.

"And, Al, I'd like you to stay here with me to speak with Maria. Depending on what she says, I may need you to follow up on some issues."

"I, too, am very anxious to hear what she says," Ali said impatiently. "Let me go and change and I'll be down in a minute."

Katie and Matt were clearing the table when they heard some rustling in the foyer. It was Carlos and Maria. Katie rushed to greet Maria and was saddened to see how pale and weak she seemed. Carlos was holding both of her arms to keep her steady. He walked her into the kitchen and gently placed her in her favorite chair at the table. Katie wrapped her arms around Maria and held her tight while the woman sobbed.

Matt tapped Katie on the shoulder and whispered, "I'll leave now for the hospital."

She took a quick look at Matt and mouthed, *Thank you*, then turned her attention back to Maria.

"I'm sorry, señora. It is my fault. I am so sorry," Maria said, trying hard to hold back the tears.

In a soothing tone, Katie said, "Maria, none of this is your fault. Do you hear me? None of this is your fault. Now, when you can, I'd like you to tell me what happened. Why did Jennifer risk leaving the house?"

Ali placed a cup of Maria's favorite tea in front of her and then sat at the counter. Katie pulled up a chair to be next to Maria. Carlos sat on her other side, holding her hand.

"Maria, do you feel up to telling us what happened?" Katie dabbed her tears away.

"I am so sorry, señora," Maria repeated.

Katie grabbed her other hand and placed it in between hers. "Maria, it is not your fault. No one blames you, I promise. But I would like to know what happened. It's important so I can help Jennifer."

Slowly, she recounted all that she remembered. "She was so insistent, señora. I just grabbed the keys and we left."

Katie listened intently but still didn't learn anything to explain their actions.

"Maria, could it have been possible that someone was at the conservatory window? Or maybe someone knocked on the door?"

"No, señora, the plants in there cover the bottom of the windows so no one can see inside, and the front door was locked. And my Carlos, he was out front, so he would have seen someone."

Carlos agreed. "No, no one came to the house."

Katie glanced over to Ali. They shared the same puzzled expression.

"Maria, would you please tell me again what Jennifer said to you in the foyer."

She closed her eyes for a deeper thought. "She repeated several times that she needed to see Mrs. Russo now. She told me to get the keys to go into town. Oh, señora, I just remembered. In the car she said she needed to see you, she mumbled something about water, and then I think she said that someone will hurt you."

"Hurt me?" Katie was bewildered. "Are you sure she said someone will hurt me?" She was so confused. Who or why would someone hurt me, and why would Jennifer think so? She wondered if Maria may have misheard Jennifer's words.

"Si, señora. I was shaking so, but I think that's what she said."

Katie could see Maria was getting tired, so she suggested she get some rest. Carlos agreed and helped Maria up from the chair.

"Carlos, we're going to the hospital, but if you need us, please be sure to call."

"Thank you, señora. I will."

Watching them slowly leave the kitchen, Katie felt a moment of guilt. None of this would be happening to Maria had she not brought Jennifer to the house. Maria and Carlos had trusted Katie's decisions, so she hoped that that trust hadn't been broken. But now she had to brush those thoughts aside and get back to the issues at hand.

Katie turned to Ali. "I don't know what to think. Any thoughts on your part?"

Ali shook his head. "I really don't know. I know the residents are angry and most likely directing their anger toward all of us. But to hurt you, that seems extreme. And, how would Jennifer even know that?"

"That's a very good question, Al, and the only person who can answer any of these questions is lying in a hospital bed. Give me ten minutes and I'll meet you at the car. Would you mind driving? I want to make some calls along the way. I especially want to call the sheriff to see how the search warrant went.

Her first call was satisfying. The sheriff said VanAnt was shocked to be served, but cooperated. The financials were turned over and, more importantly, they located the handwritten ledger.

"There was a false bottom in one of the drawers, the ledgers were in there," the sheriff said, surprised. He had not believed Katie as to its existence and was unclear why it would be hidden. "I don't see any delays, so you should have everything by end of day."

Before she could make her next call, the phone rang. It was Matt. "She's awake, groggy, but able to speak. Doctor Christian notified the sheriff's office, so I'm assuming someone will be over soon."

"Matt, we're almost there. If an officer does arrive before I do, please be sure to tell her that she must not answer their questions and that she requests legal council."

She turned her attention to Ali. "Al, Jennifer is awake and I want to be certain we speak with her before the authorities do. They know to wait until I'm there, but I don't trust them. Yesterday, they put on a good show of cooperation, but I'm not letting my guard down. I can't have her say anything that would put her back into a jail cell."

They pulled into the parking lot. There were no signs of a patrol car, but Katie noticed a news van. As soon as they arrived, a reporter and cameraman bolted from the rear of the van.

"I'm Brandon Klein from NatNews, we've heard there's been an attempt on the life of a Miss O'Neill, your murder suspect. Is it true a mob was involved?"

"I recognize you, Mr. Klein. My client was involved in an accident, not an attempt on her life."

"And I recognize you as well, Mrs. Russo. It first appeared as if this was a cut and dry case, but your presence in Keansbury suggests otherwise. What has changed?"

"Mr. Klein, I am here on behalf of my colleague and friend, Professor Kyle, who is himself recovering from an injury. Of course, I believe my client is innocent, and I am working toward proving just that. Now, if you'll excuse me please."

"Yes, of course," he yelled as she strode toward the entranceway. "I'll be here for the duration of the trial. I'd like to speak with you again." He turned to his cameraman. "There's more to this story than meets the eye. Let's get over to the police station and see what we can find out."

Katie was accustomed to dealing with the press, but now she needed to rush to Jennifer's room. She was overwhelmed with concern and anxiety at seeing Jennifer. When she arrived, Matt was standing by the door.

"Katie, I told her what you said. I'm not sure she understood. The only thing she said was for me to take you home. I don't think she meant to the Professor's house, I think she meant New York. And Doctor Christian stopped by. He said they're waiting for one more test, and if all is clear, she can be discharged this evening."

"Thanks, Matt. If you wouldn't mind, I'd like to talk to Jennifer alone." She entered the room and was pleased to see Jennifer sitting up and detached from all the equipment.

"You've had a quite a time, young lady. How are you feeling?"

Jennifer turned away from Katie and said nothing.

"I want to say something to you, and I want you to hear me. I am not leaving you. I don't know what happened, but regardless, I am not leaving you. We will see this through together. And no one is going to hurt me or you. I won't let that happen, Ali won't let that happen, Matt won't let that happen."

Jennifer turned to look at Katie. Her eyes were watery. "I made a mess of everything. I'm sorry. And Maria, I am so sorry."

"Jennifer, Maria is fine and she's waiting for you at home. I spoke with her and she's concerned about you. She doesn't know what happened that made you so frightened. Can you recall what happened yesterday morning?"

Tears flowed down her face as she shook her head no.

There was a knock on the door and the sheriff entered. Katie was expecting one of the deputies, so she was surprised to see him instead.

"Mrs. Russo, I have a few questions I'd like to ask your client."

"My client is willing to answer all of your questions at a later time. As you can see, she is still ailing and, at the moment, unable to recall the events. Sheriff, may I see you outside?" They stepped into the corridor.

"Sheriff, Doctor Christian thinks that my client can be discharged this evening. As we discussed yesterday at the station, there is no benefit to putting her in jail. I ask that you let me take her back to the house to rest and to get the care that we can provide. Hopefully her memory will return and we can finally get to the bottom of this."

The sheriff agreed. "I'll have one of my deputies bring her to the house and I'll also have a patrol car driving by on a regular basis. If she so much as leans out a window to smell the flowers, I will haul her back into jail no matter what her condition. Understood?"

"Yes, of course."

He continued. "Either myself or one of my deputies will be by tomorrow to take a statement. I expect her memory will be restored by then. Oh, and the financials will be wired to you this evening. As for the ledger..." He walked over to Matt and retrieved a large manilla envelope he had asked him to hold. He handed it to Katie. "We've reviewed the contents and it appears to be a record of some transactions, although it's not very telling. Good luck with that."

She thanked him and he left. She handed the envelope back to Matt and returned to the room. Katie explained to Jennifer that she would most likely be discharged and that an officer would be bringing her to the house. She could see the relief on her face.

"We still need to talk, but it can wait until later. Rest for now, and I'll see you at the house."

Katie drove back with Matt and Ali followed. When they returned, Matt decided to take a walk on the beach while Katie and Ali retreated to the den to pour over the ledger.

"Al, there are eight names that are listed repeatedly. Each

name is associated with a set of numbers; let's assume the numbers are dollars. We know that two of the names represent drivers, Yusaf and Franz. That's what one of the workers had told you. Do you have any operatives in the tri-state area that might be able to track down these men?"

"I do, and I'll contact them right now."

"See if they can dig up anything, anything at all, on either of them. In fact, give them all eight names, see if anything pops. I don't know how any of this fits, but I know for certain that whatever this is about, it's illegal. Why don't you work in here. I'm going to ready Jennifer's room and then look in on Maria."

She closed the den's doors and headed upstairs. The bedroom was tidy, so all Katie needed to do was open the windows to let in the fresh ocean breeze. She moved the rocker by the fireplace and turned down the bed. She then went downstairs to check on Maria. Her door was slightly ajar, so she could see that Maria was still asleep and Carlos was seated beside her reading a newspaper. He motioned to Katie that all was okay.

She heard Matt return from his walk, so she met him on the rear deck. She gave him a hug and then plopped on the lounge chair. "For one brief moment this household is quiet. How about we just sit here?"

He moved the other lounge next to hers and grabbed her hand. "Things are going to happen, aren't they?" His tone was serious, but steady. Katie and her team spent weeks buried in files and chasing leads. But Jennifer's so-called accident felt different, and Matt had a feeling she knew something vital that could shift everything.

"They will if I can find that one last piece. I keep talking about this case as a big puzzle. Think of it like a thousand-piece puzzle, and little by little you start to put all these seemingly disparate pieces together. What didn't make sense a moment ago, now makes sense. I have all these pieces, but right smack in the middle I'm missing that one piece that ties everything together. I've been working day and night and I know I'm so very close. I just haven't been able to find that one last piece. And, Matt, I'm worried. If I can't find that last piece—"

She didn't get a chance to finish. The doorbell rang. It was Deputy Wong and Jennifer, who thankfully was released earlier than expected.

Ali heard the bell and came out of the den to lend a hand. He and Matt assisted Jennifer up the stairs and into her room. She wasn't ready to sit in bed, but preferred the rocker. Katie grabbed a blanket and placed it over her lap and then turned on the fireplace. "Comfortable? Do you need anything else? Would you like something to eat or some tea?" Katie sounded like a doting mother.

"I'm fine, but if you don't mind, I'd like to just sit here alone." She started to rock back and forth.

"Jennifer, did Deputy Wong ask you any questions on the way to the house?"

"No, we didn't speak at all."

"Okay, good. I'll leave you alone for now, but I'll be checking on you later. I've left a bell for you. I can hear it in the kitchen. If you need anything, just give a ring."

Jennifer mouthed an *okay* and then continued to rock.

Matt and Ali were in the kitchen, so Katie joined them.

"This day went by so fast, it occurred to me that I haven't eaten since breakfast and I'm starving," said Matt. "I checked online and there's a Chinese place in the next town. How about I go and pick up dinner?"

"Great idea, Matt. Do you want me to go with you?" Ali asked.

"No, but thanks. I'm sure you two have more to talk about, so just get the plates ready and I'll be back in a flash."

Ali informed Katie that he had made all his calls and felt hopeful he'd get some good information tomorrow.

"Thanks, Al. Anything we get will be helpful."

"Katie, I was just wondering, what do you think will happen between Maria and Jennifer?"

"I believe they'll be fine together. Each blame themselves for what occurred. I think it will smooth over quickly. At least I hope so."

She grabbed some plates, forks, and napkins, and placed them on the table. It did seem like a flash, as Matt was already back with two bags filled with a variety of tasty morsels. She made a plate for Carlos and brought it into his room. She knew he wouldn't leave Maria to eat in the kitchen. She walked back into the kitchen and smiled at the scene of the two men devouring their meal. She, too, was hungry, so among them not a crumb remained. When they finished, Katie told them to go out on the deck and enjoy a cigar; she would clean up. She retrieved the tray from Carlos and then cleared the table. She wanted to be certain that everything was spotless for whenever Maria returned to the kitchen.

Enough time had passed for Katie to check on Jennifer. She motioned to Matt and Ali that she was heading upstairs. She brought a cup of tea, just in case. She didn't bother knocking, she just entered and placed the tea on the side table. Jennifer was wrapped in a towel and seated on the cushion near the fireplace.

"You took a bath. You should have called me, I would have helped."

"I'm fine, it just felt soothing to sit in the warm water."

"I brought you a cup of tea." She started to reach for it, but Jennifer waved her off. Katie stared at Jennifer, her cuts and bruises illuminated by the fire. She sat with a defeatist posture. Katie thought to herself how she had been so caught up with the facts and figures of the case that she didn't stop to realize the true depth of despair Jennifer was experiencing. It was heartbreaking.

"Jennifer, I can't imagine how you are feeling, but I promise you I am working hard on your case and there is hope that we can win." No sooner had Katie uttered those words did she regret saying them. It was a simplistic and an inappropriate comment. Jennifer's startled look struck Katie deeply—she hadn't meant to be so thoughtless, and the realization stung.

Jennifer lifted her head and turned to Katie. "Win?" she said incredulously. "Mrs. Russo, I've lived here my entire life. I've worked hard and no one ever gave me a thing. The only thing I ever got from my uncle was the back of his hand. I'm quiet, a loner, and awkward with people. But I never hurt anyone, ever. And then one day an awful crime was committed and one person pointed their finger at me. I was chosen, not by God or the devil, but by someone in this town. That's all it took, Mrs. Russo. Just one person said I was responsible for this awful crime, and the entire town willingly agreed. Yesterday, people that I've known my entire life wanted me gone—no, dead. I was staring at them, trying to explain, but they looked right through me. There was rage in their eyes like I've never experienced." Her voice rose in anger. "Mrs. Russo, they wanted me dead. I'm to blame for everything that's happened. Not one single person in this entire town believes me, not even the Professor. So, tell me, if by some chance I am acquitted of this charge, tell me please, what would I win?"

Katie was distraught. In an effort to lift her spirits, she did just the opposite. She had to make this right or she might lose Jennifer for good. She moved the other cushion in front of Jennifer, sat down, and grabbed both of her hands.

"Jennifer, look at me, please."

Slowly, she looked at Katie.

Katie continued. "I've spent so much time on your case, making certain I haven't overlooked anything. But, I think I've overlooked the most important part. *You.* I believe you're innocent, but I should have reminded you of that more often. This house is filled with people that believe you and believe in you. So, I'm asking you to please forgive me for not giving you the personal attention that you deserve."

Jennifer was overwhelmed. Someone was asking for her forgiveness. This was another new emotion. She could no longer be stoic; she covered her face with her hands and cried, months and months' worth of tears. Katie very carefully put her arms around her and rested Jennifer's head on her shoulder. She rocked her gently, not aware of just how much motherly instinct she had. When the sobbing stopped, Katie could feel the tears on her arms, but realized they had come from her own eyes.

"Look at us. Quite a mess," Katie said with a grin. "Here's what we're going to do. I want you to wash your face and put on your night shirt. I'm going to go downstairs and come back with some toast and a fresh cup of tea. And then we're going to do some much-needed talking. Okay?"

She stood up and nodded compliantly. Katie handed her the night shirt as Jennifer headed for the bathroom.

Matt and Ali were still on the deck arguing about some sports team when Katie returned to the kitchen. Matt stepped inside to ask if everything was all right and Katie reassured him that it was. She urged him to go back outside to continue their intellectual discussion. When the items were prepared, Katie placed them on a tray and brought them up the room. She set the tray in front of Jennifer, who had already positioned herself at the side table. While she was eating, Katie noticed the fire fading, so she added more wood and kindling. By the time she was done, she was encouraged to see that the tray was empty.

"Let's sit over here, it'll be more comfortable." They sat face to face on the lounge chairs.

"Jennifer, I want you to trust me. I won't be upset with anything that you tell me. Now, take your time, but I need for you to tell me everything that happened yesterday morning."

Jennifer began slowly. Katie thought to herself, *"I'm not leaving here until I know exactly what frightened her."*

CHAPTER 41

What had happened to Jennifer in mere minutes took her half an hour to explain. She was exhausted, and her voice trembled with the weight of it.

"The news was on the television," she began, "and I wasn't really paying attention. Then I heard the anchor say something —a single line—that made me realize I'd misunderstood what Peter said to me."

Katie leaned in, listening intently, hanging on Jennifer's every word.

"I had to tell you right away. I thought...they might hurt you." Her voice cracked, her eyes welling with tears. "I just panicked."

"Who did you think might hurt me?" Katie asked, her brow furrowed.

"The Keans' friends, their colleagues."

"And why would they want to hurt me?"

Jennifer's voice was barely a whisper. "Because you're defending me—the murderer. The Keans own this town, Mrs. Russo. They have power. I just didn't want you to get hurt."

"Ah." Katie breathed, the pieces clicking into place. "That's why you told me to go back to New York when I visited you in the hospital. You were trying to protect me."

She reached out and took both of Jennifer's hands. "No one is going to hurt me. And no one will ever hurt you again. I promise." Her voice carried the fierce protectiveness of a mother bear guarding her cub.

Katie leaned back, giving Jennifer space to continue unraveling the story at her own pace. When she finally finished, Katie drew in a slow breath, startled by the thunder of her own heartbeat. Unwittingly, Jennifer had just handed her the missing piece—the one detail that could shift her fragile alibi from fabrication to truth. And in that moment, Katie saw something else: Jennifer's transformation. She had cared—so deeply it had nearly cost her everything.

The conversation had clearly drained Jennifer, so Katie gently eased her into bed, gathered the tray, and turned off the light as she left the room. She made it only a few steps before her knees gave out. She dropped to the top stair, heart pounding, breath shallow, her mind racing like the Indy 500. Every scrap of information she'd collected since day one was now firing through her brain like a supercomputer at full throttle.

Then, clarity.

She shot to her feet, abandoning the tray, and bolted down the stairs. She ran into the kitchen, praying Matt and Ali were still on the deck. They were. She flung open the slider and grabbed Ali's arm. "I have it. I have it!"

"Are you okay? Is Jennifer okay?" Matt asked, voicing what both men were thinking.

"Geez, Katie, what do you have?" Ali asked, wincing as she squeezed his arm tighter.

Katie never cursed. She found such language offensive to her upbringing. But in this moment, no other word would do. "I have the final fucking piece of the puzzle!"

CHAPTER 42

It was late, but time was a finite commodity, so sleep wasn't an option. They had less than three weeks to prepare.

"Al, grab some coffee. We have a lot to do tonight." They retreated to the den while Matt went to bed, disappointed he couldn't be of some help.

"Matt, just being here for me is more help than you can imagine," Katie reassured him. "Don't wait up for me."

Matt laughed. "I know the drill. And please, don't let this get the better of you. Things are going to happen, aren't they?"

"I won't, I promise. And, yes." They kissed goodnight and she went back into the den. Ali was already at the computer. "Please tell me the financials have been sent."

He hurriedly scrolled through a laundry list of emails. "Yes, yes, here it is." They both hunched over the computer, quickly scanning each page of the document.

"Al, please print out two copies." Katie always preferred hard copies of any document; they were easier to read, and she was infamous for her red pen notes in the margins. The next hour was spent meticulously going through page after page. Katie was well-versed on examining financial statements, and finding the way people made creative use of the numbers was her particular skill.

"Al, take a look at this," Katie said, pointing to the data. "Compare the numbers from two years ago to just before Junior died. There's a sharp spike in profits—right when customer numbers dropped dramatically. It doesn't add up. We need help figuring out how that's even possible." She picked up her phone and called her partner, Zoe.

"Zo, it's Katie. I need help. No, I'm okay, it's this case. Yes, I know what time it is, sorry to wake you, but just listen. When you get to work, I need for you to arrange a video conference with all our partners, first thing. I need everyone's help, our overseas contacts as well. Go back to sleep." She heard Zoe make an unkind remark as she ended the call.

Ali grabbed the ledger and noted another possible discrepancy. "Katie, none of these names appear on the statements. We know at least two of the men are drivers, yet they don't appear as being compensated. Several years ago, when there were other drivers, they all appeared on the statements as payroll. Interesting. In the morning, I'll reach out to my operatives to see if there's been any progress."

Katie looked at the clock. "Al, how about we get a few hours of rest and pick up later. We have so much to do, so let's see if we can get a little shut-eye."

Ali left first and Katie promised to follow shortly. She was straightening up the papers and wondered to herself what VanAnt was thinking. Was he still awake, worrying? More likely, she guessed, he was sleeping like a baby, confident in his deception. Regardless of what he was doing, she knew she needed a few hours of rest. Not wanting to disturb Matt, she grabbed a blanket and curled up on the sofa in the den. Her last thoughts were of what Matt had said. *"Things are going to happen, aren't they?"*

She whispered to herself, "Like the Fourth of July."

CHAPTER 43

Katie was the first to awake, encouraged by the smell of coffee and bacon. She uncurled herself and stepped into the kitchen, thrilled to see Maria at the helm, but concerned for her welfare.

"Maria, are you okay? Shouldn't you be resting?"

"Señora, this is where I belong. I am okay. Now you sit down and I bring you your breakfast."

No sooner was she seated at the table, Matt and Ali appeared. "We smell food. Good food," Ali said, giving Maria a gentle hug. "Will Carlos be joining us?"

"He ate already and is in the back garden, there is much to do today."

"That's an understatement," Katie mumbled under her breath.

Anxious to start working, they ate quietly and quickly, agreeing to meet in the den in half an hour. Matt and Ali returned upstairs, but Katie stayed behind to speak with Maria.

"Maria, Jennifer is so upset that she hurt you and she blames herself for everything that happened."

"No, señora, I do not blame her. I blame me for taking her

into town and not helping her. I will make her a breakfast tray and bring it up. Then we talk."

"That's very nice of you. I'll go up now and help her get ready."

Maria instead offered. "No, señora, please let me. I will help her." Katie hugged her, then left to wash up and change.

They were soon back in the den awaiting their instructions from Katie. "Al, I know you'll keep me apprised of any name developments, but in the meantime, I'd like you to meet up with VanAnt and see if you can find anything more about his house move. I'm curious if he's staying local or, as they say, getting out of Dodge. Once you feel he's put up a roadblock to your questions, you can serve him with the subpoena. I'd love to see his reaction, but I'm guessing he'll be quite cooperative and confident. Matt, I would appreciate if you would send all the financials to Zoe at my office as well as a copy of the ledger and copies of this pile of documents. I'm going to be on a conference call with them shortly, but I'll use my phone." She stepped away from her desk to let Matt use the computer. "I'll be in the conservatory."

When Katie entered the room, she realized she had not yet cleared the fallen teacup and saucer. Still on the floor in pieces, she scooped them up before Maria noticed. She had just finished wiping the stain off the floor when the phone rang.

"Good morning, Katie. We're all here as commanded."

Katie smiled. "Okay, okay, I appreciate you all being here for me this morning."

Thomas chimed in. "Zoe told us about your late telephone call, so clearly something important is happening. What do you need?"

Katie was anxious to start, gently reminding them of the urgency. "Matt is sending over documents that I'd like you to review in detail. I'm especially interested in the eight companies listed in the financials. They're all international, and I need verification that these companies exist."

Based on what Jennifer had revealed, it was obvious to Katie that something was very suspicious at Keans Industries. "There are fewer companies but higher profits, doesn't add up. I only briefly looked into these eight companies and I haven't found any indication of incorporation. Whatever you can uncover will be an enormous benefit."

The meeting lasted another 40 minutes, ending with a promise of everyone's full cooperation.

"I can't thank you all enough. I know you're busy, so it means a lot that you are making the time to help me. Let me just say again, my entire case hinges on what we've discussed this morning. I have three weeks left to pull it all together. My client's life is on the line. Thank you, my friends."

Katie went back to the den feeling grateful for having so much support. Matt was just finishing his assignment and inquired as to what else he could do. She looked at her phone and saw several messages from the Professor.

"Matt, the Professor called, but rather than phoning I'd like to visit him in person. I want to give him an update and see what he thinks. Would you go with me?"

Before leaving, Katie stopped to see how Jennifer and Maria were getting along. She opened the door just slightly and saw Jennifer dressed and eating. Maria was tidying up the room, and she could hear her talking to Jennifer about the garden. Jennifer was responding in between bites. Katie, not wanting to disturb the flow, stayed at the door just to tell them both that everyone would be out of the house. Maria said that wasn't a problem and that she would look after Jennifer. It was a great relief to see the two of them united.

Matt yelled up to Katie that he would meet her at the car.

She said goodbye to the ladies and left. She noted that Ali's car was gone. *"He's as anxious as I am to find answers."*

They arrived at the hospital in time to see the Professor walking the hallways. Their excited expressions pleased him. "I'm ready to be kicked out of this place, finally!"

It became so routine to see the Professor at the hospital that Katie never gave thought to the fact that he'd been there for so many months. She and Matt waited in the Professor's room until he was done with therapy, and after fifteen minutes he returned, entering the room unassisted.

"Professor, Katie and I are absolutely thrilled to see your progress. As far as we can tell, you're back to the original you," Matt said with genuine caring.

The Professor smiled with pride. "It's been an incredible journey. There have been high highs and low lows; life-threatening lows. But I finally feel, as you say, Matt, back to the original me!" Just as the trio took a seat at the table, Phyllis came in. They all hugged and raved about the Professor's health.

"Did Sean tell you the good news? Hopefully, he will be discharged by the end of the week." Phyliss' face beamed.

"That's incredible news, Professor." Katie rushed to give him a hug and a kiss.

Turning to Phyllis, she said, "We'll get the house back in order so you'll both have a smooth return home."

"Kate, absolutely not!" Phyllis was insistent. "Sean and I discussed it, and we will both be staying at my sister's for the duration of the trial. You have enough to deal with, we're not going to disrupt your routine."

"Phyllis, no, we can't—" Katie didn't finish as the Professor interrupted.

"Katie, you heard the boss. Now, no more discussion."

"You're both wonderful, thank you!"

The four spent some time together before Phyllis excused

herself. "I'm sure you're here to talk about the case, so I'll run some errands and be back for lunch." She kissed Sean's forehead and said her goodbyes.

The Professor turned to Katie and Matt. "Okay, now let's get down to business. Where are we at?"

Katie spent the next hour walking the Professor through every facet of the case—what she knew, what she suspected, and what she was determined to uncover. She revisited the earlier evidence, Mr. Adams, the knife, the trail. Her tone shifted as she spoke about the port, energized and intent. "I don't have confirmation yet," she admitted, "but I'm convinced Keans Industries is engaged in illegal dealings, with VanAnt orchestrating it all. My firm is working relentlessly to bring this to light."

She laid out her theory regarding the English classes and the delivery drivers. Finally, she brought it back to Junior. "Based on what we've gathered," she said, "I believe Junior stumbled onto the port dealings and was silenced for it. Jennifer, I'm increasingly certain, has no real connection—she's being used, nothing more than a scapegoat."

When she was through, the expression on the Professor's face was apparent. He was dumbfounded.

"Katie, what you're proposing is, in my opinion, a shot in the dark. I have known the Keans for years and have even provided them with some legal advice. Their entire group is respected and, as far as I'm concerned, beyond reproach."

Now she was the one who was dumbfounded. His stance on her position was baffling. She presented a formidable argument and was confused by his loyalty to the family rather than his recognition of the work she'd compiled.

He continued. "Right now, you don't have any facts, only supposition. Until you have hardcore evidence to present in court, a guilty verdict will be the only logical outcome. Katie, you seem to be basing this on Jennifer's now recollection of what Junior said to her."

Matt remained silent, but wondered to himself if the Professor's remarks had any validity. Had Katie let her emotions overtake her reasoning?

"Katie," the Professor said gently, "you know I'm not trying to hurt you. I can see how invested you are, how much this means to you, and how strongly you believe in your interpretation of the facts. But I've said it before, and I need to say it again: Urge Jennifer to take the plea. It won't be easy—she'll still face some jail time—but it won't be a life sentence."

Before she could respond, Katie received a text message from Ali. *I have information on the drivers, let's talk asap.* She gathered up all the paperwork that was spread out on the table and placed it back into her briefcase.

"Professor, I need to return to the house, but, as always, I appreciate your unbiased feedback. I will take what you have said under consideration." Her tone was emotionless and very formal; the first time ever she had spoken to him like that.

"Katie, I—"

"It's all right, Professor. I really must go. I'll keep in touch." As she and Matt reached the door, she turned toward him. "And I really am very happy for your return to good health."

On the ride back to the house, Matt knew his wife was disappointed. If she accepted the Professor's perspective, it would render all her work invalid with virtually no place to go. Matt pulled over to the side of the road and stopped the car.

"Before we get to the house, let me just play devil's advocate. Is there any chance at all that the Professor is right? He made a very good point about Jennifer's future—some jail or a lifetime of jail."

She took a moment. "I'm an excellent attorney, and I promise you I am not gambling with this young girl's life just to prove my status. Matt, I am telling you from the depth of my soul, I am right about this. I am absolutely right about this. Professor or no Professor."

He started the car and pulled back onto the road, "Okay, then let's roll up our sleeves and get moving, Professor or no Professor!"

CHAPTER 44

Ali greeted them at the door, anxious to share his news.

"Al, I hope that grin on your face is indicative of good news," Katie said, almost pleadingly.

"It is, Katie. At least I think it is," Ali said, hoping he wasn't about to let her down.

"Give me just a minute," she said. "I want to quickly check on Jennifer. Why don't you and Matt wait in the den and I'll be there shortly."

Katie first stopped by the kitchen to tell Maria they were all back, then headed upstairs. She quietly entered the room and was relieved to see Jennifer sitting by the window, book in hand. "Hi, Jen. Feeling better, I hope?"

Jennifer closed the book and turned to Katie. "I do feel a little better. The medicine helps, although it makes me very sleepy."

"Okay, I'll let you rest, but if you need me, I'll be in the den."

Jennifer nodded, then closed her eyes.

Katie took the book from Jennifer's lap and placed it on the side table, then quietly left the room. Matt and Ali were talking about the Professor when she came into the den. Ali was equally surprised by the Professor's reaction, but was hopeful that what he learned might sway his perspective.

"I'll leave you two alone," Matt said as he got up from the desk chair.

"Matt, I feel so guilty for taking you away from your business, your work, but very selfishly, I am so happy to have you here with me. I would really like you to stay. Besides, at this point, I think you can try this case yourself."

"I agree," Ali offered.

"Okay then, I'm part of the team!" Matt turned to Ali. "So tell us what you've got!"

Ali began. "Two things. First, I went to VanAnt's home, but only the maid was there, who told me he was at work. I drove to the port, where I found him alone in his office. I noticed that there were several moving boxes in the corner. Anyway, he danced around the housing question. The most he offered was that they were considering all options. I then handed him the subpoena to appear in court and, as you predicted, he was cool and confident. He also said that you didn't need to get the sheriff to issue a warrant for the company's finances, he would have readily made them available if you had asked. Katie, he may have appeared nonplussed, but I have a strong feeling that lava was boiling just beneath the surface."

Matt interjected, "Is that good or bad that he feels confident?"

Katie responded quickly. "I like when they're confident, almost arrogant. When I start breaking down their testimony bit by bit, they begin to crumble. It's not what they expected, so they become disoriented, in a way. If I have everything I need when the trial starts, that's exactly what will happen. You can count on it."

Ali smiled and nodded, then continued. "On a hunch, I stopped at the travel agency. There was an *out of business* sign on the door, which was locked. However, I could see there was someone inside, so I knocked. It was the owner. Her name is Toni, and she was cordial enough to invite me in. She was packing up her office for a move up to New Hampshire. I told her a white lie, I said I just wanted to confirm that Mr. and Mrs. VanAnt had made upcoming travel plans. She wasn't hesitant to respond to say that Mr. VanAnt had inquired about one-way fares to Monaco. However, if he did actually make reservations, it wasn't through her."

"Great work, Al."

Matt questioned what the second thing was that Ali had to offer.

"Katie, it's only one response, but my operative was able to track down one of the drivers. Goren Vertic. He drives exclusively for Pixie Furniture. The way it works... He gets a call from Pixie as to when to be at the port for pick up. He gets the cargo loaded onto his truck, then transports the goods to a distribution center in Ohio."

Katie was extremely intrigued. "Is he aware of the cargo? How does he get paid?"

Ali continued. "He claims he does not examine the cargo, he just delivers it. And, when the cargo is unloaded, he is handed an envelope with cash." Ali laughed. "He made a point of telling me he reports all the money on his taxes."

"Do we know anything about the distribution center? Is it legit?" Katie wanted to know.

"It's a legally registered business. As far as I know, they send furniture all over the continental US. We're checking with some of those stores to see if, in fact, they are receiving the furniture."

Matt was a little confused. "I'm new to all of this, but, Ali, you talked about VanAnt and then you talked about the driver and the distribution center. Does all this make sense?"

"It's music to my ears," she said enthusiastically. "It seems unconnected, but as I've said, these are all puzzle pieces falling into place."

Just then the phone rang. It was Thomas from the office.

"Katie, we got lucky. One of our contacts happened to be in Thailand on vacation. He did us a favor and checked out the Paulson Company. It exists on paper, but, Katie, the location…it's a dilapidated warehouse." They spoke for another fifteen minutes.

Katie hung up and turned to Ali and Matt.

"I don't think this day could possibly get any better!"

CHAPTER 45

They worked all through the day, stopping occasionally to stretch their legs and get a bite to eat. Calls were coming in with vital information, so taking long breaks was impossible.

It was early evening when the sheriff stopped by to interview Jennifer. He had been apprised of the events, but needed to hear directly from her. With Katie at her side, she recounted what prompted her panic and concern for Katie's welfare.

"Sheriff, I realized that Peter Jr. wasn't talking about himself that day in the library. That's when I panicked. I knew Mrs. Russo was alone in town, and I just became alarmed. I know I should not have left the house, and I certainly know I should not have gotten Maria involved. All I can say is I was scared and not thinking about the consequences."

The sheriff was satisfied with the explanation, but cautioned her about no second chances. Katie walked the sheriff out, but stopped to speak with him as he entered his patrol car.

"Sheriff, where do you stand with charging any of that mob with attacking my client?"

"Mrs. Russo, we went through this already. There is no evidence suggesting that anyone was responsible for your client's injuries. The information we have suggests it was an accident. I think we're done now."

Katie was livid, but controlled. "This town is toxic, Sheriff. A town whose umbilical cord was tied directly to Keans Industries. Once it was cut, this town, *your* town, died. It seems these citizens never learned to stand on their own two feet. My client is like a square peg trying to fit into a round hole. I'm going to fight like hell to get her acquitted and out of this suffocating place. Have a good night, Sheriff." She turned away.

"Before you continue to bellow, I think you should know that there is press in town now. They got wind of this case and your involvement and now they are scouring the town digging for information. I just thought you should know."

Katie managed an *okay*, then repeated her goodnight. Matt waited at the front door for her.

"Everything okay?"

She let out a sigh. "Yes, all is okay." She wanted to get the hell out of this town too.

"Your office called, I think it was Zoe. Ali took the information." They reconvened in the den and worked till nearly midnight. Expediency was critical, so information was pouring in from colleagues and contacts. They were just about to call it a night when Matt asked a significant question.

"I see how all the information that you've gathered is falling into place, but what I don't see is how exactly this relates to Jennifer." Katie and Ali looked at one another. It was a question that wasn't lost on either of them.

Katie spoke first. "I know, it isn't quite a direct line to her. I'm working on a theory, but I think it involves her tenuous relationship with Junior. Let's call it a night and we can discuss it further tomorrow."

It felt comforting to Katie to finally be in bed, next to Matt, after a long and tiring day.

Matt was curious. "Hon, I'd like to ask you just one last question before we both pass out."

She rolled over and kissed him. "Of course, what's on your mind?"

His tone was serious. "You have so many puzzle pieces coming from so many places. How many witnesses are you planning on putting on the stand?"

She was struck by the way he asked, wondering what he was imagining. "Just one, VanAnt. He's my only witness, my entire case." It was the first time Katie had said it out loud and it sounded daunting.

"Wow, just one," was all Matt could muster. He was clearly surprised, but much too tired to follow up.

He wrapped his arms around her, and they were both sound asleep in minutes.

CHAPTER 46

The time leading up to trial was like the movie *Groundhog Day*, reliving the same day over and over... All they did was work, eat, sleep, repeat. There was no time for distractions or relaxation. Thankfully, Maria did her part by tending to Jennifer. Her wounds began to heal, and so did her mood. Given the circumstances, she managed to be present and alert. Matt's question about linking the decline of Keans Industries to Jennifer was not lost on Katie. Initially, she had a few ideas as to what may have occurred, but the more they discussed the evidence, one theory rose to the top of the list.

Katie explained to both Ali and Matt that she was entirely confident that Jennifer was a scapegoat. "If I'm correct, I think Mr. Adams may have shared what he heard in the library with several people. If VanAnt was one of those people, he may very well have used that information to frame Jennifer."

She needed to speak again with Mr. Adams, the librarian, so it was her first stop of the day.

"Excuse me, Mr. Adams, I'd appreciate a moment of your time for just one question."

Initially, he refused to speak with Katie, but she let it be known that he could answer her now, in the library, or, uncomfortably, on the witness stand. It took only a moment before he relented.

"Mr. Adams, you've already made it known as to what you believe the conversation to have been between my client and Keans Jr. Despite the size of this community, I know it's tight-knit. Understandably, people want to share their opinions. Do you recall at any time discussing with anyone what you believe you heard?" She tried to make certain that neither her words nor tone appeared accusatory.

"I suppose I did. We were together and I probably shared what I had overheard."

"Mr. Adams, you said *we*. Do you remember who was part of that discussion?"

"Let me think. I know we were eating at Spanish Gardens for dinner. If I recall correctly, it was Ricardo Rodrigues, he's the owner of the restaurant, Miriam Kurtz, she's a member of the town council, Mr. VanAnt, and, of course, you know the Professor."

"As I said, that's totally understandable. One last question, Mr. Adams. Do you recall when you may have had this discussion?"

"Now that you ask, I do recall. It was April 6th. It was Kristen's birthday, that's Ricardo's wife. He gave everyone in the restaurant some birthday cake."

"Thank you, Mr. Adams."

Not wanting to wait, Katie called Ali from the car. "Al, he said April 6th. That's about two weeks before Junior's murder. Two weeks, Al. That's plenty of time."

When she arrived back at the house, Katie grabbed a quick bite, then met with the team in the den. It took into the wee hours, but she, Ali, and Matt finalized all the data that had been provided by her office colleagues and Ali's operatives.

Every box was finally checked, every step in the entire legal process was finally completed. Subpoenas, warrants, meetings; every i was dotted and every t was crossed. She rewrote her opening statement. It now embodied the power and confidence she was determined to deliver. Not content to end the night, she enlisted Ali in some roleplay. He portrayed VanAnt while Katie put him through the paces. She launched question after question. His heart and pulse were racing; he could only imagine how VanAnt would feel. As they wrapped up for the night, Matt was again curious.

"I promise this is my last question. This was impressive, but everything rests on your examination of VanAnt. What if he refuses to answer? I think you call it taking the fifth. Where does that leave us?"

Katie smiled when Matt said *us*. She was pleased that he recognized his contributions to the case.

"That's a great question. I'm pretty good at reading people, and I know VanAnt to have self-assured hubris. The gallery will be filled to the rafters with residents of Keansbury, all of whom hold him in high regard. His reluctance to answer my questions would be tantamount to an admission of guilt. And above all else, he is steadfastly loyal to Keans Sr. He will attempt to defend the indefensible. And with every lie, there is a straight line to Junior's death, his murder."

Ali and Matt stood quietly, impressed with Katie's passion and commitment.

"Katie, it's taken months and months of hard work, determination, and some good luck to get to this point," Ali interjected. He turned to Matt. "To quote an Alicia Keys song, 'this girl is on fire.'"

Matt put his arm around Katie. "Why don't we all get some well-deserved rest."

CHAPTER 47

It was Tuesday morning, and everyone was in motion preparing for the Wednesday afternoon trial start. It was originally scheduled for Monday, but the main water pipe burst, making the entire courthouse unusable. Katie surmised that the late start tomorrow would allow time only for opening statements by herself and the prosecutor. Witness testimony would most likely commence on Thursday. She worked with Jennifer for days, getting her ready and prepared for what she was about to see and hear. Today, she wanted to review one last time.

"Jennifer, bear with me, let's go through this again. The prosecutor will be presenting witness after witness who will testify to your character, your behavior, your lies. It is critical that you do not respond to any of it. All eyes of the jury will be on you, evaluating your facial expressions, your demeanor, your outbursts. I am asking the impossible of you. Don't react. Let me deal with it. I'm asking you to trust me. It may not seem so, but I have a definitive plan. Can you do this for me?"

Jennifer took a deep breath. "Yes, I understand. I trust you."

When they were done, Katie decided to run some errands.

She asked Ali to review some of the potential derogatory and inflammatory testimony with Jennifer. As painful as it would be to hear, Katie hoped that it would help minimize the ignominy of listening to it in court. "I'll see you both later."

She and Matt drove up the coast. At this point Keansbury, was persona non grata. They stopped at a few shops, then decided to revisit the La Mare Café. The quiche, wine, and ocean breeze were a welcome relief. Just as dessert was offered, Brandon Klein, the reporter, interrupted to ask a few questions.

"Mr. Klein, have you followed us here?" Katie asked, obviously bothered.

"Mrs. Russo, I apologize for interrupting your meal, but it's been impossible to get you to respond to my requests for an interview. I've spoken to just about everyone in Keansbury, and it's as if they all rehearsed the same answer. She's guilty...end of story. You're a well-respected attorney and I don't believe for a minute you've taken this case intending to lose. So, I want to know what you know that no one else does!"

"Listen, I understand you have a job to do, but you have to realize I'm not going to reveal any of my strategy to you before the trial begins. I will tell you this, and you can quote me: My client is innocent."

"Ah, come on. I did find out that you have been poking around Keans Industries. Is there some connection there between your client and the business? Perhaps a personal relationship between your client and the father?"

Katie had had enough. "The trial starts tomorrow. Everything you want to know will be said in court. Now, if you'll excuse us, we'd like to finish our dessert."

He rose to leave. "There's going to be more press here tomorrow. My articles have generated interest, and please know that they've been fair and accurate reports. I am not the paparazzi; I am a news reporter. I hope I can speak with you in the future."

Katie had worked with the press for many years, so she understood their role. Most were legitimate, some were just looking for titillating stories. She remarked to Matt that she wasn't sure why, but she liked him. Klein was kind of charmingly quirky and, from what she knew of his work, "fair."

She and Matt returned to their chocolate desserts.

"Katie, I wanted to tell you something. I've never been involved in your cases, certainly not like this. I always knew what you did was important, but I'm seeing things from a different perspective. You always talk about keeping a separate line between the client and the legalities of the case. With Jennifer, I think you've crossed that line, but in a good way. This girl has had an awful life and she's scared, never so much as right now. Of course she needs an attorney, but she also needs a mother, a father, a friend. I've watched you be all of those, and you've seemed to instinctively know which one she needed."

Katie sat quietly for a moment. "I can't deny there's something about her life that just reached me in a personal way. I told you when I first started that her emptiness hit home. I had parents, but they were never there for me. I didn't feel really connected until I met you and the Professor. She hasn't yet had that opportunity. I guess I tried to fill in that gap. But, Matt, I am her attorney first, second, and third. I haven't lost sight of my role."

He held her hand. "I have no doubt about that." He grinned. "You're a beast, but seriously, I've seen a natural and instinctive warmth in you that you often doubt. I will say this only once and then will drop it. You are not your parents, thankfully." He leaned over and gave her a kiss and wiped away a tear with his paper napkin.

The ride back was quiet, as was the house when they

entered. Jennifer was asleep in the rocking chair, Ali was playing football with several boys on the beach, and Maria was helping Carlos in the garden.

"I think everyone just needs some alone time," Matt said. "Would you mind if I sat on the deck for a while? I'd like to finish the magazine article I started several days ago."

"Of course not. I think I'll sit in the hot tub."

Without articulating, everyone found a way to relax and, in a way, to prepare for what was to come. The remainder of the day was low-key, but Katie did request that everyone gather for dinner, including Maria and Carlos. The conversation was light, with no mention of the upcoming trial. When they were through, Katie went upstairs with Jennifer while the men stayed to help Maria clean up. Katie helped Jennifer change into her night shirt.

"Your bruises seemed to be healed nicely. Are they still painful?"

"Just a little," Jennifer murmured. "But I've stopped taking the medication—it leaves me so drained." She hesitated, then looked up at Katie with a fragile seriousness. "Mrs. Russo, may I tell you something?"

"Of course, you can tell me anything." Katie stopped straightening up the room to give Jennifer her full attention.

"I'm scared. I'm scared of what I'm going to hear and scared to see all those people from town."

Katie sat on the edge of the bed, turned to her, and spoke softly. "It would be foolish of me to tell you not to be scared. I understand. But let me say this. I have represented big, burly, mean-looking men that weren't nearly as brave as you have been. You have endured unimaginable hardship, yet you never gave up, you never stopped believing in yourself. That takes a great deal of bravery. And, anytime you start to feel scared, you look at me, you look at Ali. We will be by your side throughout the trial. Okay?"

"Okay."

"Now get some rest, and I'll see you in the morning." Katie bent down and kissed her on the forehead.

When she got to her room, Matt was already there, waiting.

"How's she doing?"

"Matt, she's scared. I tried to comfort her, but to tell you the truth, I'm a bit scared myself. This is a case like no other."

He wrapped his arms around her. "You'll be fine, I know it."

Just then, her cell phone rang. "I better check." She sighed. "It's the Professor again. This is the fourth time he's called me today."

"Are you not speaking with him?"

"Matt, I can't. I just can't take his disappointment in my decisions. I don't want to start this trial with his words in my mind. He said my whole case was a shot in the dark. I love him, Matt, but he's wrong."

"He'll come around. Now, let's not think of the Professor. I love you and I believe in you. Let's just get a good night's sleep."

"You're my world, Matt. Don't ever forget that."

CHAPTER 48

It must have seemed like an eternity to Jennifer, but the day had finally arrived. Matt remarked that despite what was about to happen, the household was remarkably calm. Everyone met for breakfast, then retreated to their respective corners to get ready.

Promptly at noon, the doorbell rang: it was Deputy Wong. The sheriff had assigned the deputy with transporting Jennifer to and from the courthouse each day. Maria escorted Jennifer down the staircase, steadying her with each step.

"Miss O'Neill, I'll be taking you to the courthouse. Please come with me." The deputy retrieved her handcuffs, but Katie intervened.

"Is that really necessary, Deputy? I promise you, my client won't give you any cause for concern."

"It's protocol," the deputy responded, but then gave a huge sigh and relented. "Mrs. Russo, I swear you keep trying to get me fired." She grabbed Jennifer's arm. "Let's go."

Katie and Matt soon followed. Ali went in his own car. Not wanting to endure the ordeal of seeing anyone, Maria decided to remain at the house with Carlos. Arriving at the courthouse,

Katie wasn't surprised to see the large crowd of Keansbury residents gathered on and around the front steps. The parking lot was at capacity, swelled with cars and several chartered buses. Matt noted that the entire town was most likely in attendance. Fortunately, the courthouse was equipped with an underground garage, making it easy and safe for Jennifer. However, Katie, Matt, and Ali entered through the front of the building. It was like the parting of the Red Sea as they climbed the steps. Initially, everyone was silent, but little by little some derogatory comments were hurled, followed by slight pushing and shoving. The trio finally made their way into the lobby.

"This is crazy. We need police presence or access to the underground parking."

"Matt, I agree." She turned to Ali. "You okay?"

"I'm good, but I can't help thinking what Jennifer went through in town, facing that mob. It's damn scary."

Katie wanted to refocus. "Let's shake this off and we'll deal with it later."

The courtroom itself was standard, although the rear benches in the gallery were replaced by folding chairs and several ceiling tiles were missing; a byproduct of the broken water pipes. Katie and Ali seated themselves at the defense table, with Matt securing a spot directly behind. Shortly, the prosecutor arrived with his team and greeted Katie before wheeling himself to their table.

"Good luck, Mrs. Russo. Plea deal?"

Katie shook his hand, smiled, but said nothing.

Jennifer was escorted by the bailiff and took a seat between Katie and Ali. He placed a reassuring hand on her arm, but could feel her trembling. As the attorneys settled in, Katie noted that an additional bailiff entered the room. It was obvious that more protection was needed in anticipation of a highly charged crowd.

Within moments of opening the doors, a throng of anxious viewers descended on the available seats—a scene reminiscent of a game of musical chairs. Katie cast a brief glance toward the gallery. A few seats had already been reserved for the noticeably frail Mrs. Keans and Mr. VanAnt. The sight of Mrs. Keans gave Katie pause. She had initially suspected that her doctor might be exaggerating her condition to shield her from questioning, but it was now painfully evident that her health was in serious decline. With the background she'd already gathered, Katie had concluded that pressing for a personal meeting was unnecessary. She also noted the absence of VanAnt's wife, whom she had expected to attend in a show of moral support.

Once all seats were occupied, the doors were closed and the remaining crowd waiting grudgingly on the outside grounds. The room was now under control and silent. The judge entered and all rose. Prior to the jury's presence, the judge gave a brief but stern instruction. Being fully aware of the potential powder keg of emotion, he reminded everyone of his expectation for decorum and respect throughout the proceedings. Next, the jury took their seats, and within minutes, it began. The agonizingly long wait that Jennifer had had to endure was finally over.

The prosecutor wheeled himself in front of the jurists and presented his opening statement. He was slow and deliberate, outlining every step of his case. He spoke eloquently about the disparity between what he characterized as facts and Jennifer's initial statement. Jennifer stared straight ahead, emotionless, as she listened to herself being branded as a conniving, manipulative, and deadly spurned lover. He finally thanked the jurists, and it was Katie's turn to do what she did best. The Professor had taught her well.

Katie started by praising the prosecutor's delivery of his fantasy fairytale and then proceeded to tell them the truth of what occurred: Jennifer had unknowingly become the scapegoat in a criminal scheme on a staggering scale. Katie deliberately withheld key details, choosing instead to maximize the impact of her witness examination when it mattered most. She alluded to a different perpetrator, deliberately omitting VanAnt's name at this stage. It was nearly five o'clock when she finished. "Thank you, ladies and gentlemen, for your time and patience."

With that, the judge adjourned for the day, ordering them to reconvene Thursday morning at ten.

Katie turned to Jennifer. "I have a few things to finish here, so I'll see you back at the house. Are you okay?"

Jennifer could only respond with a fake smile and a nod. Katie and Ali had done their best to prepare her for what to expect, but the prosecutor's words were like a scalding blade slicing through her soul. One of the bailiffs came for Jennifer while the other approached Katie.

"Your deputy asked that I escort you and your colleagues to your cars. There's still quite a crowd out there. Why don't you all follow me, we'll go this way."

Katie was gathering up her paperwork when Matt tapped her on the shoulder.

"Hon, look." He motioned to the back of the room. Walking toward her was the Professor. Katie was shocked.

"Professor, you're only recently out of the hospital. My goodness, what are you doing here?"

"You didn't return my calls. I know you're very busy, but I was unhappy with how we ended our last visit."

"Professor, I—"

He interrupted. "Listen, I know you need to go, I just wanted to tell you that you were wonderful today, very convincing. What I personally think about your strategy is irrelevant. You try your own case."

"Thank you, Professor." She gave him a quick hug.

"Mrs. Russo, this way please. We need to get going," the bailiff said forcefully.

They managed to return to the house with little disruption. Everyone was exhausted, but surprisingly hungry. All but Jennifer gathered in the kitchen.

"The señorita was tired, so I brought her some food to her room. Was that okay to do? I wasn't sure if you wanted her to be at the table."

"Maria, that was perfect, thank you. I'll run up to see how she is and then I'll be back for whatever you made that smells so scrumptious."

Katie knocked and walked in to see Jennifer propped up in bed with the tray on her lap.

"I know this was a very hard day, but I can only ask you again to do your best to ignore what you will hear from the prosecutor's witnesses. Tomorrow their lies and misconceptions will begin. Is there anything I can do to help you more?"

"No, but thank you. I'm going to finish eating and then turn in." It was Jennifer's way of saying she wanted to be alone. Understandably, it was a difficult day for her.

Katie had begun to turn away when Jennifer spoke again.

"Mrs. Russo, you did everything you could to prepare me for what I'd hear in court, but it still hurt. I've always known how this town sees me, but hearing the prosecutor say it out loud—it cut deep. For the first time, their judgment had a voice. And despite what people might believe, I'm not some emotionless machine."

"Of course you're not," Katie replied gently, hoping to offer comfort.

"These past few months with you... I've learned what feelings really are. You showed me trust, compassion, and hope. But those come hand in hand with fear, pain, and disappointment. It's a balancing act I'm not sure I'm ready for—not yet. I just don't want to let you down. I'm trying to be strong."

Jennifer's vulnerability moved Katie deeply—it was both encouraging and heartbreaking. "You haven't let me down. Not for a single moment. Now please get some rest."

With that, Katie quietly excused herself and returned to the kitchen. She was still turning over Jennifer's words when Ali's voice pulled her back to the present.

"That was quite a surprise to see the Professor. Did you have any idea he would be there?"

"No, not at all. But I'm glad he was."

Energy was draining quickly, so they finished eating and called it a night.

Matt and Katie sat in bed for a while, talking about the afternoon.

"You were very impressive. It's not often I get to see you in action."

Katie grabbed his arms and wrapped them around her. "The real work starts tomorrow. I just finished telling Jennifer to try to ignore what she'll hear about herself. She'd have to be made of stone to ignore the hurtful lies."

"Katie, this may be asking a lot, but is there any chance you can let everything go for a while and just focus on us?"

She turned to him. "At this moment, there's only us. I love you."

CHAPTER 49

The phone rang very early in the morning. It was the clerk informing Katie that the trial would be delayed until 1:00pm, due to the judge experiencing a personal emergency. More delays. Katie wasn't certain if the few extra hours were aiding or hindering Jennifer's emotional stability. She decided to let her sleep in while she and Matt took a brief, but much appreciated, walk on the beach.

"Katie, how are you feeling this morning?"

"I'm ready, Matt. I'm ready to prove Jennifer's innocence. I'm ready to get home and back to our life." She paused and looked into his eyes.

"Matt, these past months with Jennifer have stirred something in me I wasn't sure existed. It's strange—just yesterday she told me I'd taught her how to feel, but the truth is, I've been thinking the same about her. I care about her deeply. I want her safe, protected, happy, healthy...all the things a mother wishes for her child. I used to worry that my parents' coldness might be part of me too, that maybe I wasn't capable of being the kind of mother your mom is. But I've come to like these feelings —this tenderness, this hope—and I want to share them with a child. Our child. When all of this is behind us, I think we should finally do what we've talked about for so long... Start a family. I know, it's insane to be saying this now, in the middle of a murder trial. But Jennifer had the courage to speak her truth, and I owe it to myself—and to you—to do the same."

Matt grabbed her hand. "You know I've always supported your decision, whatever it was, but I won't lie, I've prayed that I'd hear you say these words."

They hugged. "Some timing," she said sarcastically. "Let's get back and we can revisit this once the trial is over."

The morning went quickly, and in no time Deputy Wong was at the door to collect Jennifer. At the courthouse, a crowd was again assembled, but confrontation was avoided, as both the prosecutor and defense teams were given permission to enter through the garage. Once in the courtroom, Katie watched as the long line of attendees were escorted to the available seats. The same two chairs were already reserved for Mrs. Keans and VanAnt. Katie, still curious, had earlier questioned Deputy Wong as to the whereabouts of VanAnt's family. According to the deputy, he had them quietly spirited off to his Vermont timeshare, hoping to shield them from the emotional strain of the trial. Katie found herself wondering if this was, in fact, more likely an escape strategy. She then scanned the room for the Professor, but he didn't appear to be present. Quickly refocusing, she took her position at the defense table alongside Jennifer, Ali, and the new addition of Matt. The judge soon entered and apologized for the delay. Next, the jury took their seats, and within minutes, the trial began.

"Is the prosecution prepared to present its case?"

"We are, Your Honor."

"Please call your first witness."

The prosecutor began by calling several witnesses who knew Jennifer as their student, employee, or classmate. Each recalled a specific incident where it appeared that Jennifer was, among other things, sullen, depressed, and contrary. Despite Katie's frequent objections, the impression he was attempting to relay to the jury was starting to take hold. The last witness for the day was Mr. Adams, the librarian. He relayed, probably for the 100th time, how he heard Jennifer and Junior arguing about being together, and how she grabbed him as he attempted to walk away. He heard her clearly say, "Please don't go, come back." His interpretation was one of a lover's quarrel.

It was Katie's turn to cross examine. She started by asking him if he wore a hearing aid, which he adamantly stated he did not. As she began the next few questions, she turned her back to him and walked toward the defense table. She spoke loudly, but he interrupted her to ask her to repeat the question, as he was unable to understand.

She turned to face him. "Mr. Adams, I was speaking in a loud voice and I was closer to you than my client and the decedent were in the library, yet you claim to have heard their conversation. At the time of their meeting, you had previously indicated that the area was empty but for the two of them, so extraneous noise was not an issue. I ask you, is it possible that you may have unintentionally inferred their conversation from their body language rather than actually hearing their words?"

He was a proud man and was uncomfortable with being challenged. He didn't respond.

Katie continued. "Is it possible that they were discussing a non-romantic issue at which time Mr. Keans Jr. walked away and my client was asking him to return to continue the conversation? Mr. Adams, is that possible?"

He took a moment to answer. "Yes, I guess it is possible. I'm not lying, but I may not have actually heard what they were saying."

"I never believed you were lying, just mistaken. Thank you,

Mr. Adams." Turning to the judge, she said, "I'm through with my cross examination, Your Honor."

The judge acknowledged the lateness of the hour and adjourned for the day.

Jennifer was escorted out quickly, but Ali and Matt remained at the defense table to debrief.

"Hon, that was great. You punched a hole in his testimony."

Ali agreed. "You did a good job of creating an out for him without him feeling attacked. His concession seemed more believable."

She turned to them. "It was only a very small start, but it did tell the prosecution that we are going to fight for every inch of this trial. Let's get back to the house, I have a few details to review with you both."

Maria had a light dinner prepared for their return, which they ate in the den. They knew Friday would be an important day. The prosecution would be calling the sheriff, who would be presenting the most damaging of evidence. Unfortunately, when first questioned, Jennifer had declined council, so her complete account of the event was on the record.

"Matt, would you generate a few computer pictures of the knife? And, Al, I know it's last minute, but would you go over to Lamberts Trail and snap a few pictures of the bottom portion?" Katie explained in detail what she needed from them both, hoping that these visuals would be an impactful way of undermining the credibility of the prosecutor's evidence. With Ali on his way and Matt at the computer, she went to check on Jennifer.

"Jenn, tomorrow is going to be hard. The prosecutor is going to take everything you had said and attempt to discredit it one piece at a time. There are a few things I can challenge, but the jury will hear what everyone really believes happened that day.

Now, don't forget, the trial is far from over. We still get our chance to tell the truth."

Jennifer walked over to Katie. "Mrs. Russo, in the courtroom, you stood up for me, you fought for me. No one has ever done that, certainly not since Peter's death. I trust you."

Katie smiled and nodded. It felt like a breakthrough. "Get some rest now."

She returned to the den to find Ali and Matt already working on the pictures Ali had taken. Another hour, and everyone headed to bed.

"A big day tomorrow," Matt whispered to Katie.

"Yeah, a big day."

CHAPTER 50

Friday morning and everyone was back at the courthouse.

"The prosecution calls Sheriff Michaels."

Katie knew his testimony would be damaging, as he was the first person to interview Jennifer following her arrest. The prosecutor's strategy was to take each part of Jennifer's account of the day and refute them one by one. Clearly, her declining council was an immutable mistake, but one Katie was prepared to confront as best she could.

The prosecutor began. "Sheriff Michaels, when did your department first encounter Miss O'Neill?"

"On April 19th, at approximately 9:00pm, my deputies observed Miss O'Neill running on the northbound side of Highway 22. They approached her and noticed she was covered in blood. They pulled over and engaged the defendant."

"Sheriff, you mentioned she was running. Did your deputies observe her running toward Keansbury or away from Keansbury?"

"Away."

The remainder of the morning was spent with the prosecutor meticulously dissecting each claim made in

Jennnifer's initial interview. The sheriff, often referring to his notes, was composed as he disputed her account of the events, replacing, as the prosecutor noted, fantasy with facts.

"Sheriff, were the cabin light and telephone malfunctioning?"

"No, they were functioning."

"Sheriff, were the window curtains opened, allowing light from the full moon?"

"No, they were closed."

"Sheriff, did the murder weapon, the knife, belong to the defendant?"

"Yes."

"Sheriff, was the Rahway Road trail blocked?"

"No, it was clear from the cabin to the highway."

"Sheriff, were drugs found in Mr. Keans' body?"

"No, not now or ever."

The list went on and on, with Katie taking notes while observing the jury's facial expressions. She knew what testimony was expected, but hearing it live was still jarring. As for Jennifer, she did her best to sit stoically, although occasionally she leaned forward with her head down. The prosecutor finalized his examination of the sheriff at the noon hour, so the judge adjourned until 1:30, at which time Katie would begin her cross.

Matt wasn't certain what normally happened during lunch break. "Shall we grab a bite? I could use a bit of nourishment."

Katie was reviewing her notes. "Why don't you and Al go, I want to stay and go over a few things. I could use a coffee though."

They returned shortly, each consuming a protein bar. "Why are you eating that, and where's my coffee?"

"The two closest restaurants were packed, and recognizing us, no one was willing to let us step in. We got these from the snack machine down the hall. Tomorrow, we're bringing a Maria special. And sorry, the coffee machine is broken."

"That's okay, but let's hope this isn't a sign of things to come this afternoon.'"

Promptly at 1:30, the judge entered and the proceedings continued. The sheriff was instructed to return to the stand.

"Mrs. Russo, are you ready for your cross examination?"

"Yes, thank you, Your Honor.

Sheriff Michaels, you stated that your deputies first saw my client on Highway 22. How did they happen to be on that highway at that time of night?"

"That stretch of the highway is on the outskirts of town and somewhat desolate, often used by young couples. We routinely patrol that area. On that night, we received a call that a deer was dead and blocking the northbound side, so we responded. As they approached the area, they spotted your client."

"Who placed that call?"

"It was an anonymous call, and when we listened to the tape, the voice was garbled."

"Sheriff, if the call was anonymous, the voice was garbled, and there was no way to verify the legitimacy, does your department consider such calls reliable?"

"I didn't see any reason not to act on the call. As I indicated, we routinely patrol the area, so it would not have put us out of the way."

"Quite good fortune, wouldn't you say, Sheriff?"

The prosecutor objected, but she got her point across.

Katie opened her briefcase and took out a photo of Lamberts Trail for the sheriff to view. "Sheriff, you stated that my client was observed running away from Keansbury. I ask you to please look at this photo of the last 20 yards of Lamberts Trail. Would you please describe the direction of the path."

"Proceeding downward from the cabin, it makes a sharp left, exiting onto the highway."

"So, Sheriff, following the natural path of the trail would bring a person onto the highway facing away from the city, is that correct?"

"Yes, it would."

"Then is it possible, Sheriff, that in a frantic state after just witnessing the decedent, my client was just following the flow of the trail rather than fleeing?"

He hesitated. "Yes, I suppose it's possible."

Katie walked over to the exhibit table to retrieve the knife.

"Sheriff, the victim was stabbed in the chest. Based on the location and direction of the entry wound, would you please demonstrate for the jury how this knife would have been held."

The sheriff wrapped his hand around the handle of the knife and made several downward strokes, simulating the action needed to inflict the mortal wound.

"Sheriff, was the knife inspected for fingerprints?"

"Of course it was."

"Were my client's fingerprints on the handle?"

"Yes, they were."

"Were my client's fingerprints on the handle in the location you just demonstrated?"

"No."

"Where were my client's fingerprints?"

"They were on the handle consistent with someone holding the knife to slice bread or a tomato."

"Well, Sheriff, how do you account for this?"

"There was an obvious attempt to wipe clean the handle."

"Sheriff, are you telling me that my client had the wherewithal to wipe the knife of fingerprints and managed to remove only those that mimicked the downward thrust, but left those that mimicked slicing bread? Is that what you're telling me?"

The sheriff paused a moment. "I guess, yes, that's what I'm saying."

"More good fortune for you, wouldn't you say?"

Another swift objection.

Katie pressed forward with her cross-examination of the sheriff, aiming to chip away at the jurors' confidence in the evidence. It was late afternoon when she asked her last question and the judge adjourned for the day.

Once the courtroom emptied, Ali turned to Katie. "You did some damage today. Even the sheriff looked as if he was second-guessing some of the evidence."

"Al, it wasn't much, but if I've planted even a seed of doubt in the jury's mind, it'll make a difference when I go up against VanAnt."

Katie took a quick look at the gallery and saw Klein in the back row. He nodded and gave her a thumbs-up. She didn't respond, but smiled to herself.

On the drive back to the house, Matt was buoyant. "I know I said this before, but, hon, you were amazing. I watched the faces of the jury and the gallery, and you could tell you got them thinking, wondering. And Jennifer seemed a little less stressed."

"I really appreciate your enthusiasm, but I'll remind you, we have a long way to go." Katie turned to him and, with a sly grin, said, "How about you show me some of that enthusiasm tonight."

The day started and ended on a good note.

CHAPTER 51

The weekend was calm and uneventful. Katie remarked that it was a much-needed break for Jennifer—a chance to decompress after enduring such intense criticism. Unable to leave the premises, Jennifer once again found comfort sitting by the open window and reading. Confident that she was safe in Maria's care, Katie and Matt decided to set off to explore some of the more tucked-away towns, meandering through antique shops and cozy little cafés.

Ali passed his time with some of the fellows from the port—his new "buddies," as he liked to call them—kicking around a soccer ball by day and bonding over a steaming bowl of mussels in white wine by night. Among the household, not a word was said about the trial—there was no need. They were steady, composed, and fully prepared for what Monday would bring.

With the weekend behind them, and with little fanfare, they were all reassembled back at the courtroom on Monday morning. Katie scanned the attendees, noticing a few different faces. She had heard that residents camped out overnight to ensure a coveted seat. Their desire to be present was understandable, but it nevertheless made Katie upset to know that many were involved in the incident in which Jennifer was injured. After a few minutes, the judge entered, a stickler for promptness. He again reminded everyone of proper courtroom decorum and then instructed the prosecutor to begin.

Similar to the previous Friday, the prosecutor began by calling a parade of witnesses, seemingly everyone that knew Jennifer from the time of her birth. There was no denying that Jennifer was quiet, shy, even reserved, all traits that somehow were interpreted as conniving, manipulative, dishonest, unfeeling. Even her beauty and intelligence were viewed as arrogant and pretentious. Several of the more seasoned residents who knew her callous uncle claimed that the "apple didn't fall far from the tree." The prosecutor was clever in tying character testimony to relevant facts, but some responses were clearly more opinion-based.

Katie objected strenuously. "Improper character evidence, lack of foundation, prejudicial." The judge sustained her objections and at one point even more formally warning the prosecutor.

He apologized, but his attempt at character assassination had played well with the jury. Katie noticed some nods of agreement and even a few skeptical glances directed toward the defense table. She knew very well that jury perception can be as powerful as evidence.

The judge called for a lunch break, which was welcomed. Katie had done her best to deflect the harsh characterizations, but Jennifer was obviously affected. Her eyes were red and her cheeks tear-stained. Both Katie and Ali reached out to hold one of her hands, trying to reassure and comfort her. She would have had to be made of stone to ignore being portrayed as "the devil incarnate."

The afternoon session began with the prosecutor calling the medical examiner. In Jennifer's initial statement, she had insisted that the deceased indicated he was a drug user. The sheriff previously testified this was unfounded, but the prosecutor wanted a more detailed explanation from a medical perspective. The examiner meticulously explained that the toxicology report confirmed that he was completely substance-free at the time of his death. Furthermore, there was no sign whatsoever that he had engaged in substance abuse at any time in the past. When the prosecutor completed his interview, Katie declined to cross examine. She already knew that the victim was clean and that Jennifer had misunderstood their conversation. She intended on addressing this issue during her direct examination of VanAnt.

The prosecutor called just two more witnesses to refute claims that Jennifer had made. The last was the public service energy company, which indicated that both the lights and telephone were in working order. Once this testimony was concluded, the prosecutor informed the judge, "Your Honor, the prosecution rests its case." Due to the lateness of the hour, the judge adjourned for the day, informing Katie that the defense could present its case in the morning.

The group retreated to the safety and calmness of the house and Maria's welcome dinner. Jennifer attempted to dine with the group, but midway through she began to cry. Ali and Matt picked up their plates and moved to the patio, giving Katie and Jennifer some alone time.

"Jennifer, I can't even begin to know how painful it was for you to hear those untruths about yourself. But despite that, you stayed strong in court. I'm sure the prosecutor expected you to lash out, to make a scene, but you didn't. Your tears only showed your humanness."

Jennifer turned to Katie, but looked down. "Mrs. Russo, but what...but what if what they said about me is true? What if I am some of those things they said?"

Katie gasped. "Jennifer, look at me. Absolutely none of what they said is true, none of it. Being quiet or shy does not make you an evil person. Hear me, please. I've told you this before, but it's definitely worth repeating. I believe in you, Matt and Ali believe in you, Maria and Carlos believe in you. And I'm asking you to trust me to make the prosecutor believe in you, the jury believe in you, and this God-forsaken town believe in you. I'm asking you to muster up every ounce of strength you have and hang on just a little longer. Tomorrow is our turn, and I promise you, tomorrow is the day you have been waiting for. Tomorrow, we take control."

Jennifer nodded and grabbed a napkin to wipe away her tears.

"Are you okay to finish dinner?"

Again, Jennifer nodded.

Katie waved for Ali and Matt to return. "Anyone for seconds?"

"Of course," Matt responded. "Let me get us all a fresh plate."

They sat together eating while keeping the conversation light. After dinner, they retreated to their rooms.

"Tomorrow's the day, isn't it?" Matt asked.

"To put it in the Professor's poker term, tomorrow, we're all in." Katie switched off the light. Another night in which sleep came easily to the household.

CHAPTER 52

I t was Tuesday morning. The judge queried, "Is the defense ready?"

"We are, Your Honor."

"Please call your first witness."

"Your Honor, the defense calls Mr. Aaron VanAnt.

Katie turned to watch him rise from his usual seat. Mrs. Keans gave a tender squeeze to his hand and a thoughtful nod. He walked tall and confidently to the stand, ensuring that each step told Katie he was prepared for her offensive. As he took his seat, she recalled the moment she first met him. He was calm and polite, a gentle giant, she had thought. That façade was about to be exposed.

She began the questioning establishing his forty-year position as vice president of Keans Industries.

"And for the record, what type of business is that?"

"Essentially, we're a port of call for domestic and international imports and exports. We are certainly minor in size compared to the New York/New Jersey port, but we're very conveniently located and we're able to offer a more economical passageway for smaller ships."

Katie turned her attention toward the decedent. VanAnt confirmed that he knew and loved the young man and established that he had worked at the business for three years, mostly in training on a part-time basis.

"Mr. VanAnt, who was his supervisor?"

"I was his supervisor."

"And would you please describe the specific nature of the decedent's responsibilities."

"Peter Jr. was responsible for imports. When a ship arrived at the port, I received the manifest detailing the contents of each container and compiled the necessary paperwork for its release. Once a container was offloaded, he conducted an inspection to verify that the cargo numbering matched the manifest. When the truck drivers arrived to pick up the cargo, Peter Jr. coordinated with the crew to ensure proper discharge."

Katie further established that these were the victim's only responsibilities and then thanked VanAnt for providing a clear and concise overview of his work role.

"Mr. VanAnt, you previously explained the nature of Keans Industries, but I'd like to delve a bit further. Up until two years ago, the company had been doing very well, is that correct?"

He paused momentarily, wondering to himself why she specified two years ago. "Yes, up until two years ago, Keans Industries had been a very profitable company for two generations, since its inception."

"Mr. VanAnt, I recall when speaking with you previously, the company was very generous to its employees. You mentioned offering free meals and free English classes. Who implemented these employee perks?"

Again, he wondered about the questioning. "I did, but with Keans Sr.'s approval, of course. The company was profitable and we wanted to share in our good fortune."

The prosecutor announced sharply, "Your Honor, this

information is incompetent, irrelevant, and immaterial. Where are we going with this?"

Katie didn't wait for a ruling. "Your Honor, my client is on trial for her life. I'm asking for the broadest possible latitude in my examination. I assure you I will reach a logical conclusion— if you'll allow me just a bit more time to finish my questioning."

Judge Grayson leaned forward. "Mrs. Russo, I, too, am uncertain of your direction, but I'll allow you to proceed. Please get to your point soon. The objection is overruled."

Katie continued. "Mr. VanAnt, are these programs still in place?"

"The meals are still provided, but not the English classes."

Katie questioned the reasoning for the discontinuation, to which VanAnt indicated that the instructor, Mr. Parkence, had retired.

"Mr. VanAnt, we spoke with Mr. Parkence, and he was adamant that he did not retire, but was, in fact, dismissed by you. Is that correct?"

"I suppose so."

She noticed a very slight shift in his seat, and she could tell he was wondering why she was pursuing this line of questioning. Katie looked over at the jurists; she knew they, too, were wondering, but she was confident that they would fully understand when all was revealed.

"Mr. VanAnt, who is responsible for the hiring and firing of employees?"

"I am."

"Two years ago, over the course of three months, seven men from the crew were dismissed, as well as Mrs. Maccia, your administration secretary. Would you please tell us why."

"I don't recall specifically, but I would imagine that at the time their positions were no longer necessary."

"When you and I met some time ago, you told me

emphatically that the dock worker positions were not refilled, and yet, according to your payroll records, soon after, you hired four new men. Would you explain that please."

"I, I don't recall. I'm sure they would have been hired for different jobs."

"Mr. VanAnt, what about Mrs. Maccia? Was her position no longer necessary?"

"Well, no. I mean, yes, her position was necessary, but I guess I was having Peter Jr. take on some of those responsibilities."

"Mr. VanAnt, you just testified that the victim's only responsibility was to work on the dock, checking cargo."

"I'm sorry, I just don't exactly recall at the moment. I think my intention was to have him also become involved in office work."

"It surprises me, Mr. VanAnt, that someone in your position wouldn't recall something so central." Katie's tone was calm and respectful; she was trying to gently challenge the witness's credibility without outright hostility. It was a subtle way to signal to the jury that the forgetfulness may not be entirely genuine. He shifted again.

Katie continued. "Mr. VanAnt, do you recall the names of the seven men that were dismissed by you?"

There was no response.

The prosecution kept interrupting with objections, even going so far as to accuse her of badgering her own witness. Thankfully, the judge overruled most of them, and granted her leeway to treat the witness as hostile.

"Mr. VanAnt, please tell me if you recall these names: Anthony Walton, George Tilton, Antonio Reyes, Santiago Cruz, Miguel Torres, Diego Martinez, and James Vega."

"Yes, now I do."

"Mr. VanAnt, other than working for Keans Industries, do you know what these men have in common?"

"No, I don't. I can't imagine."

"With the exception of Mr. Walton and Mr. Tilton, the other five men all took advantage of your generosity and successfully completed the English classes. Interestingly, that means all seven men and Mrs. Maccia were all English-speaking and all were fired within a three-month period. Would you explain that please."

His discomfort was becoming evident. He was shifting and clearing his throat more regularly. He was caught off guard underestimating Katie; she had uncovered something he thought was undetectable and inconsequential to any outsider.

"I'm sorry, I don't know what you mean. I guess it's just a coincidence." His reply carried the weight of rehearsed sincerity.

The prosecutor leaned over to his assistant and whispered that he also didn't understand what she meant. He was perplexed as to the line of questioning, but decided not to object, preferring to let her dig a deeper hole for herself.

"Mr. VanAnt, in the past two years, your total employment has consisted of ten men, all working at the docks. Of those ten men, would you please tell me how many are fluent in English."

He reached for his handkerchief to wipe his brow. "I don't know."

"Well, Mr. VanAnt, the answer is zero. All your employees in the past two years are Spanish-speaking only."

The prosecutor had enough. "Your Honor, I must repeat my earlier objection. The counselor is seemingly taking us down a road that is as far away from this case as possible."

Katie responded quickly. "Your Honor, please, if you will allow me to complete my examination, I promise you that everything I'm asking will all come together at the end. I promise. I just need to finish my questioning."

The judge paused for a moment, mindlessly tapping his pencil on the desk. "All right, Mrs. Russo. I expect to see relevance. I will hold you in contempt if you are taking us down the rabbit hole."

Katie breathed a sigh of relief. She was confident in her overall strategy, but needed the freedom to execute it, especially with the next series of questions. She slowly walked toward the jurists as she continued. "Let me ask you about the overall business. I've had the opportunity to review your financial records and up to two years ago, the company, since its inception, has performed consistently well. I've mentioned two years ago several times during your testimony because it was a critical time for business in this country. Do you follow what I mean?" Katie was starting to circle the wagons, and he knew it.

"Sorry, no, I don't know what you mean."

"Well, then let me inform you. Two years ago, the entire US economy was in a recession, one of the worst in decades. Despite this fact, your financial records indicate that Keans Industries had its most profitable year. In fact, these past two years have been remarkable. How do you account for this?"

He loosened his tie; beads of sweat appeared on his brow. Katie noticed a few of the jurists leaning forward, hopefully a sign of increased interest. He cleared his throat before answering. "Ahh, I can only say that we are fortunate to have very good and loyal customers."

He responded exactly as Katie had hoped. "I'm glad you mentioned your clients. Would you please tell this court the names of these good and loyal customers."

"There's Pixie Furniture, Golden Dragon Trading, ah, oh, I'm sorry, I can't seem to recall the others at the moment."

"Please let me refresh your memory. In addition to the two you mentioned, there is Paulson Clothing, Sol Energies, Casa Pottery, Aaranya Innovations, Andes Natural, Café Bruma... Do you recall now?"

He could only nod.

"For the record, would you please respond verbally."

He was defiant. "Yes, I recall now."

"Mr. VanAnt, prior to two years ago, you were doing business with approximately twenty-four companies and profits were good. Two years ago, during the recession, your client base dropped to the eight we've just mentioned, and your profits were the highest since inception. Can you please explain that."

"I can only restate that we have very good and loyal customers."

"Would you please tell me what these good and loyal customers export."

"Um, clothes, furniture, household goods, coffee, items like these."

Katie turned to the judge. "Your Honor, if you please, as we discussed in chambers, I'd like to take a few minutes to show several slides."

Judge Grayson nodded. "Proceed."

Katie then turned to Matt and gave him a signal. He positioned a large screen near the bench so everyone, especially the jurists, had an easy view. He placed the laptop on the defense table and displayed an empty slide; it was perfectly positioned on the screen, so Katie continued.

"Mr. VanAnt, a few minutes ago you acknowledged the names of your eight good and loyal customers." Katie handed him a paper with the names of each customer. "Would you please read the first company name on the list and its location."

He was trembling, his voice weak and shaking. "Pixie Furniture, Philippines."

"Mr. VanAnt, I'd like to draw your attention to the screen. This is a picture of the company you just mentioned and its location. As you can see, it's a parking lot. Would you please read the next business name."

His voice was barely audible. "Paulson Clothing, Thailand."

"As you can see, this business is a dilapidated warehouse, with three walls and no roof. The next please."

"Sol Energies, Brazil."

"Mr. VanAnt, this business is a soccer field."

Katie continued with the remaining five businesses, each displaying non-existent locations. When the final slide was shown, VanAnt rested his head in his hands and began to weep.

"Mr. VanAnt, would you please explain to the court how not one of your good and loyal customers exists." She handed him a glass of water and tissues and waited a moment for him to compose himself before continuing. He could only respond that he didn't know.

Katie continued. "Mr. VanAnt, are you familiar with the name Goren Vertic?

"I don't recall."

"Mr. Vertic is one of eight dedicated truck drivers who pick up cargo from your port. I mention eight. There is one and only one truck driver permanently assigned to each one of your eight good and loyal customers. All eight of these drivers have been hired by Keans Industries, and they receive cash payment from you. Mr. VanAnt, isn't that unusual? Isn't it the obligation of the exporters to hire their own drivers to deliver their merchandise?"

He was dumbfounded. How could she possibly know about them? He was in a daze of confusion and appeared unaware of what was happening.

"Your Honor, would you please instruct the witness to respond."

The judge ordered VanAnt to respond.

"I can't explain," was the best he managed to utter.

Katie took a deep breath before continuing. The next few minutes would be the defining moments to this entire saga. She was going to finally expose the truth, which her client so desperately deserved.

"Mr. VanAnt, you've said you can't explain. That you don't know how it all unraveled. But the ledger recovered during the warrant—a ledger in your own handwriting—tells a story. During the recession, Keans Industries was bleeding. The company was on the brink. You and Mr. Keans Sr. were near financial ruin. Lavish lifestyles at risk. The town's economy hanging by a thread. That's all accurate, yes?"

"Yes."

"And then, somehow, your operations shifted. Not just clothing and home goods. Shipments began arriving and leaving at odd hours. More security. Fewer paper trails. Is this correct?"

"Yes."

"Mr. VanAnt, were *drugs* part of that transition?"

There was a long and painful pause before he had to respond, "Yes."

The gallery gasped and the judge ordered silence.

"Did it start as desperation—and spiral into something you couldn't stop?"

He tried to speak, but his throat was dry and his body was shaking. He took another sip. "We didn't have any other choice. We didn't have a choice. The town would have died."

His words drew chatter of disbelief from the gallery, at which time the judge once again issued a warning to remain silent, this time threatening to clear the courtroom.

Katie took a moment to walk to the defense table to retrieve some papers and noticed Mrs. Keans obviously agitated and crying at what she was hearing. Before turning back to VanAnt, she locked eyes with the Professor, who was seated in the corner. His expression yielded no clue as to what he was thinking. She looked away, not wanting to be distracted by his opinion one way or the other. She had a job to do.

Returning to VanAnt, Katie continued. "Mr. VanAnt, you worked exclusively with the same eight so-called companies and the same eight drivers, drivers you claimed to trust. Trust enough to move cargo worth hundreds of thousands of dollars, correct?"

"Yes."

"And yet, several of those drivers are now in federal custody. Are you aware of that?"

He shook his head. "No I am not."

"Were you aware that the FBI, in coordination with other law enforcement, secured warrants and conducted searches at the port?"

He was defeated. "No."

"Did you know drug-sniffing dogs were used?"

"No."

"Would it surprise you to learn that traces of narcotics were found throughout the property? That residue was consistent with long-term, repeated trafficking?"

"We didn't have any other choice."

"Mr. VanAnt, did you fire everyone that could read, write, and speak English in an effort to keep this illegal operation concealed?"

"Yes, yes!" He was screaming now. "Please, you must understand, if the company died, the town died. We didn't have any other choice."

"A noble thought." It was a sarcastic remark she couldn't resist. "Mr. VanAnt, you had previously testified regarding the decedent's work responsibilities. Against your instructions, did he open a cargo crate for inspection?"

"Yes, he was told never to open crates."

"Did he find the crate to contain drugs?"

"Yes."

"Mr. VanAnt, please tell the court what happened after the

victim opened that crate."

He was visibly shaken. "He wasn't supposed to. I yelled, I panicked, but then... I told him we'd handle it. I said I'd speak to his father, maybe even the police. I begged him not to act until we sorted things out."

"And what happened next?"

"I guess that wasn't good enough. He started digging—asking questions. He came to me later, said he thought his father was involved in smuggling drugs. He was crushed. Said he didn't know who to trust."

Katie walked toward him, leaning in. "Was that the moment you realized the truth coming out would shatter everything? That your name, your fortune, everything you'd built, would burn down with it? Is that when you decided..." She paused, and then said the words he feared would be forthcoming. "Is that when you decided Peter Keans Jr. had to be silenced?"

He exploded, "No! No, God, no! I loved that boy like he was my own. Yes, I handled the shipments. I ran the operation. I kept the books. But I swear to you, I didn't touch him. I didn't kill him!"

Katie waited a moment before continuing; she wasn't through yet. "But he wasn't your own, was he? Mr. Adams, the librarian, previously testified that he discussed with you the so-called lover's quarrel he had observed between my client and the victim. Is that when you decided to silence the victim and frame my client for the crime?"

He could barely speak. "No."

"Mr. VanAnt, you heard testimony describing my client as quiet, shy, friendless. Did you decide, based on the perceived fight with the victim and my client's character, that she would be a logical scapegoat?"

"No, no."

"Mr. VanAnt, did you lure the victim up to the cabin and

have him call my client to arrange a meeting there?" She didn't wait for a response. "Did you then kill Peter Keans Jr. and manipulate the scene so that an innocent young woman would take the full blame?"

He was near collapse. Before her eyes, this giant of a man transformed into a young boy who had been caught telling a lie. He could only stutter. "I, I, I don't know, I don't know anything anymore. I just... I don't know what I did..." His voice trailed off.

Katie turned to the judge. "Your Honor, the defense rests."

"Mr. Prosecutor, do you care to cross?"

"No, Your Honor."

And with that, the judge dismissed the jury, informing them he would reserve jury instructions and closing arguments for the morning. He then instructed the bailiff to take Mr. VanAnt into custody.

Just then, a scream was heard from the gallery. It was Mrs. Keans, looking directly at VanAnt. "No, oh God no!" she screamed in disbelief. "How could you?" "You—"

She never finished her words, collapsing to the floor from the weight of her sorrow. She continued to moan and wail, the sounds resonating from a place deep within. They came to her aid, trying desperately to console her, but the almost unrecognizable screams only intensified. Even the blare of the ambulance siren couldn't drown out her anguished cries. Racing to the hospital really didn't matter. No earthly medicines could ever heal her despair.

CHAPTER 53

They all arrived back at the house in silence. The morning's testimony and Mrs. Keans' collapse were overwhelming, and they needed time to process. Jennifer retreated to her room to rest while the others found comfort sitting around the kitchen table. Maria had prepared a light fare, not knowing if or when they would return. The meal and several cups of coffee were a welcome respite.

Ali finally broke the stillness.

"Katherine, I've seen you in court many times, but I have never seen you present such a powerful performance. Against all odds, you solved the insolvable. The faces of the gallery were painted with shock and disbelief. How it must have felt to witness their hero crumbling."

Matt chimed in immediately. "I wanted to say something to you, but just couldn't find the words. I've *never* witnessed anything like I saw this morning. Your work isn't only important, it's lifesaving. You were absolutely amazing."

Katie never accepted praise well. "Thanks, you two, but it isn't over yet. We need an acquittal from the jury, and I never presume to know how they will vote. However, let me say this.

The morning went as I hoped it would; that being said, I didn't take any joy out of humbling VanAnt. What he and Keans Sr. have done to this town is abhorrent and it needed to be exposed. I did what I had to do to save my client's life. And by the way, I didn't do it alone. I could never have uncovered the evidence I needed without your help and the help of my colleagues. You all worked tirelessly. Geez, I sound as if I'm giving an acceptance speech after winning an Oscar!"

Matt gave her a hug and whispered, "I love you," which made her smile.

"By the way," Katie said. "That reporter, Klein, cornered me as I was leaving the restroom. He begged me for an exclusive interview when the case is over and, I don't know why, but I agreed. I've been reading his columns and he's actually been very fair and accurate. It's a bit funny to think back to when I first arrived and no one outside of this town had any interest."

"It's really not surprising, Katie," Ali commented. "Your reputation, the Professor, the nature of the crime. You must admit, it makes for a very entertaining story."

"I know, you're right. I just don't like Jennifer being a headline. Speaking of, I'm going to check on her." Katie squeezed Matt's hand, then headed upstairs.

"I could use a run on the beach," Ali said, trying to sound casual but not quite masking the need in his voice. It was an overwhelming morning. "You up for it, Matt?"

"Sure, let me just change and I'll be down in a sec."

Katie knew they all needed time to decompress from the tumultuous court setting. She intentionally didn't say much to Jennifer, wanting to give her time to reconcile her thoughts. Katie knocked on the door, but didn't wait for a response. Jennifer was standing in front of the open window, the light breeze gently tossing her long hair.

"Jen, are you okay?"

She turned toward Katie; her eyes were red and her face tear-stained.

"Oh, Jennifer, come here." Katie wrapped her arms around Jennifer and held her tight for a few moments, then led her to the lounge chair. "It was a lot to absorb, wasn't it?" she said. "We still need to hear from the jury tomorrow, but it did go well today. Tell me how you're feeling."

"Mrs. Russo, honestly, I'm scared. If the verdict goes against me, I know I won't be able to endure this anymore."

Katie reached for her hands. "I sound like a broken record, but I need you to stay strong just a little longer. Nothing is guaranteed when it comes to a jury, but I have my closing argument tomorrow, and I promise you, I will knock it out of the park!"

The remark made Jennifer smile. "Okay, just a little longer."

"Jennifer, I have some work to do, so if you need me, I'll be in the den. And please, try to eat something." Katie rose and headed to the door.

"Mrs. Russo, today... What you did for me today. Thank you."

Katie smiled and left. She walked into the den, wondering how many more times she would be sitting in the oversized leather chair behind the oak desk. The Professor hadn't been in the room for months, but she could still smell the sweet cherry aroma from his pipe. There was no mistake, his presence permeated the room, and Katie found it to be of great comfort.

Ali tapped on the door. "We're back from our run, can I help you with anything? You looked like you were a million miles away."

She smiled. "I was just thinking about the Professor, the case, a little bit of everything."

"I noticed the Professor in the gallery, has he reached out to you?"

"No, I noticed him too. He probably wants to give me some time. I'm sure he'll call me. Where's Matt?"

"He's taking a shower, but I can stay and help if you need to go over your closing argument."

"Thanks, but I'm good. And, don't think I didn't notice that earlier you called me Katherine. The last time someone called me that was Sister Margaret when she caught me carving my initials in my desk, only there were a few more poignant words that followed!"

Ali laughed. "What's the plan for the remainder of the day?"

"I'm going to review a few more things, then just relax. I'll see if Matt wants to take a drive. If not, I'll watch a few movies and call it a day."

"Okay, but if you need me, I'll be reading my book on the deck."

Katie smile and nodded. "Thanks, you just relax."

The remainder of the day was met with mixed activity. Everyone found a private corner in which to retreat and unwind in their own way. The hectic day had finally taken its toll on the mind and body, and, a sense of sereness enveloped the household. But Katie knew there was still more to come.

CHAPTER 54

It was the final day of the trial. Katie and Jennifer were in the kitchen discussing how things would unfold in the morning's court proceedings. "The prosecutor has the burden of proof, so Mr. Ryan will present his closing argument first. I will close after, highlighting all the weaknesses in his case. If there's no prosecution rebuttal, which I doubt there will be, the judge will give instructions to the jury. He will provide legal guidance on how they should evaluate the evidence presented and how they should apply the law."

Jennifer sighed, "And then we wait."

"Yes, and then we wait."

The doorbell rang. "Ah, Deputy Wong, right on time."

Katie walked Jennifer to the door.

"Good morning, Deputy."

"Good morning, Mrs. Russo. Before we leave, the sheriff asked me to let you know that Mrs. Keans died early this morning."

"Oh, damn it. Another poor victim." Katie was genuinely upset by the news. By all accounts, Mrs. Keans had no involvement in any of her husband's dealings, but was forced to pay the ultimate price of losing a son and, consequently, her own life.

"Mrs. Russo, for what it's worth, you changed a lot of minds yesterday. It's been quite a lot to absorb."

"I'm afraid it's too little, too late, but I appreciate you sharing." Turning to Jennifer, she said, "I'll see you shortly." Katie watched as the police car pulled away, praying these rides would soon end. She turned to see Matt and Ali coming down the stairs.

"Are you ready, Katie?"

"Let me just get my briefcase."

They rode together in silence. They arrived to see a large but subdued crowd; Katie correctly surmised that the news of Mrs. Keans passing had become public knowledge.

While everyone waited for Judge Grayson to enter, Katie scanned the room. With the notable exception of Mrs. Keans and Mr. VanAnt, everyone was positioned exactly as the day prior; even Klein managed to secure a seat. She was very glad to see the Professor. He gave her a smile and nodded, hopefully a sign of approval. Closing arguments were one of his specialties, so she learned from the best. For a brief moment, she couldn't help but feel as if she was that same college student seeking his approval. Her thoughts were quickly interrupted by the entrance of the judge. He wasted no time in reminding the jury that closing arguments were not evidence, but rather summaries of each side's case.

"Mr. Prosecutor, you may proceed."

He wheeled himself in front of the jury and began. He concluded thirty minutes later, at which time Katie began her remarks, countering each of his points. As the minutes passed, her words flowed like a symphony. She was poised, confident, and in control.

Ali leaned over to Matt and whispered, "They look mesmerized. What she's saying is resonating with the jury."

When she finished, Matt half-expected the gallery to erupt with a standing ovation. He was bursting with pride. Katie turned to walk back to the defense table. She quickly glanced over to the corner of the room to see the Professor's reaction, but was disappointed to see his seat vacant. Her focus, however, was on Jennifer, who leaned over to say thank you.

Before adjourning, Judge Grayson proceeded with the jury deliberation instructions. "Members of the jury, you are now exclusive judges in this case, and it is your duty to determine the facts from the evidence presented. You must apply the law, regardless of your personal opinion." He spoke for an additional 15 minutes, concluding with a reminder that their verdict must be unanimous. Upon completion, court was adjourned, and the group returned to the Professor's home.

Becoming a ritual, they were once again sitting at the kitchen table consuming a light fare. Maria, Carlos, and Jennifer joined in.

"How long will it take to find the answer?" Maria inquired.

"I honestly don't know, Maria. It could take hours, days, even weeks. I know it's hard waiting, but you really want the jury to discuss the evidence in the hope that they make the right decision."

Jennifer listened to the table chatter, then finally spoke up. She was unaccustomed to speaking, and certainly not in a group setting.

"Mrs. Russo, I want to say thank you." The group went silent; it was an unexpected occurrence. "Regardless of the outcome, I want to thank you for all that you have done for me. Everyone, thank you. No one has ever helped me, and…" Her voice trailed off as she began to tear up. Maria rushed over to give her a motherly hug. Even Ali's eyes began to water. Matt looked at

Katie with a wide grin, knowing this was a major breakthrough for her. Katie walked over to join in the hug. She realized that unique circumstances had brought them all together, and she, too, wanted them to know how she felt.

"Everyone, we have spent so many months together. We are quite a crew, an amazing crew," Katie said with deep sincerity and appreciation.

Like the previous afternoon, everyone found something to keep them occupied. The anticipation of a verdict was palpable; all movement ceased with each ring of the house phone. Katie knew any news would be sent to her cell phone, but that still didn't reduce the overall household anxiety.

It was early evening when the Professor called. Katie was so pleased to finally hear from him. He apologized for not contacting her sooner, but insisted he didn't want to be a distraction, especially after their last meeting. Of course, he assured Katie of how proud he was and remarked several times about how he, along with the entire town, was so shocked by the drug revelations and its consequences.

"Katie, your instincts were sound from the beginning. I repeatedly urged you to accept a plea, and yet you held firm. In hindsight, I'm grateful you did. My phone hasn't stopped ringing —colleagues and friends alike are stunned by everything that's unfolded. It's humbling, and frankly, we owe you a debt of gratitude."

The Professor took a moment, then continued, "I've known and worked with Senior and VanAnt for years and was totally in the dark. And Junior's death, I don't even know what to say."

They spoke for another half-hour, ending with the Professor informing Katie of his plans. "I'm finally well enough to take Phyllis on that long overdue vacation. We're leaving in a few days, and I wanted you to know that you are welcome to stay at the house for as long as you like. Regardless of the outcome, you and Matt may want to stay on and enjoy the beach, although you're probably more than eager to return to your normal life. Katie, I know you sacrificed so much to get to this point in the trial. I feel guilty for having involved you in this, for taking you away from your law firm and your home. And if the verdict comes back guilty, or if there's a mistrial, I will find another attorney to work with Jennifer. I don't want you to spend another moment on this case. And I'm being firm on this."

Katie responded affirmatively only to placate the Professor. Up to this point, she hadn't discussed any contingency plans with Matt. Her focus was on an acquittal; no other option was even considered. Katie placed her phone on the desk and started to walk away when it rang. She thought for a moment it was the Professor again, but the number was unfamiliar.

"Good evening, Mrs. Russo. This is Barbara Stanhope, the clerk for Judge Grayson. I'm calling to inform you that the jury has reached a verdict and court will reconvene tomorrow at 10:00am for its reading."

The relatively brief deliberation caused Katie to pause momentarily. Her silence was deafening.

"Mrs. Russo, are you there?"

"Oh, I'm sorry. Yes, I understand, and we will be there promptly at 10:00. Thank you, and have a good evening."

"The same to you, Mrs. Russo."

Katie sat still and took a long, deep breath. Tomorrow, she knew, would be the culmination of months and months of blood, sweat, and tears. This case was different than any other she had ever tried. It tested her knowledge, her endurance, and, unexpectedly, her emotions. After a few minutes, she called Ali and Matt into the den and told them the news.

"Katie, that was so quick. What does it mean? Is that good, bad, what?"

"Matt, I hate saying I don't know, but I don't know.

Ali asked if Katie had spoken to Jennifer yet. "I'm going to tell Maria and Carlos, text the Professor, and then go speak with Jen."

Katie didn't bother to knock. She gently opened the door to find Jennifer at her usual spot in front of the open window.

"Jennifer, I just received a call from the clerk. The jury has reached a decision and we are to be back in court tomorrow at 10:00."

She just looked at Katie and nodded.

"Do you want me to stay and talk about it?"

Again, not saying anything, she just shook her head, indicating no. Katie decided it was best not to press her into a discussion, so she turned to leave. As she was about to close the door, Jennifer spoke, almost whispering.

"Mrs. Russo, do you want to know what I've been wondering? I've been wondering if I'll ever be able to feel the ocean again."

Katie's heart ached at the question.

"You will," Katie said, her voice soft but certain.

That simple yearning—to feel the ocean—was almost too much. It wasn't just about waves or water; it was about freedom, healing, and the hope for something beyond pain. Katie wanted that for her. She wanted everything for her. She lingered for a moment, then quietly closed the door and walked away.

Matt was just coming up the stairs. "How is she?"

Katie grabbed his hand. "Are you up for a walk on the beach? I think we have some things to talk about."

"Sure, hon."

They walked and talked for several hours, returning to the house as the sun was setting. They made a tray of snacks and decided to relax in their room for the remainder of the night.

"Katie, I know this is part of your job, but I don't know how you do this. I'm actually nervous about tomorrow. I'm a tough guy, but my insides are rumbling."

She gave a short laugh. "Some cases are harder than others, but I'd be lying if I didn't say I'm a little nervous too. I want so much for this girl." She changed the subject. "How about we put on *The Honeymooners* that you love so much. I could use a few hours of just plain silly. I'm done thinking!"

Matt was happy to see that the streaming service carried every episode recorded. He plopped down next to Katie and pressed play. "Hey, how about sharing some of the cheese and crackers." They laughed and munched on the snacks until sleep found them both.

Just as Katie closed her eyes, she thought to herself, *"Yeah, I'm a little nervous too."*

CHAPTER 55

Katie didn't think it was possible, but the courthouse crowd was the largest yet. It seemed that every citizen from Keansbury and the surrounding towns was in attendance. Contrasting with the previous day's sereness, Ali remarked that it looked like a circus. Food carts peppered the perimeter with reporters abound, interviewing citizens seeking their 15 minutes of fame. Extra law enforcement made their presence known, trying desperately to keep civility.

Once inside, some degree of normalcy prevailed. Defense and prosecution were seated at their respective tables; the gallery was in place.

Matt turned to Ali. "Am I mistaken, or is the courtroom air feeling thick with anticipation?"

"That's an understatement!" he whispered.

Katie looked over at Jennifer. She reached for her hand only to find it unsteady. She was just about to say something comforting when the judge entered. As with the start of each court session, everyone rose. The judge took his seat, called the session to order, and requested the bailiff to summon the jury.

All eyes focused on the twelve men and women as they

entered, each one of them knowing they carried the weight of their decision. The judge reminded the courtroom to remain silent and respectful.

"Mr. Foreman, have you reached a decision?"

"We have, Your Honor." His voice wavered slightly.

"Would you please hand your verdict to the clerk."

The clerk handed the form to the judge, who read it silently, then gave a small nod. The clerk returned the form to the foreperson. The judge continued, "Will counsel and the defendant please rise."

Ali quickly put his arm around Jennifer, who could barely hold herself upright. Her heart was pounding and her breathing became more rapid. He held her tightly. "Hold on, hold on."

The judge turned to the jury, "Mr. Foreman, what is your verdict?"

The foreman briefly glanced at Jennifer, then read from the form. "In the matter of the State versus Jennifer O'Neill, we the jury find the defendant Not Guilty."

There were gasps and cries from the gallery. The judge banged his gavel several times to restore order. Jennifer collapsed into Ali's arms, and both he and Matt helped her back into her chair. For a few moments, she was oblivious to all sights and sounds; she prayed it wasn't a dream. Katie put her arm around her and then turned her attention to the judge.

"Ladies and gentlemen of the jury, this has been a highly emotional case, so I want to thank you for your time, attention, and service. On behalf of the judicial process, I am grateful for your commitment. This court is now adjourned." He banged his gavel one last time and it was over.

The crowd raced out of the courtroom, each wanting to be the first to relay the news to the outside gathering. A few attempted to speak with Katie, but Matt served as a bodyguard. This was Jennifer's moment, and no remorse or congratulations on the part of anyone was wanted. Katie looked at Jennifer, who was just getting the color back into her face.

"Honey, it's over."

Jennifer still looked somewhat disbelieving. "Did he say not guilty?"

Katie chuckled. "He sure did!"

She turned to Ali and Matt. "Please take Jennifer back to the house and I'll follow shortly. I have some paperwork to finish here. I won't be long."

Before leaving, Matt grabbed Katie and gave her a hug. "You did it, you really did it!"

"*We* did it. I was never alone."

After they left, the prosecutor asked for a minute of Katie's time. "Mrs. Russo, you did an incredible job and I must admit that I am regretful that I dismissed your input. I have no excuse for not conducting the investigation that this case warranted. What we did to your client was reprehensible."

Those were words she was not accustomed to hearing from a prosecutor, but she was also not one for *I-told-you-so*.

"Mark, you're a good attorney, and I can understand how you were dubious about my client's initial statements. But you, law enforcement, and the town never looked beyond that. You were all so convinced of her guilt that you looked no further, even after I shared developing information."

He looked defeated, both professionally and personally.

"Has VanAnt detailed how he arranged Junior's death?" she wondered.

"No, not yet. He's confessed to the drugs, but he's insistent that he didn't kill the boy. We'll stay on him. It'll come eventually."

"I imagine the FBI has been in touch with your office."

"Yes, we have a meeting scheduled for tomorrow morning. From what I understand, they've been investigating drug trafficking on the East Coast and were a bit surprised by the big role we played. I'm saying 'we' as we are all somewhat culpable."

She turned to retrieve her briefcase and jacket.

"Mrs. Russo, I don't know if this town will survive. There are a lot of good people who did the wrong thing. Regardless, we have a lot to make up for with your client. I hope she'll allow us to do that."

"That's up to Miss O'Neill." And with that, she left the courthouse for the final time.

On the drive to the house, Katie sent an audio message to the Professor, then called her father. He mustered, "Good job," followed by, "What a waste of talent." She said goodbye and disconnected even as he was still speaking. Next, she called her office colleagues, who were huddled in the conference room. Their cheers and screams erased any negativity left by her father. She thanked them over and over. She knew their last-minute hard work saved the day. Finally, she called her mother-in-law, who may have possibly screamed the loudest. Contrasting with her own parents, Matt's mother was so excited and proud.

"We miss you and Matteo. When you come home, we will have a feast in your honor. You bring Jennifer too." His family had a wonderful way of making her feel special and loved.

By the time she finished her call, she was arriving back at the house. When she entered, it was surprisingly silent. She walked into an empty kitchen, but was relieved to see they had assembled on the deck. She slid the doors open and was greeted by a bearhug from Maria. Carlos handed her a glass of champagne.

"I see you started the celebration without me."

Carlos handed her a second glass. "You will catch up, señora."

They all laughed as she gladly consumed the two glasses she

had in her hands. It took Katie a moment to realize Jennifer wasn't with them. "Matt, where is Jennifer? Is she okay?"

Matt pointed to the water's edge. It made Katie smile to see Jennifer standing knee-deep and getting soaked with each crashing wave.

"That child looked out the window every day wondering if she'd ever get to feel the ocean again. What she had to endure..."

Matt reached for Katie's hand. "It's okay. Let's just enjoy now, and we can worry about the rest of our lives tomorrow."

"Deal," Katie said as she finished the last drop of champagne.

Carlos handed Katie another glass, which she took willingly.

Maria then announced, "And now we eat!"

Ali turned to walk down the beach to retrieve Jennifer, but Katie interrupted him. "Al, I think she needs some time by herself. She'll come up when she's ready."

"Yeah, you're right." He reached over and they hugged tightly.

"You know, Al, I could never have done this without your incredible hard work." He jokingly assured her that she was right again.

Perhaps for the last time, they assembled around the kitchen table and ate, laughed, and drank more champagne. Jennifer finally came in, drenched, but hungry. They sat for hours just reveling in the moment. The conversations were light and often silly—champagne has a way of doing that. All serious topics and thoughts could wait until tomorrow.

"Carlos, you clear the table. Make room for three desserts." Maria outdid herself, and despite cries of, "I can't eat any more," all three desserts had disappeared before the night was over.

CHAPTER 56

Katie quietly slipped out of bed, not wanting to disturb Matt. After dinner last evening, he, Carlos, and Ali sat on the deck smoking cigars and drinking cognac. She wondered if any of them would even wake up today.

"Good morning, Maria."

"Good morning, señora. I have a big pot of coffee ready. I think we all will need it today."

"Matt and Ali are still sleeping. Is Carlos?"

Maria laughed. "Señora, I thought he was not living. I poked him many times and he only rolled over."

"I don't expect we'll see any of them until this afternoon. Has Jennifer been down?"

"Si, I make her tea and eggs. She asked for a towel and she is on the beach with her book. I keep checking on her. The beach is very empty."

"Thank you, Maria. I imagine everyone is still in their homes shocked at all that has occurred. If you wouldn't mind, I would love some eggs too, and a very big cup of coffee."

After breakfast, Katie brought her third cup of coffee with her to the den. It was time to start packing all her case files.

Unlike her colleagues, her idea of backing up her computer data was to print important documents and place them in a three-ring binder. In college, a computer glitch had erased an important term paper, and since then, she always kept a hard copy of essential files. Consequentially, she required a dozen boxes in which to store her notebooks. She was meticulous, numbering and dating each one, ensuring easy retrieval if and when necessary. After she finished taping the lid on the last box, she began removing all the sticky notes, papers, and pictures that adorned almost every inch of the walls. Each paper reminded her of her very first days in Keansbury and her very first steps into the Professor's den.

"May I be of any help? Although your response should be no thank you."

She laughed as she turned to look at Matt, a little disheveled and clearly not yet ready to face the day.

"Ah, no thank you. I'm doing okay on my own," she said with a smile.

"Ali and Carlos are joining me in the kitchen for some coffee, coffee, and perhaps more coffee. Seriously, hon, could you use some help?"

"Seriously, I'm fine. This organizing is really something I need to do on my own. Of course, you fellows can help when it's time to load up the cars." He gave her a quick peck on the cheek and left her to finish. When all was done, she stacked the boxes in the foyer and, against Maria's protests, she vacuumed the carpet and dusted the desk and bookcases. She surveyed her fine work from the Professor's chair, melting in its plushness most likely for the very last time. She sighed deeply. Something was giving her pause, like a grain of sand in her eye; nothing serious, but just enough to be annoying.

Ali finally came in and was taken aback at how neat and clean the den appeared.

"Wow, it's so much larger when all our work has been removed. And who knew there was wallpaper?!" he said jokingly.

Katie gave a half-smile. "Is Jennifer okay?"

"She wanted to go for a walk along the beach, so Matt and Carlos have gone with her. The beach is still as empty as yesterday, but they wanted to be certain no one bothered her, just in case."

"Oh, that's great. She stared at the ocean for months. She equates it with freedom."

Like a hundred times before, Ali pushed his favorite chair to the front of the desk. "I know you, Katie. Something is not right. Tell me what's bothering you."

She shook her head. "It's probably nothing, but I keep thinking about VanAnt's testimony. I dislike the man and I think he's reprehensible, but I don't know. He just seemed so genuine about loving Peter. The prosecutor said he confessed to everything but the murder, although he was confident that admission would be forthcoming."

Ali looked a bit shocked. "Katie, you can't possibly think that Jen—"

She cut him off immediately.

"Oh no, absolutely not. That never entered my mind. I'm just overthinking it all. That murder was so meticulously planned, and there's no one else who even had a motive. He alluded to it, but I guess I just wanted him to definitively say it in court."

"Katie, I'm going to say something harsh, and it's only to bring you back to the facts. Your job was to get an acquittal for your client, and you did that. There's no question in anyone's mind that she's innocent. Now, whether or not VanAnt is guilty, that's not your concern. Let the law deal with that."

She knew Ali only had her best interest in mind, so she listened to what he had to say.

"I know, you're right. Let's close the door on this room once and for all."

Ali pushed the chair back to its proper place, then they slid the doors closed.

"Al, what are your plans? Will you be leaving today? You know you can stay for as long as you want. Matt and I will be here for a few more days. I want to speak with the Professor and, above all else, I need to help Jennifer get settled. I haven't spoken with her yet as to her plans."

"I think I'll leave later this afternoon. It's time I get back home, and I want to visit my mother over the weekend. I don't have much to pack, so I'll shower and then get on the road."

"I'm going to miss seeing you every day, but I know we'll work together again. I've said it before, but I swear, Al, I never could have done this without your skill, your commitment, and your friendship."

He gave her a hug. "You know what I'll miss the most? Maria's cooking."

She pushed him away and laughed. "Make sure you don't leave before seeing Matt and me."

When Ali went upstairs, Katie decided to relax on the deck. She moved the lounge chair into the sun and grabbed two pillows. She had intended on reading a magazine, but sleep took over after only a few minutes.

She stirred when she heard voices; the trio had returned from their long walk. It was now mid-afternoon, and Ali was ready to leave.

He said his goodbyes to everyone, especially Jennifer. "I'm so happy for you and so glad I was a part of your journey to freedom. If I can ever be of help to you, please reach out anytime." Jennifer hugged Ali and thanked him for all that he did.

As he started for the door, Maria intercepted him. Not

surprisingly, she had packed a bag of snacks for him in case he got hungry on the drive home.

"Maria, if you weren't already married, I'd propose to you right now!"

"Oh, señor, you make me blush."

He gave her a hug and said goodbye.

Matt went up to the room for a long overdue shower, which left Katie and Jennifer alone on the deck. Katie had hoped to speak with Jennifer about what lay ahead, but before the moment presented itself, Jennifer—clearly weary—had quietly excused herself for a nap. Katie suspected her emotions must be too raw and she likely needed space to absorb it all. She could only imagine the whirlwind inside her: the lightness of newfound freedom mingled with the uncertainty of what comes next. There was no need to press the matter; they would talk soon.

"Señora, do you have a minute for me?" It was Carlos asking Katie to follow him to the greenhouse. In all the time she was at the house, she realized she had not visited the greenhouse since she had first arrived in Keansbury, so many months earlier. She recalled that she had been amazed at its size and the variety of plants and flowers.

"I know how much you like the Sirenacus plants, so I prepared three for you to take home, two small and one large. The señor said you have a balcony, so they will do well there. They are very hardy plants. Keep them wrapped for one week. After, you only need to trim them in the warmer months. Don't forget, señora, they perfume only three weeks the entire year. The fruity aroma is only in June. You can leave all your windows open and the house will smell beautiful."

"That's so thoughtful, Carlos. Thank you so much. I remember the first time I arrived in Keansbury, I was captivated by their perfume. Thinking back, it was in June."

He had wrapped and crated them for easy transportation. Between their two cars, she knew there would be plenty of space for her boxes and the plants.

"You and Maria have been so wonderful to us, I will never forget your warmth and kindness."

"It has been our pleasure, señora. We are so happy that the señorita is free."

"Carlos, I'll let you get back to work, and thank you again." Katie started to walk back to the deck when she stopped dead in her tracks, becoming weak. She quickly grabbed one of the support poles to steady herself. She muttered out loud, "No, oh God, no."

She collected herself and raced into the house, frantically searching for her cell phone, to no avail. Not wanting to waste a minute, she grabbed the house phone and called Ali. "Where are you? I need you to come back to the house. Yes, right now. No, Jennifer is okay, but please just get back here. I'll explain later."

She ran up the stairs yelling for Matt. He was in the bedroom, dressing from his shower. "Matt, I need your help. Please hurry, come downstairs. I'll be in the den."

"What's the matter? Is Jennifer okay?" She appeared to Matt as if she had lost all the color in her face.

"Jennifer is fine. Please, just come downstairs. I called Al, he's on his way back. I need both of you to help me." She spotted her phone on the night table, grabbed it, and raced back down the stairs, not responding to any more of Matt's questions.

In the foyer, she tossed aside her file boxes until she reached box one, at the bottom of the pile. Lifting it with some difficulty, Katie went into the den and dropped it heavily on the desk. She reached for the scissors in the side drawer and cut the tape that secured the lid. As she was peering through the contents, Matt entered the room.

"Please, Katie, what is going on?"

"Give me a few minutes and I'll explain."

He watched as she found the right binder, then flipped through several pages until she found what she was looking for. She moved her finger across the paragraph, reading the passage out loud, but too quietly to be understood by Matt. When she finished, she closed the binder and fell into the chair.

"Shit, shit, shit," was all she could mutter.

She grabbed her cell phone and made a call. "This is Katie Russo. Let me speak to Mr. Ryan. It's an emergency. I don't care, I said it's an emergency."

Matt was getting more concerned by the minute.

The prosecutor answered the call, curiosity piqued.

"Mark, it's Katie Russo," she said, her voice firm. "Please, listen—I need to meet with you and the sheriff immediately. I will be coming into town shortly. Would you please contact the sheriff and let him know we will be meeting him at the police station. Listen, I need to speak with you both. And, Mark, I will need to have a few words with VanAnt. Please, just do as I ask. I will explain everything when I get there. Yes, thank you."

Perfect timing; when she ended her conversation, Ali walked in. He looked at them both with anxious confusion. "What has happened?"

She briefly explained what occurred with Carlos and the Sirenacus plants. "I know who killed Peter Keans Junior." With that, she handed them their respective assignments; there were several sources she needed them to reach for further explanations. "I don't care who you must call or disturb, I need this information immediately. There's no time to waste."

They both looked shell-shocked, but determined to fulfill their assignments. They took separate cars into town, not knowing where their searches would lead. After they left, Katie informed Maria that they would be out of the house and asked her to keep an eye on Jennifer. She grabbed her jacket and phone and sped into town to the police station. When she arrived, the two men were waiting impatiently in the rear conference room.

The sheriff was the first to speak. "Mrs. Russo, what in the hell is going on? Isn't your case over?"

"I know this is highly unusual, Sheriff, but I promise you this is all for a very good reason. I'm going to ask you to indulge me just a little longer. I would like five minutes with VanAnt. There are a few questions I need to ask."

He practically screamed, "What?! We've accepted your client is innocent, what else do you possibly need to know?"

Mark cut in before she could reply. "Sheriff, let her have five minutes. She's been right about everything, so if there's more that we need to know, I trust her."

Katie met with VanAnt in his cell. She was surprised to see how he had morphed into an almost childlike state. It took a few minutes for him to focus, but he was finally able to give Katie all that she needed. When she returned to the conference room, her phone rang twice; first it was Ali, then Matt. Both had the information she had requested, so she instructed them to meet her at the station.

When they arrived, she asked them all to be seated as she explained her theory. They were words she never imagined speaking, and she was shaking terribly with each utterance. After she finished, there was momentary silence. She prayed that someone would tell her she was crazy, that this wasn't possible.

Mark spoke first. "Unfortunately, it appears that your theory is most likely a reality. Now, what do we do about it?"

The group spent the next half-hour formulating a course of action to be implemented tomorrow morning. As they were dispersing, Katie told Matt she was too upset to drive, so she would be going back to the house with him. Overhearing this, the sheriff had her leave her keys and said he would arrange for the return of her car. She tossed them on the table and left.

They all returned to the house, and Ali told Maria and Jennifer a white lie, that he had forgotten that some unfinished business needed to be addressed in the morning. With the excuse accepted, Ali, Matt, and Katie spent the rest of the day staging a flawless act of normalcy—one that could rival any well-rehearsed play. Katie, in particular, made a point to reassure Jennifer that once she wrapped up a few last-minute tasks that evening, she'd sit down with her the following day to talk through their plans for the future.

Unaware of the weight the trio carried, the household moved through the evening undisturbed. Dinner passed without incident, and at last, nightfall offered its quiet reprieve. One by one, they withdrew to their rooms.

Katie's emotions finally got the best of her, and tears flowed easily.

"Do you want to talk about it?" Matt said, trying to comfort her.

"Matt, I can't. I just can't. I hate this, and I hate myself for what's about to happen."

He grabbed her tightly. "Don't you say that, don't you think that. None of this is your fault."

"Matt, I want to go back in time. More than anything, I just want to go back in time, to before I ever heard of Keansbury." They lay in bed, Katie never closing her teary eyes. It was the longest night of her life.

CHAPTER 57

The phone rang at 10:00am.

"Katie, it's Mark." All formality had been dispensed.

"Mark, was she picked up?" Katie asked nervously.

"Yes, we picked her up this morning and she's resting comfortably in my office. I told her we needed her help and we would explain everything later."

"And, Mark, was he told?" Katie's voice was shaking.

"Yes, Deputy Wong did her part. She explained that her cell phone was broken, so she had asked the deputy to relay the message to him. It all went smoothly."

Katie ended the call, unable to breathe. She went to speak with Jennifer, then Maria and Carlos.

"I need to ask you both for a favor. I have an important meeting here soon and I don't want Jennifer on the property. I would appreciate if you would take her to lunch. Do you know La Mare Café? It's on the beach and it's private."

"Si, señora, we eat there on special occasions," Maria offered.

"I don't want Jennifer to know that I want her out of the house. I told her that you just wanted to take her to lunch and she agreed."

"Of course, señora, we would be happy to help."

Katie handed them money, but they refused.

"Señora, it would be our pleasure to take the señorita to lunch."

"Thank you both so much. Jennifer will be down shortly; can you be ready?"

"We will need only five minutes."

Katie was relieved to watch the car pull away; this would not be a scene she wanted Jennifer to witness. Her heavy thoughts were disrupted by a familiar ringtone. The call came as expected.

Katie answered immediately, "Yes, of course. Everyone is out at the moment, but I'll be here. Fifteen minutes. I look forward to seeing you again."

She stood there frozen. She could barely breathe. She waited in the kitchen. Sure enough, fifteen minutes later, Katie heard the front door unlock followed by the opening of the sliding doors to the den.

"Katie? Katie, I'm here."

Her name seemed to echo throughout the huge empty house. Her legs felt numb, unable to move, but she had no choice. She walked to the den and entered.

"Hello, Professor."

"Well, there you are. So good to see you. I want to tell you again how proud I am of you and what you've accomplished. Katie, I wish we could spend more time together, but I'm in a bit of a rush. We are leaving for Switzerland tonight and Phyllis misplaced her passport. I'm hoping it's in one of my file cabinets."

Katie swallowed hard. "That's okay, Professor. We can spend time when you return. Matt and I will be leaving tomorrow. I wanted you to know that Maria and Carlos have been so kind to us." It took all her strength to make it sound routine.

He nodded his head, not fully listening as he was focused on finding the passport.

"You know what that sweet Carlos did? He wrapped up three Sirenacus plants for me to take home to the city."

He again only nodded, and she noticed he was becoming slightly irritated at not uncovering the passport, slamming each empty drawer.

She continued. "Do you know about these plants, Professor? The fascinating part is that they emit the most beautiful scent, it's a fruity, cherry scent, but only for three weeks in June. Isn't that interesting? The scent is only in June."

He paused for a moment to look at Katie, wondering why she was going on about some plants. "I'm sorry, I really can't talk right now. I must find her passport." He slammed another drawer. "Where is that damn passport?"

"Professor, when you first asked me to come to Keansbury, it was in June, and I remember that lovely cherry aroma from the Sirenacus plants. And then I met with Jennifer at the jail to hear her account of what happened. She was very detailed, omitting nothing. And you know what I just remembered yesterday? She had told me that when she entered the cabin, the first thing she recalled was the scent of the Sirenacus plant. She recalled that cherry scent. But, Professor, she was wrong. She didn't lie; she was just mistaken. You see, she did sense the cherry aroma, but the murder was in April, so it couldn't possibly have come from the plant. It came from your cherry pipe tobacco."

He stopped cold. "Katie, what are you talking about?" He was shocked by her words.

She tried not to cry, but her eyes started to well. "You're a terrible gambler, always have been according to your own words. It didn't take much digging to find out that two years ago you were in serious debt. You were on the brink of losing your house, your reputation, and possibly even Phyllis. You were so desperate that you went to Keans Sr. and he made you a deal you couldn't refuse. According to VanAnt, in exchange for paying off your massive debt, you would be the attorney for their drug business. He mentioned you created non-existent companies, prepared illegal contracts, and did anything else they asked of you. I'm going to surmise that once the debt was paid off and the money started rolling in, you became hooked on that lifestyle."

"Katie, what are you saying? This simply isn't true." He now sounded like someone scrambling to conceal what was already out in the open.

She took the edge of her sweater to dry the tears that wouldn't stop flowing. "I asked VanAnt if he had told you about Junior and the open crate, and he said yes. That young boy was too honest. He would never have ignored what was happening at the company. You must have panicked. Then, one day at lunch, fortuitously, Mr. Adams told the gathering about what he believed was the exchange between Junior and Jennifer in the library. Was it then that you became desperate enough to develop a plan to get rid of Junior and blame Jennifer? My God, Professor, I can't believe I'm even saying these words."

"Then think about what you're saying, Katie. That isn't me and you know that."

She was shaking now. "Professor, this plan must have been so easy for you to arrange. The number of criminal trials you've been involved with, you've seen it all. How long did it take you to develop this? An hour? A day? Two days?!" She was screaming.

He just shook his head.

"And thinking back, you used me like a puppet on a string. I'm sure you got hurt somehow, possibly when executing the cabin set up. I'm guessing you had planned on representing her, ensuring she would be found guilty. But when you were hospitalized, you called upon me, the one person you knew you could manipulate, the one person you knew would keep you in the loop. The one person who loved you unconditionally."

She dropped to her knees, sobbing, but she had to continue. He walked over to help her, but she waved him off. "Don't touch me. Don't you dare touch me! You were as guilty as Senior and VanAnt, but you cleverly stayed in the background. VanAnt never even mentioned you at trial. It most certainly never occurred to him that you could be involved with the young boy's death."

"Katie, please." His voice cracked with desperation, begging her to let the accusation go.

"Oh, there's more, Professor. We checked with the foreman working on your home renovation. He said your checks had bounced and you were unable to adequately fund the work, so he had no other alternative than to cease. We also checked with Toni, your travel agent. You had made reservations for Switzerland two days prior to the murder. You probably wanted a quick getaway should anything go wrong. You cancelled only after you were hospitalized. Mr. Paultz at the tobacco shop says he orders Captain Black Cherry for you on a regular basis. I'm sure if we keep digging, we'll find more and more incriminating evidence."

He sighed. There was no denying it anymore, not to her. "Katie, please let me explain."

She grabbed the arm of the chair and helped herself up, managing to sit on the edge of the cushion. "Explain? Did you just say explain?"

"Katie, I got caught up in my own ego. I am the Professor. Successful lawyer, prominent teacher, sought-after lecturer. I moved here permanently to our summer home because I knew Keans and VanAnt and this was a tight-knit community. I thought I could live off my reputation, which I did for a few years. But this gambling addiction just wouldn't let me go. I could no longer borrow on my reputation, so when Senior offered me a way out, I took it. Reluctantly at first, but then my debts were cleared, I was getting money, and I could continue to gamble, worry-free. Of course, you know what a poor card player I am, so I never really had money saved, but that was okay. Then that silly boy had to go and open a crate. He was going to take us down, all of us. Katie, I swear, I didn't mean for this to happen, I just became desperate."

"Didn't mean for it to happen? His murder wasn't an impulse or a spur of the moment thing. You devised a very clever and intricate scheme."

"Yes, it was clever. And, Katie, it was so easy. I had years of listening to my clients' attempts to circumvent the law. It almost became a game to see if I could pull it off. When Jennifer worked here at the house, I went to her apartment and got the knife. As for the cabin, I was there before and after her and rearranged everything. And you were right about hurting myself. After she went up to the cabin, I pulled a heavy log onto the Rahway Road bridge, making it impassable, forcing her to take Lamberts Trail. Then I went back and removed it. However, I got my foot caught in some twigs and I went down hard on my hip. I dragged myself to my car and made it back to the house. I then lay at the bottom of the stairs and called to Phyllis. Everyone thought I fell down the stairs. Then, of course, my condition deteriorated due to my diabetes, and I wasn't certain I would even survive."

Katie kept shaking her head, hoping this was all a dream.

"I know human nature. Once I pointed the finger at Jennifer, I knew the town would do the rest, and they did."

Katie was traumatized. "I don't even know who you are. You were my father, my mentor. Was all that a sham? Professor, this wasn't an exercise in ingenuity. You murdered an innocent young boy and blamed an innocent young girl. This boy's father is permanently comatose, his mother died of a broken heart, and this town has essentially imploded. The suffering you caused is incomprehensible. And Phyllis, what about Phyllis? How could you do this to her?"

He became defiant. "She has nothing to do with any of this. I kept all of it from her."

He looked at his watch and realized he was running out of time. As if nothing Katie said had mattered, he turned his attention away from her and back to the steel file cabinets. "Ah, finally, here it is." He grabbed the passport and hurried toward the sliding doors. She rose up to block his path.

"Do you think you can just walk away from what you've done? I know everything now. Do you plan on killing me too?" She was a wreck; her eyes were blurred from crying, her legs began to buckle, and her breathing became sporadic.

"Of course not, I would never hurt you."

"Oh, but you have. What you've done to me is worse than death. I will never forgive you."

He was desperate; there was nothing left. "Katie, I'm asking you to let me leave. I am begging you to give me time to get on that plane with Phyllis, never to return. For all that I've ever meant to you, for all that I've ever done for you, please, Katie, step aside." It was his final closing argument.

She turned her back to him. "Professor, this will be the last time we will ever see one another. May God forgive me." And with that, she stepped aside.

He thought twice about saying anything further. He slipped the passport into his jacket pocket and placed his hands on the doors. With great force, he slid them apart and took two fast-paced steps, only to stop dead in his tracks. Like a concrete wall, he came face to face with ADA Ryan, Sheriff Michaels, Deputy Wong, Ali, and Matt. He was dumbfounded, having believed he'd successfully procured his escape.

It was the sheriff that spoke. "Professor Kyle, you are under arrest for the murder of Peter Keans Jr. You have the right to remain silent." When he finished giving him his rights, he was handcuffed and led away.

"Phyllis. Please, my wife will be worried waiting for me." He pleaded for understanding.

"Your wife is safe at the district attorney's office," the sheriff said. "We brought her in a few hours ago."

The Professor thought for a moment. "You arranged this, didn't you? You took her passport knowing I would come here to look for it."

The sheriff half-smiled. "You're not the only one who can be manipulative."

The siren signaled their departure, so Matt raced into the den to be with Katie. She was curled up on the floor, sobbing and rocking back and forth. He wrapped her in his arms and gently stroked her hair. His tone was soothing. "It's going to be okay, it will all be okay."

Ali apologized for interrupting. "Maria called, she wants to know if they should come back."

Matt nodded yes. "I'll take Katie upstairs. Would you please tell Maria and Carlos what's happened? But let's not say anything to Jennifer yet. We'll talk to her later."

While Matt helped Katie up the stairs, Ali helped Mark, wheeling him to his car.

"Mark, what will happen to the Professor?" Ali wanted to know.

"He will be arraigned before end of day and prosecuted to the fullest extent of the law. We have his confession on tape, so there's no wiggle room on this one. Mrs. Russo did a fine job of getting him to admit to the murder. Thanks for your help."

Ali walked back into the house, contemplating all that had transpired in just two days. He hated seeing Katie so distraught;

it broke his heart. He went into the den to straighten up and then headed to the kitchen to wait for Maria and Carlos. He knew what he had to tell them would be upsetting and would certainly impact their lives.

Thirty minutes later, he heard their car pull into the driveway. He dreaded the conversation to follow. Matt came down to the kitchen to get Katie a cup of coffee. He hadn't realized Maria and Carlos had returned. Maria's tears and Carlos' shocked expression signaled that Ali had broken the news to them. He put his arms around Maria's shoulders, trying to be of comfort. "*Two more victims*," he thought. He then looked around the room quickly, then to Ali.

"She's on the beach. I didn't say anything to her."

"Okay. Maria, I'm going to be upstairs with Katie. She's obviously very upset. I know you and Carlos are as well, but we'll all come through this together. Katie will talk to Jennifer later."

Matt returned to the bedroom to find Katie sitting by the open window, watching Jennifer wading in the water.

"Matt, everywhere I look there's another victim of his heinous crime. There isn't anyone in this entire town that hasn't been affected."

He handed her the cup of coffee. "The Professor wasn't solely culpable for all that's happened, but he was the linchpin. If he hadn't murdered Junior, I suspect that Keans Industries might have continued in drug trafficking for a couple of years before being exposed."

She turned to him, tears streaming down her face. "Matt, I...I just can't believe it was the Professor I was talking to. I thought I knew him. Knew him well. Oh, Matt, was our entire relationship a lie? Did he not care about us?"

He grabbed her face in his hands. "Listen to me. The man we both loved and trusted did exist. He was a friend, a mentor, and a father figure to you. I believe he genuinely cared for both of us. But now we must accept that he's gone. The Professor we loved is gone. This Professor now, he's a stranger, someone we won't have contact with, ever."

They sat together until Katie regained her composure.

"I think I'm cried out. I should be able to get through the conversation with Jennifer. She needs to know the truth."

"Let's do it together. Come on, I'll go with you."

Katie sat on the deck while Matt walked down the beach to retrieve Jennifer. When they finished updating her, she moved close to Katie. "I'm not sure how I feel. He's a smart man, and I guess he saw how weak I am and knew I would be the perfect pawn."

Katie shook her shoulders. "Don't you say that. You are a brilliant young woman who became the Professor's second victim. You are not weak. In fact, you're one of the strongest people I've ever known. All that you've been through and you fought to survive. That takes a great deal of strength and courage."

Matt turned to them both. "It's been a long day for all of us. Let's make Maria happy and grab a bite to eat. We can sort everything out tomorrow. I think we've been through enough for today."

They all sat together sharing an unanticipated meal. The mood contrasted sharply from the congratulatory spirit the day of the acquittal. Matt leaned over to Katie and whispered, "Don't worry, we'll sort it all out tomorrow."

CHAPTER 58

The morning sun seemed to wash away the shadows of yesterday. It was time to move on. For everyone. Ali was getting ready to leave, this time permanently. He was with Matt in the driveway, helping to pack the cars.

"Matt, have Maria and Carlos decided what they're going to be doing?"

"As far as I know, their son rented an apartment for them, so they'll be living in New York, at least for the short term. Like so many, they'll need some time to think things through. We said our goodbyes early this morning. They left to meet their son at the train station. He'll spend some time here helping them with the move."

Katie arrived just as Ali was ready to depart. She had borrowed Maria's car so that Matt could finish packing their two cars. Neither of them wanted to spend any more time on the property than necessary.

"Al, I hope you weren't planning on going without saying goodbye." Katie put her arm through his, holding him tight. "I'm going to miss you, at least until our next adventure."

He held her arm closely. "Of course I wouldn't leave without saying goodbye. Matt said you were on your way back, so I waited. He mentioned you went to visit Phyllis. How is she?"

He and Matt were anxious to hear. "Understandably, she's upset, confused, embarrassed, angry, heartbroken...just about every available emotion. She was with her sister and some other family, and the sheriff was there too. I only spoke with her briefly. She kept apologizing for what the Professor did. She said she knew he had a serious problem and had begged him to get help. As far as she believed, he was regularly attending Gambler Anonymous meetings, but as we now know, he was not. As for the house, she was adamant that it would go on the market as soon as possible. She doesn't want to live here any longer. Matt, I did tell her that if she needs us, we'll be there for her."

"Of course. She's been a trusting victim like the rest of us."

They said their goodbyes to Ali and he drove off, knowing confidently he would never be returning.

"So, Matt, where's my friend?" she said a bit sarcastically.

"He's in the conservatory. I gave him a cup of coffee and told him to stay put. Jennifer is out of the house, and I told him she is off limits."

"Good. Let me fulfill my promise, and then I'll talk to her later."

"Good morning, Mr. Klein. I'm here as promised." Katie spent the next half-hour answering every question posed. He was particularly curious as to what prompted her to investigate the drug angle.

"Mr. Klein, that's a very good question, and one I am happy to answer. It was actually Miss O'Neill who unknowingly led the way. Up until recently, she believed young Mr. Keans had indicated he was a drug addict. As you know, the medical evidence proved otherwise. I knew something illegal was happening at the port, but all I had was a puzzle box full of bits and pieces. Then, not too long ago, Miss O'Neill was sitting right where you are now, mindlessly watching a news program. As she related to me, it was a brief story about one brother saving the other from a frozen pond. The mother of the boys said they always fought, so she was happy to know they really cared for one another. The anchor ended the story by saying something about how it proved that blood is thicker than water."

Klein interrupted. "I'm intrigued, but I don't see what any of this has to do with drugs."

"You see, it triggered a mistaken memory Miss O'Neill had of her conversation that day in the library. She thought Junior had said it was in his blood, and she interpreted that as him telling her he was an addict. However, what he really meant was that it was in his *bloodline*. She realized he was telling her he was so distraught because his family was involved with drugs. That's why he rejected any assistance she was offering in terms of rehab and meetings. Once I had that knowledge, all the other pieces fell into place."

"That's an incredible story and an incredible bit of luck. But, what made her risk jail by going into town? Why not wait until you returned here?"

"Because she panicked and feared for my safety. She knew the Keans and their associates were powerful, so she was concerned that while I was in town, they may try to reach out and hurt me in some way. By doing what she did, Mr. Klein, she came terrifyingly close to losing her life for the sake of mine."

"Mrs. Russo, I know you were very fond of Professor Kyle, so I am sorry how things turned out. You were convinced that Mr. VanAnt was the murderer; what made you realize it was the Professor?"

Katie went on to explain the turn of events regarding the Sirenacus plant, at which he remarked that luck seemed to play an important part in solving this case.

"Well, Mr. Klein, let me say this. We all worked very hard on this case, and I think luck was a result of that. I think I've answered all your questions. We're anxious to leave today, so I am going to thank you for your fine reporting, and I look forward to reading your final installment."

"You were very generous with your time, and I very much appreciate your candor. For what it's worth, I think you're a damn good attorney!"

As she watched Klein depart, the ADA pulled up.

"A busy morning here," Matt remarked.

Mark rolled down the window to speak to them both. "May I have a minute?"

They walked over to his van.

"I know you're leaving soon, so I just wanted to touch base with you before you left. There's a West Coast company expressing interest in buying Keans Industries and rebuilding the port. If they do, I suppose there's a chance that the town can rebuild and perhaps even find its soul. Mrs. Russo—Katie—I just want to say, on behalf of the town, I am so very sorry for everything that's happened to Miss O'Neill. There's been an attempt by some of us to apologize to her in person, but understandably, she declined. Anyway, that's all I wanted to say."

She took a moment before responding. "Mark, I appreciate you driving out here to tell us that. But let me say that rebuilding starts with more than apologies. It starts with accountability. That young girl lost nearly a year of her life, and no apologies or good intentions will vanish that. I hope you and the town will truly understand what you did, and I pray that it never happens again to anyone else."

He nodded. "I understand. By the way, the Professor has again asked to see you, but I told him you aren't available, at least for now. Have a safe trip home." And then he left.

Katie turned to Matt. "I'm going to finally have that talk with

Jennifer. Do you know where she is? Never mind, silly question. Beach?"

"Yeah, the beach."

Matt continued packing the cars while Katie walked on the beach looking for Jennifer. She found her sitting on the remnants of a jetty which only made itself visible during low tides. She looked deep in thought.

"Jen."

She turned to face Katie.

"Mrs. Russo, you know what I was thinking? I was thinking that I've had so much pain in my life—my uncle, my loneliness, this nightmare. But none of that is as painful as having to say goodbye to you."

It caught Katie off guard, and she swallowed hard.

"Well, I appreciate that, but before we part, there is this little problem regarding my fee."

"Mrs. Russo, I promise I will pay you every cent I owe. I will get two, three jobs and send you money every week and—"

Katie cut her off. "Well, that's not good enough. I'll tell you what I propose. I've been away from my law firm for quite some time, and when I return, I'll need help. I propose that you come live with Matt and me and work as my intern at the firm. You'll have free room and board, and I will pay you a stipend for your work. I propose that you will also need to enroll in the local community college for a year while you get settled. After which time, we will help you apply for a scholarship to any top college in the country. So, that's my proposal, would you—"

Katie didn't get a chance to finish. Jennifer jumped up and hugged her so hard she nearly knocked her over. Katie held her. "It's going to be all right. I promise you, it's all going to be all right."

They both were teary.

"Matt and I will drive over with you to your apartment and

collect anything you want to take. We have plenty of room. Is that okay with you?"

"Yes, of course. I don't know how to thank you. I promise I won't be a bother, I'll help you at work and at the apartment." She was so excited that she rambled on and on. It made Katie smile.

"We'll work it out, I know it, so please don't worry."

Katie looked up at the deck to see Matt standing there, waving to them both. She put her arm around Jennifer's waist.

"Come on, let's go home."

EPILOGUE

Katie and Matt welcomed their first child—a boy, Vito Russo, named after Matt's grandfather. They were both wonderful parents, especially Katie, whose motherly instincts came so naturally.

Jennifer settled in to her new life with great appreciation. She thrived at the local college, and will attend Princeton in the fall. Hoping to make a meaningful impact, she chose to study sociology, aiming to become a social worker. She met a young man at Katie's law firm, and they have been dating for six months.

Ali has helped Katie with two more cases since Keansbury. He's the baby's godfather.

Not surprising to anyone, Maria and Carlos have opened a small café in the East Village. Full house each night. More importantly, the "crew," as Katie has named them, unfailingly meet once a month for dinner. They talk about the present and future, nothing of the past. The six of them have an unbreakable bond.

Phyllis moved in with her sister, still not able to fully process the events.

Since that fateful day, no contact has been made with the Professor. They learned through Phyllis that since his incarceration, his health has deteriorated. No trial is planned; he accepted his fate and will remain imprisoned indefinitely.

The FBI contacted Katie to thank her for her assistance and to let her know that VanAnt has been "singing like a bird" in an effort to lessen his sentence.

As for the fate of Keansbury... No one cared enough to inquire.

ACKNOWLEDGMENTS

What's the expression...it takes a village? Well, this book took an entire country!! What started as a germ of an idea for a murder mystery grew rapidly with the help and support of so many wonderful family, friends, and professionals.

As a first-time author, I was eager for critical feedback, good or bad, and forthcoming it came. Thanks especially to my initial fans, Stacey Delvecchio and Barbara Rinaldi. Their encouragement was boundless.

I have great appreciation to so many others who were my ground floor readers. They provided critical insight and some very good common sense: Cathy Stickles, Tracy Noone, Toni Deis, Tessa Verga, Muffy Basile, Ruby Verga, Barbara Catterall, Marie Titus, Peggy Perrochino, Bertha Gleaton, Marlene Klein, Ellen D'Amato, Jennifer Pereira, Annie Basile, Marissa Garabedian, Jeanette Criscione.

Thank you to my editors, formatters, designers and promoters: Juliette Townsend, Sean Leonard, Alex Dickson, Danna Mathias Steele, Marie Force Formatting Fairies, Derek Garabedian.

To say I was overwhelmed by the thought of actually publishing my book would be a vast understatement. I was frozen on the spot until I received the warmth of kindness from Eva Natiello, author and publishing consultant. She held my hand throughout the entire process, patiently answering my seemingly endless list of questions and guiding me to the mountain, so to speak! Thank you, Eva.

And last, but not least, a special thanks to Kathy Taylor. As our session ended, you looked at me and said, "you need to write."

This journey was entirely unfamiliar to me, which made the process fun, exciting and sometimes hair pulling. However, I learned a lot and got the opportunity to meet and collaborate with amazing people.

Grazie a tutti!!

QUESTIONS AND TOPICS FOR
BOOK CLUB DISCUSSION
FOR TRIAL BY TOWN BY
SHARON FERNICOLA

In order to provide discussion topics for reading groups and book clubs, important plot points may be revealed. You may wish to explore these questions only after finishing Trial By Town.

1. As far as Keansbury is concerned, Jennifer is the one and only one guilty of the murder. How does Jennifer's isolation shape the town's willingness to believe she's guilty? And what does her steadfast insistence on innocence reveal about her character?

2. Keansbury depends on the Keans family business. How does this economic dependence influence the town's behavior during the investigation? Do you think their collective morale eroded from the time of the murder to the trial?

3. Katie is a wife and well respected and successful attorney. However, she struggles with an internal conflict throughout. Discuss the reasoning behind the conflict and how it impacted her decision to represent Jennifer.

4. In what ways do Katie and Jennifer mirror each other emotionally despite their dramatically different backgrounds?

5. The Professor was a mentor to Katie from college throughout her adult life. How does this mentorship influence her behavior and complicate her decisions?

6. As the story progressed and clues were uncovered, Katie determined VanAnt to be the killer of Junior. What does his breakdown on the stand reveal about guilt, pressure, and complicity?

7. The Sirenacus plants only bloom for three weeks in June. Was there any point in the story where you believed their reference was significant?

8. At what point did you begin to suspect the true killer – if at all?

9. Katie's discovery of the Professor's betrayal is devastating. How does this moment reshape the story's emotional core? Do you see the Professor as villain, a tragic figure, or both?

10. Were you satisfied with the book's ending?

11. How satisfying is the resolution for Jennifer, Katie, and the supporting characters and what does it mean that no one cares how Keansbury is doing after the trial?

ABOUT THE AUTHOR

Sharon Fernicola is a writer drawn to layered mysteries, emotional realism, and characters who challenge assumptions. Her fascination with crime and justice began early, watching Perry Mason with her father and falling in love with the genre's blend of intellect and drama. Her debut novel, Trial by Town, explores the fragile line between perception and truth in a small town desperate to preserve its legacy.

In her 70s, Sharon completed three triathlons, obtained dual Italian–American citizenship, and wrote her first book—living proof that bold dreams don't come with an expiration date. She brings a poetic sensibility to her storytelling, blending suspense with empathy and nuance. When she's not writing, she's mapping out her next adventure or putting in time at the gym, always chasing the next challenge with curiosity and grit.